Dangerous Deception
at
Honeychurch
Hall

Hannah Dennison

CONSTABLE

CONSTABLE

First published in Great Britain in 2018 by Constable

Copyright © Hannah Dennison, 2018

1 3 5 7 9 10 8 6 4 2

The moral right of the author has been asserted.

A CIP catalogue record for this book is available from the British Library.

ISBN: 978-1-47212-849-2

Typeset by Initial Typesetting Services
Printed and bound in Great Britain by Clays Ltd, Elcograf S.p.A.

Papers used by Constable are from well-managed forests
and other responsible sources.

MIX
Paper from
responsible sources
FSC® C104740

Constable
An imprint of
Little, Brown Book Group
Carmelite House
50 Victoria Embankment
London EC4Y 0DZ

An Hachette UK Company
www.hachette.co.uk

www.littlebrown.co.uk

Hannah Dennison was born and raised in Hampshire but moved to Los Angeles to pursue screenwriting more than two decades ago. She has been an obituary reporter, antique dealer, private jet flight attendant and Hollywood story analyst. Hannah writes the Honeychurch Hall Mystery Series and Vicky Hill Mystery Series, both of which are set in the wilds of the English countryside. She currently divides her time between California and the West Country.

www.hannahdennison.com

To my *absolutely fabulous* and very best friend,
Faustina Gilbey

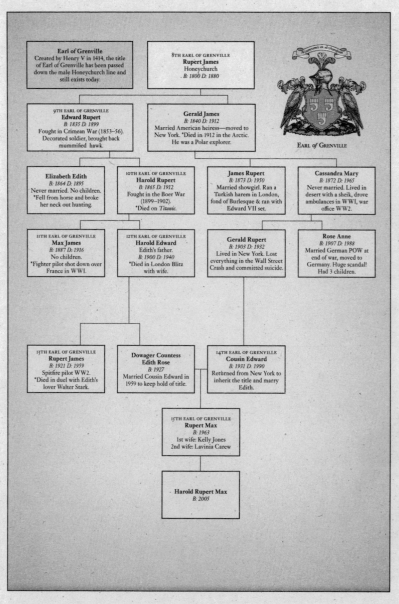

Earl of Grenville
Created by Henry V in 1414, the title of Earl of Grenville has been passed down the male Honeychurch line and still exists today.

8TH EARL OF GRENVILLE
Rupert James
Honeychurch
. B: 1800 D: 1880

EARL of GRENVILLE

9TH EARL OF GRENVILLE
Edward Rupert
B: 1835 D: 1899
Fought in Crimean War (1853–56). Decorated soldier, brought back mummified hawk.

Gerald James
B: 1840 D: 1912
Married American heiress—moved to New York. *Died in 1912 in the Arctic. He was a Polar explorer.

Elizabeth Edith
B: 1864 D: 1895
Never married. No children. *Fell from horse and broke her neck out hunting.

10TH EARL OF GRENVILLE
Harold Rupert
B: 1865 D: 1912
Fought in the Boer War (1899–1902).
*Died on *Titanic*.

James Rupert
B: 1873 D: 1950
Married showgirl. Ran a Turkish harem in London, fond of Burlesque & ran with Edward VII set.

Cassandra Mary
B: 1872 D: 1965
Never married. Lived in desert with a sheik, drove ambulances in WWI, war office WW2.

11TH EARL OF GRENVILLE
Max James
B: 1887 D: 1916
No children.
*Fighter pilot shot down over France in WWI.

12TH EARL OF GRENVILLE
Harold Edward
Edith's father.
B: 1900 D: 1940
*Died in London Blitz with wife.

Gerald Rupert
B: 1903 D: 1932
Lived in New York. Lost everything in the Wall Street Crash and committed suicide.

Rose Anne
B: 1907 D: 1988
Married German POW at end of war, moved to Germany. Huge scandal! Had 3 children.

13TH EARL OF GRENVILLE
Rupert James
B: 1921 D: 1959
Spitfire pilot WW2.
*Died in duel with Edith's lover Walter Stark.

Dowager Countess
Edith Rose
B: 1927
Married Cousin Edward in 1959 to keep hold of title.

14TH EARL OF GRENVILLE
Cousin Edward
B: 1931 D: 1990
Returned from New York to inherit the title and marry Edith.

15TH EARL OF GRENVILLE
Rupert Max
B: 1963
1st wife: Kelly Jones
2nd wife: Lavinia Carew

Harold Rupert Max
B: 2005

Ad perseverate est ad triumphum

EARL *of* GRENVILLE

Chapter One

Edith Honeychurch abruptly stopped her chestnut mare in the middle of the bridleway. With a snort of protest, Tinkerbell shied, nearly unseating the eighty-six-year-old dowager countess, who still insisted on riding side-saddle.

'Edith! Are you OK?' I called out, only just managing to avoid barging into her mount with my own. She gave a wave of acknowledgement but did not ride on.

I'd been daydreaming – astonished at how life could change so drastically. Just last August I was living and working in London as the host of a television show called *Fakes and Treasures*. Just over a year later, here I was riding Jupiter, a beautiful horse, in the wilds of the Devonshire countryside.

'Kat! Come and look.' Edith gestured for me to join her alongside. 'This is outrageous! Why would someone do that?'

I immediately saw the reason for her dismay. A bulging black bin liner had split open, spewing household waste, sodden paper and broken glass across the bridleway.

Mr Chips, Edith's little Jack Russell terrier, bounded

forward and dragged out a grubby blue-and-white-striped sock that for some reason looked familiar.

'Leave it!' Edith commanded, but the dog kept his prize and bolted through a gap in the hedge.

'Fly-tipping,' she said with disgust. 'First Bridge Cottage and now up here on Barton's Ridge. It's getting worse and it seems that there is nothing we can do about it.'

She was right, of course. Illegal dumping of domestic and industrial rubbish, particularly on private property, was on the rise despite the promise of crippling fines and prison sentences for repeat offenders. To add insult to injury, the landowners had to pay to clear the rubbish away, otherwise they would be fined too. It seemed most unfair.

'Rupert should just get a shotgun and shoot the scoundrels on sight,' Edith went on. 'That would be a real deterrent.'

I regarded her with horror. She seemed perfectly serious.

'We'll have to retrace our steps,' she said. 'I'm not risking injuring these horses with all that broken glass.'

Our morning ride had been fraught with problems from the start. Jupiter had cast a shoe, but luckily hadn't gone lame. Then she'd tripped and I'd fallen off into a muddy puddle. I'd been riding in wet jodhpurs for the past hour and it wasn't very pleasant.

Shortly after *that* fiasco, Tinkerbell refused to pass a giant bale of hay covered in a black tarpaulin that snapped and crackled loudly, and we were forced to take a different path. It was the first time I'd ever seen Edith give in to a horse and it reminded me that although her mind was as sharp as a tack, she wasn't as physically strong as she used to be.

Fifteen minutes later, we rejoined Barton's Ridge higher

up the hill. From this vantage point, the view of the sprawling Honeychurch Hall estate – and now my home – was not as attractive as the one seen from Hopton's Crest on the opposite side of the valley.

A tangle of scaffolding encased the east wing, which was awaiting repairs to the roof that would probably never be done. There was a bird's-eye view of the kitchens and servants' quarters, which were in dire need of a coat of paint, and the line of ramshackle potting sheds, broken glasshouses and abandoned hothouse furnaces in the Victorian walled garden gave the property a sad and neglected air. Only one of the three adjoining estate cottages seemed to be cared for, with its window boxes filled with red geraniums – a nice touch by the new housekeeper, who had recently arrived at the Hall and who I had not yet met.

It was then that I noticed the stranger in a gateway just a few yards further down the hill.

Standing alongside a dirty black Citroën CX was a man in jeans and a black leather jacket, looking through a pair of binoculars across the valley. A camera with a telephoto lens hung about his neck.

He must have heard us coming because he quickly jumped down, wrenched open the car door, turned the ignition and sped away. I got a glimpse of a European Union sticker – gold stars on a blue background – but the number plate was too dirty to make out.

There had been something odd about the car, and then I realised what it was. 'Did you notice that Citroën was left-hand drive?' I said to Edith.

'I believe it was,' she said. 'Someone knows you have come out of retirement. What do they call those frightful newspaper photographers? The paparazzi?'

'I hope not.'

'Or perhaps someone has discovered Iris's true identity.' Edith cracked a smile. 'Although he doesn't look the type to read racy bodice-rippers.'

It was possible – but unlikely.

Just before my father died, he had made me promise to keep an eye on my mother, Iris. Little did I realise that this promise would change every aspect of my own life.

Mum's new-found freedom had led her to recklessly buy a dilapidated carriage house hundreds of miles away without so much as a whisper of her intentions to me. Even more shocking was the discovery that she had been writing romance novels under the pseudonym Krystalle Storm for decades. And all the time Dad and I had thought she was suffering from bad migraines! He passed away before he knew the truth, and even now, her identity was a closely guarded secret.

So now we both lived on the estate – although fortunately not together – where the closest village boasted just one general store, a post office, a church and the Hare & Hounds pub.

I had to admit that like Mum, I too had enjoyed my new-found freedom, and seeing a man with binoculars and a camera brought my old life rushing back – the constant public scrutiny, the criticism of what I said, and of course, the countless wardrobe malfunctions that I was famous for.

'I can't imagine my appearance at tomorrow's BearFest would generate international appeal,' I said.

'Why ever not?' Edith replied. 'These past few weeks your shining star has been very difficult to ignore.'

This would be the first year that the Dartmouth Antique Emporium would be holding a one-day festival dedicated to the teddy bear. It had been given masses of publicity. Advertisements had been taken out in all the trade magazines, as well as national and local newspapers. There had been continuous plugs on a mind-boggling number of radio stations, and naturally, giant posters of my face – perfectly airbrushed, thank God – had been dotted around the country announcing my role as valuation expert, auctioneer and keynote speaker.

'Or perhaps he was doing a spot of twitching,' said Edith thoughtfully. 'Hmm. We do have a fine pair of peregrine falcons. We should alert the police just in case.'

'About the cameraman? No need. I can handle it.'

'Not him, dear,' said Edith. 'The police work closely with the RSPB to stay aware of potential thieves who are out to steal our protected birds' eggs.'

'I had no idea,' I said.

'That's because you're a city girl,' Edith teased.

'Not any more! I could never live in London again. The Devon countryside has spoiled me for life.'

'I'm glad to hear it. Of course, the nesting season is over now, but even so, we should tell them,' she said. 'As for the BearFest, I'm sorry to say I have a prior engagement.'

I laughed. 'I didn't think it would be your cup of tea.'

'Nonsense. I have some Pony Club business to attend to. Perhaps your participation might generate some new business for you. I know it's been a struggle.'

'Yes. It takes a while to get established.' It was thoughtful of Edith to acknowledge this. I had launched Kat's Collectibles & Mobile Valuation Services at the beginning of the summer, but business had been slower than I had expected, and since I was still paying the mortgage on my flat in London, money was tight.

All thoughts of the BearFest and the possible egg thief vanished when we both became aware of raised angry voices close by.

'Oh dear,' said Edith. 'The earls are quarrelling again.'

Rounding the corner, we saw a black Range Rover that belonged to Rupert, Edith's son, the 15th Earl of Grenville, and a battered grey Volvo owned by Aubrey Carew, the 12th Earl of Denby and Rupert's father-in-law.

Their vehicles were parked on the gravel drive of Bridge Cottage, which was now a blackened shell. Last October a terrible fire had gutted it – one from which my mother and I had barely escaped with our lives.

In the past few weeks, the ruined site had become a major spot for fly-tipping. Hardcore rubble, a mess of electrical cables and nondescript steel poles jostled with boxes of old clothes and photographs, mounds of tyres and abandoned kitchen appliances. Muddy tracks criss-crossed the old garden, flanked by mattresses and an assortment of broken furniture.

The place gave me the creeps.

We caught snatches of the argument: 'This is your responsibility' coming from Aubrey, and 'I refuse to spend another penny for something that is not my fault' from Rupert.

'Oh dear,' said Edith again.

'Have you any idea how much I've already paid to get this removed?' Rupert raged. 'I'm damned if I am going to build a ... a ... what do you call it? A bund? Anyway, I fail to understand why this is my responsibility.'

'It's duty of care, you imbecile!' Aubrey exclaimed. 'Bridge Cottage is on your land!'

'Good morning, gentlemen!' Edith called out cheerfully. 'Lovely day for a ride.'

Both men spun around to face us.

They were dressed in the traditional garb of upper-class landowners: namely corduroys, tweed jackets and Woodstock boots – although Aubrey was wearing a particularly garish orange tweed flat cap this morning. He was also sporting a fluorescent green badge that said *EcoChamp*, the name of his latest environmental campaign to clean up the countryside.

Aubrey was a local legend and lived on the neighbouring Carew Court estate. As well as being a fierce conservationist, he was a renowned expert on antique weapons and armoury, and a ruthless magistrate with a notorious reputation for enforcing the maximum penalty regardless of how petty the crime.

The earls' dislike for each other was tangible and came off them in waves, but good breeding seemed to prevent them from arguing in front of the fairer sex, so they both forced smiles and uttered courteous greetings.

'Edith, my dear,' said Aubrey smoothly. 'Can you talk some sense into your son, who clearly does not understand the law?'

'I am fully aware of the law,' Rupert spat.

'He may be lackadaisical in other areas of his life – notably his marriage vows – but it is the landowner's responsibility to remove fly-tipped waste and dispose of it legally.'

'Oh for heaven's sake,' said Edith. 'Stop pontificating, Aubrey!'

'Really, Edith? You surprise me,' Aubrey declared. 'Rupert faces a five-thousand-pound fine and a further five hundred pounds a day until this waste is removed, and I shall be only too happy to enforce it!'

'*Really*, Aubrey. You surprise *me*,' said Edith drily. 'Don't you have real criminals to put away?'

Rupert bristled. 'Stay out of this, Mother.'

'I'm not asking him to get his hands dirty,' Aubrey went on. 'There are many reputable companies that dispose of waste. All one needs to do is make a phone call—'

'And open a chequebook,' Rupert fumed. 'Damned expensive they are. What's more, I have cleared this area three times in the past two months. Good God, man, do you think we're made of money?'

'You could start by erecting a CCTV surveillance system … and …' Aubrey made a grand sweep of the area. 'Where is your caution sign?'

Rupert was getting redder in the face by the minute. 'The sign was stolen!'

'If there is no caution sign, it's an open invitation for fly-tipping,' Aubrey went on. 'Surely you must be aware of that.'

'Don't patronise me!'

'I am merely informing you of your legal duties.'

'And I am informing you that if you don't back off—'

'Rupert! Aubrey!' Edith said wearily. 'Is this really necessary?'

'No, let Rupert finish, Edith,' Aubrey exclaimed. 'Are you threatening an officer of Her Majesty's government?'

Rupert muttered something incoherent, threw up his hands and stalked back to his Range Rover.

'You'll receive a summons!' Aubrey shouted after him. 'I'll look forward to seeing you in court!'

There was a hollow clunk as Rupert viciously reversed the Range Rover into Aubrey's Volvo and sped away. Unfortunately, the damage would have been worse for Rupert's car than Aubrey's, Volvos tending to have bodywork as thick as a Sherman tank.

'Really, Aubrey,' Edith scolded. 'I do think you are being unreasonable.'

And I totally agreed with her. My dealings with Aubrey in the past had been based on a shared interest in antiquities, and this was a side of him that I had never witnessed before.

Aubrey drew closer, chest puffed up with indignation. 'I see you aren't wearing your EcoChamp badges.' He pointed to his own. 'It's critical that the general public are made aware of the deterioration of our countryside.'

'I'm afraid it didn't quite go with my habit,' said Edith mildly. 'Good day to you. Come along, Kat.' And with that, she urged Tinkerbell into a brisk trot.

As we rode home side by side, Edith mused, 'I wouldn't be surprised if one of these days Aubrey's heavy-handedness is going to be the death of him.'

Chapter Two

Edith seemed lost in her thoughts for the remainder of the ride, and mine were filled with the busy afternoon ahead.

We reached the main entrance to the estate, marked by a pair of towering granite pillars topped with stone hawks with their wings extended. The words *Honeychurch Hall* were engraved on one, lending a grandiose air that was echoed by the pair of eighteenth-century gatehouses. It was from here that I ran my antique business. I used the West Gatehouse as a showroom and the East as a workshop and for storage.

Each arched front doorway bore the family crest and motto carved in stone: *Ad perseverate est ad triumphum* – To endure is to triumph. In the Honeychurch clan's six hundred years of existence, they had certainly endured: plagues, wars, tragedies and all manner of titillating scandals. I suspected that the trials and tribulations of twenty-first-century fly-tipping would seem rather tame to their ancestors.

Even though Edith was renting the properties to me for a nominal amount, I'd spent a fair bit on repairing gutters and broken windows. I'd also redecorated the interior, put in blinds, installed display shelving and updated the little kitchenette and loo in the West Gatehouse. They looked lovely. All I needed now was customers!

As we continued up the mile-long drive, we passed a wrought-iron archway that straddled a pair of wrought-iron gates, topped by a metal cast of a galloping horse. This was the equine cemetery, filled with beloved horses from both distant and recent past. Just last week, Willow had died in her sleep at the astonishing age of thirty-seven. Her death had hit Edith hard.

Ahead were the soaring chimneys and mullioned windows of the old house peeping through the trees. Another break in the shrubs on my left revealed glorious parkland and an ornamental lake. The drive forked in front of a horse chestnut tree, and we took the right fork, riding uphill, past the post-and-rail paddocks. One side harboured a small outdoor sand dressage arena; the other was laid out with cavaletti jump poles. Ahead was a range of red-brick buildings with neat white trim and green roofs. An impressive archway with a dovecote and a clock tower registering the right time in Roman numerals – 11.45 – marked the entrance to the stable yard. Parked against an outside wall was a large silver horse lorry with living accommodation over the cab, and a hunter-green Land Rover.

Compared to the rest of the estate, the stables were luxurious.

Built around a stone courtyard, three sides of the quadrangle housed four loose boxes each, with the fourth being divided by a second archway that linked up to the service road behind. Horses peered over green-painted half-doors.

Alfred Bushman, the stable manager and Mum's step-brother, greeted us and took Tinkerbell's reins. He led her over to the stone mounting block. Edith gracefully lifted her right leg over the front pommel and slid on to the top step, adjusting her habit as she did so. She had taught me to ride side-saddle, but I never felt completely safe.

'Good ride, your ladyship?' Alfred asked politely.

'Yes, thank you,' Edith said. 'Other than Jupiter casting a shoe.'

'I'll call the blacksmith. Do you want to turn Tinkerbell out?'

'I'll do it,' said Edith. 'I like to do these things whilst I still can.'

As I dismounted, Alfred turned his attention to Jupiter. 'Which foot is it?'

'Off fore.'

I held her bridle and Alfred gently ran his hand down her foreleg and lifted her hoof to inspect it. 'No damage done,' he said. 'That's good.'

It had taken me a while to get to like this mysterious, wiry character with his thatch of white hair, wire-rimmed spectacles and mouth with very few teeth. With his heavy jaw, he always reminded me of a bulldog. Over these past few months, however, I'd grown to admire his gift with horses as well as his uncanny intuition, which he attributed to his Romany blood.

Even though over a year had passed since my mother had

told me the real story of her life, and how she had come to regard Alfred as family – namely, that she'd been adopted by a travelling fair and boxing emporium – I still found it hard to reconcile her prim and proper persona from my childhood with the irrational and somewhat wild romance writer. Her novels were steamy to say the least.

As I took off Jupiter's tack in her stable, I felt a wave of affection and gratitude for Edith. She had told me to regard the bay mare as if she was my own – something that thrilled me beyond measure.

I had ridden a lot as a child, but we had never been able to afford a horse, let alone keep one in the middle of London. Being given Jupiter was like a dream come true for a townie like me, and another reason why I could never imagine returning to live in the city.

Hearing the sound of voices, I looked over the half-door and saw eight-year-old Harry Honeychurch, sole heir to the earldom, hurrying into the yard. As always, he was dressed as his World War I aviation hero, Squadron Leader James Bigglesworth, complete with flying helmet, goggles and a white scarf. He was chattering to a girl of his own age who I did not recognise. Dressed in a coat that was far too large for her, she wore her blonde plaits under a beret, and was sporting sunglasses, despite the leaden sky and bouts of rain that had plagued us all morning.

'Don't run!' chided Alfred. 'Walk around the horses!'

'Sorry!' Harry yelled. 'We're looking for Stanford.'

'In here, sir!' I called out.

'Excellent, excellent!' Harry grabbed the young girl's hand

and they advanced. 'Allow me to introduce the newest member of our team. This is Special Agent Felicity – Fliss – Ridley.'

I stepped out to shake Harry's friend's hand. 'Very honoured to meet you, Special Agent Ridley.'

'*Bonjour.*'

'Is that French?' I asked.

'*Oui,*' she said. '*D'accord.*'

'You're French?'

Harry hooted with laughter. 'She's not French. She's pretending to be French because she's a double agent – working for us, of course.'

'Well, she fooled me,' I said.

'Fliss is top in her French class.'

'Are you at school together?' I asked.

'Yes, I recruited her,' said Harry. 'We've been working on a special assignment for ages – code name Operation Bridge Cottage.'

'Oh? Is it on a need-to-know basis, or can you give me a clue?'

Harry whispered in Fliss's ear. She whispered back in his. Then he nodded. 'We're conducting a surveillance operation from Falcon's Nest.'

Of course I knew Harry was referring to his tree house not far from Barton's Ridge, where Edith and I had been riding only this morning. It would afford an excellent view of Bridge Cottage and the dumpsite.

'We've been watching enemy movements at the … er … *ammunition* dump.' Harry withdrew a sheet of paper from the back pocket of his trousers. 'Here are our instructions.'

I scanned the list: date, time, location, description of ammo, number of boxes, physical description of enemy, enemy vehicle (if any), to include make, model, colour and number plate, proximity to crime, and weather (visibility).

'That's a very thorough list.' I was impressed, but also a little concerned. Even though I was sure the children would be safe in Falcon's Nest, not all fly-tippers were just regular householders wanting to get rid of an old sofa. There were serious criminals in the area who might do anything to avoid getting caught. It could be dangerous. I was surprised that Rupert would even suggest such a thing.

'I assume these are orders from the top?'

'That's right.' Harry nodded. 'It was Special Agent Kitten's idea.'

'A kitten?' I said. 'One of the cats has had kittens?' The yard boasted at least five feral cats that kept the rats at bay. 'Where are they?'

'No!' Harry hooted with laughter again. 'She's not a cat!'

'I'm confused,' I said.

'Here she is!' Harry waved, and I turned to see the most beautiful woman stride through the archway, accompanied by Harry's mother, Lady Lavinia.

The pair couldn't have looked more different. Whereas Lavinia's boyish frame was clad in muddy jodhpurs and her blonde hair was crushed under an unsightly slumber net, her tall, willowy companion wore skinny jeans and a stylish thigh-length white turtleneck knitted tunic bearing the EcoChamp badge.

I guessed her to be around the same age as Lavinia. She had perfectly highlighted blonde hair with a striking pale pink streak. A row of tiny stud earrings graced one of her ear lobes, and she wore EarPods connected to an iPhone that she held in her hand.

'Biggles! Good morning!' the beauty called out.

Alfred materialised by my side. 'That's Cassandra something-or-other,' he said in a low voice. 'You've got a rival there. Be careful.'

Chapter Three

I knew immediately who Cassandra was, though I had never met her. Not only did she have a space at Dartmouth Antique Emporium, she specialised in antique bears and dolls like me. She was also a former girlfriend of Lavinia's brother, Piers Carew – Aubrey's son – a man who I was currently dating, although it was early days and I was still very cautious about having *any* relationship at the moment. There had been a rumour that Piers and Cassandra had been betrothed at birth, but Piers had dismissed it as something their parents had hoped for when they were children, and I believed him.

Cassandra just radiated elegance and gorgeousness. I suddenly felt very untidy. My jodhpurs were still wet from my fall, I never wore make-up when I went out riding, and I had followed Lavinia's example of trapping my trademark Rapunzel-like locks under a slumber net.

I was about to introduce myself when Edith emerged from the tack room. 'Someone actually answered the phone at the police station this morning. What a miracle— Oh! Kitten!'

She broke into a broad smile. 'What a lovely surprise! When did you arrive?'

'Late last night, darling.' Cassandra kissed Edith on both cheeks. 'Caught the train from Paddington to Totnes and Lavinia picked me up from the station.'

'How was Greece?'

'Full of Greeks,' Cassandra quipped. 'Such delicious men.'

Lavinia looked at her friend with rapt adoration.

'Vinnie said I could stay, Edith,' said Cassandra. 'Do hope that's all right.'

'Of course,' said Edith. 'Although you'll be lowering your standards by staying at Honeychurch.'

'Rubbish!' Cassandra cried. 'As you know, I usually stay with Piers, but …' she paused to look directly at me, 'apparently not any more. *Tant pis.*'

'Oh, Kitten!' wailed Lavinia. 'But you *do* have the best guest room here. It has a storage heater that works and also a washbasin!'

'Which room have you given her, Lavinia?' Edith demanded.

'The Blue Bedroom.'

Edith winked at me. 'Is that the haunted one?'

Cassandra pretended to be scared. 'Please! No! Anywhere but the Blue Bedroom.'

Harry hurled himself into her arms. 'I'll protect you. So will Fliss … I mean Special Agent Ridley!'

'Oh goodness, you are too adorable for words.' She looked at Lavinia. 'Don't they remind you of Piers and me when we were their age?'

'Yes.' Lavinia nodded. 'You even wore plaits!'

'All in the past now, Vinnie,' said Cassandra. 'But Edith, I insist on paying my way.'

'Nonsense!' Edith exclaimed. 'You are our guest.'

'No, I *insist*. Besides, I've already told Mrs Cropper to take the weekend off. If I need any help, I'll use the housekeeper – what's her name?'

'Delia Evans,' said Lavinia. 'She's jolly good. Her hair is such a lovely colour. Like an aubergine.'

'They're all good until they become overfamiliar,' said Cassandra. 'Don't you agree, Edith?'

'Well, we're hoping this one will stay,' Edith said.

'Oh, I love your cooking, Kitten!' enthused Lavinia. 'Will you make your venison casserole?' Lavinia turned to me, eyes shining. 'Kitten was a chalet girl at Klosters. She is an incredible cook, Kat. Oh! Kitten and Kat! How funny is that!'

Cassandra ignored her. 'Edith? Where is your EcoChamp badge?' She pointed to her own. 'Aubrey won't like it if you don't wear one.'

'I'm wearing mine,' chipped in Lavinia. 'Oh, I was. It must have fallen off.'

'Did you know that we have broken the five thousand friends mark on our EcoChamp Facebook page?' Cassandra declared.

'Should that mean something to me?' said Edith.

'Oh, I forgot,' said Cassandra. 'You don't have the Internet here.'

I was about to say that I had a signal at the top of the drive, but decided against it.

'Golly. Five thousand friends!' Lavinia was agog. 'Does Daddy know?'

'Not yet. I can't wait to tell him.'

'You're so clever.' Lavinia turned to me again. 'Daddy adores Kitten.'

'Oh good,' I said.

'I see you don't have a badge either, Kat,' Cassandra went on. 'You'd better not let Aubrey see you without one. I'll give you a few.'

Harry and Fliss begged to be given badges too.

'Yes, yes, of course, darlings,' said Cassandra. 'Now, aren't you supposed to be on surveillance?'

'Yes!' they chorused.

'Do you have your two-way radio transmitters?' said Lavinia.

'Yes!' they chorused again and brandished their Motorola walkie-talkies.

'They've got a range of twenty-three miles,' Harry said. 'When can we get headsets like yours?'

'These?' Cassandra pointed to her EarPods. 'I'll see what I can do.'

'Wicked!' Harry exclaimed.

'Run along now, kiddies,' said Lavinia.

The children scampered off and Edith called to Mr Chips – who was still carrying the grubby sock – and followed them out of the yard.

'Radio transmitters?' Cassandra sounded impressed. 'Rupert must be feeling flush.'

'Oh no,' said Lavinia. 'It was Kat who bought them, for

Harry's eighth birthday. Mobile phone reception here is ab-so-lutely useless unless you are either on high ground or up a tree. Harry tends to wander off for hours. Now we can keep in touch with him all the time.'

'I am so sorry I missed his birthday, Vinnie,' said Cassandra. 'What a terrible godmother I am.'

'You were busy!' Lavinia exclaimed. 'You have such a busy life. Not like us here.'

'Speaking of which,' said Cassandra, 'aren't you going to formally introduce us?'

'Yes! So sorry,' said Lavinia. 'Kat Stanford, this is Cassandra Bowden-Forbes. She's my oldest and very best friend in the world. We call her Kitten—'

'Let me explain.' Cassandra rolled her eyes. 'Piers had a frightful lisp when he was little and couldn't pronounce my name properly. One day he just announced he'd call me Kitten, and the name has stuck.' She flashed a perfect smile. 'It's so good to meet you. I've heard a lot about you, and of course I am one of your biggest fans. In fact, I think watching you on *Fakes and Treasures* was what got me interested in becoming an antique dealer myself.'

'Kitten has been on the television too,' Lavinia put in. 'Did you see her? She starred in *Made in Monte Carlo*.'

Cassandra rolled her eyes again. 'A hideous reality TV show, but the producer was a friend and begged me to do just one season. I know *you* know what it's like being in the public eye.'

'I do,' I said. 'And I honestly don't miss it.'

'I'm sure we'll be firm friends.' Cassandra extended a hand

for me to shake. Her nails were perfect. Mine were grubby, but I took it all the same.

'Sorry, I'm a bit horsey,' I said.

'How is Jupiter?' Cassandra asked. 'Vinnie told me you'd been riding her. Isn't she divine? I've missed her so. We'll ride this afternoon, Vinnie. Excuse me ... Hey! You!' She snapped her fingers at Alfred, who was walking across the yard carrying two buckets filled with water.

'That's Alfred,' Lavinia said.

'Alfred!' Cassandra shouted. 'Get the horses ready. We'll be riding at two.'

'Jupiter has already been ridden this morning,' I said. 'She's also cast a shoe.'

'Oh.' A flicker of annoyance crossed Cassandra's flawless features. 'I was really looking forward to going out on her.'

Lavinia looked distressed. 'I'm sorry, but Kat ... well, Edith ... um. What about Duchess? She'll give you a good ride.'

Cassandra scowled. 'I always ride Jupiter when I come here. She won't mind a second ride. Can't the blacksmith come out today?'

'Not until Monday,' said Alfred firmly.

'Anyway, I thought you were going to the BearFest in Dartmouth tomorrow.' Lavinia was beginning to sound desperate. 'Isn't that why you came to Devon? Kat's the main presenter. She's doing valuations and everything, aren't you, Kat?'

'That's right,' I said.

'Piers is going to take Harry along,' Lavinia went on. 'It's going to be frightfully good fun.'

'I'll be there off and on,' said Cassandra lazily. 'Aubrey begged me to oversee the EcoChamp membership table we're setting up by the entrance. You'll give me a lift, won't you, darling?'

'Oh golly, Kitten, I can't. Edith and I have a Pony Club thing. I thought I told you.'

'Silly me!' Cassandra gave Lavinia a punch on the arm that I presumed was a sign of affection, but Lavinia cried out in pain.

'Ouch, I hate it when you do that.'

'All that ouzo has fried my brain.' Cassandra laughed. 'Don't worry. I suppose I could take a taxi – unless you can persuade Rupert to let me borrow that old Land Rover.'

Lavinia looked uncomfortable. 'Um. I'll see what kind of mood he's in.'

'I promise I won't hit anything. If someone hits me, well … No, don't worry. I'll probably go with Aubrey.'

'I can take you,' I said. 'But I'll be at the festival all day.'

'Thanks, but no thanks,' said Cassandra. 'There didn't seem much point in hiring a car since I'll be flying back to Athens on Wednesday.'

'Where in the Greek islands did you go?' I asked politely.

'Cruised around on Spyros's yacht.'

'He's her new man,' Lavinia declared. 'He's quite scrummy and frightfully, *frightfully* rich. A much better catch than silly old Piers.'

'Vinnie, *please*!' Cassandra said. 'It's OK. Really.' She gave a heavy sigh. 'Poor Vinnie still thinks there's something between her brother and me, but I can assure you, I moved on aeons ago. Four months – no, that's not true – *three* months, three weeks and four days ago, if we're actually counting.'

I didn't know what to say, so I said nothing. But I distinctly heard an alarm bell in my head. *Four months!* That would have been around the time Piers first asked me out for dinner. I wondered just how serious they had been prior to that, and why he hadn't told me.

'It was nice to meet you,' I said. 'I've got to get to the Emporium. There's a committee meeting this afternoon.'

'Ugh.' Cassandra pulled a face. 'I can't think of anything worse.'

Any further conversation was prevented by the arrival of a red van emblazoned with the words *Courier Parcel Service* on the side. The van stopped next to Cassandra and the driver opened the window. 'Looking for a Stanford?'

'Look no further,' said Cassandra, pointing to me. 'This is she. I'll take that.'

'Been driving around for hours trying to find this place,' he grumbled as he passed over a package. 'Half the signposts are missing on these country lanes … Here, print and sign your name, please.' He passed her a clipboard, which she handed on to me. I scribbled a signature, and the van sped away.

Cassandra studied the package. 'Good Lord! Ann *Summers*. Well, well, well – Piers *is* lowering his standards.'

For a moment I didn't know what she meant, but then I remembered that Ann Summers was a lingerie company with something of a saucy reputation – some of their lines catered primarily to the exotic.

I was mortified. 'I didn't order this.'

'Piers used to be more of an Agent Provocateur man,' said Cassandra. 'I suppose people change.'

'Excuse me,' I stammered. 'I need to get home and change.'

'I would if I were you,' said Cassandra. 'You'll catch your death in those wet jodhpurs.'

As I hurried away, I heard Lavinia say, 'Who is Ann Summers? Did she go to school with us?'

I'd left my Golf parked beyond the archway next to the service road and couldn't get there quickly enough. Could this really be from Piers? I was flustered and confused. I pulled out a Swiss Army penknife from the glove compartment and sliced through the tape.

Nestled in mounds of red and black tissue paper was a sheer black negligee trimmed with ostrich feathers and a matching thong. A pair of feathered mules dotted with Swarovski crystal beads completed the outfit.

I was dumbfounded. It was so not my style. Was this really how Piers saw me?

But then I spotted a black envelope embossed in gold. It must be a gift card, and it wasn't sealed.

I opened it and gasped.

To Iris, it read. *From your most ardent admirer.*

Chapter Four

My mother had an admirer? Not only an admirer, but someone who had actually gone to the trouble of buying her sexy lingerie.

I felt rather sick, and more than a little bit shocked.

It had been eighteen months since Dad had passed away from cancer. Mum had sworn she would never look at another man; that Frank had been the love of her life.

Besides, she was seventy now. Wasn't she too old for that kind for thing? Maybe she had bought the negligee for herself. But that made no sense. She would hardly send herself a card! However, I had noticed that she'd been taking a lot more care over her appearance the last few weeks. She'd told me that just because she didn't have much of a social life didn't mean she had to let herself go. Perhaps she was lying? Perhaps she did have an admirer, but who?

My mother rarely went to the Hare & Hounds pub, and when she did, it was with me. She spent her days writing and was always in a state of panic over her deadlines. On the regular occasions she and I went out together to see a play at the Northcott Theatre in Exeter, or a movie at the Barn Cinema at Dartington Hall, I'd never once seen her talking to a man.

Online matchmaking was not a possibility. Regardless of the fact that Mum did not have the Internet – the West Gatehouse was the only place on the estate where it was installed – she flatly refused to use a computer.

There was the Women's Institute, but I usually went along with her to meetings, and as far as I could recall, men were scarce.

I was really puzzled.

Now I had a problem. It was obvious that I had opened her parcel. I decided to wrap it back up again and claim it had been delivered damaged.

First, though, I had to nip back home for a quick shower. I zipped along the service road that ran parallel to the estate. Before World War I, most service roads were screened from the 'big house' by hedgerows, so that visiting guests would not see the amount of work required to keep them going.

The road ran past Honeychurch Cottages and the ivy-clad Victorian walled garden. The terrace of three had been built towards the end of the nineteenth century for the gardeners when the Hall was in its heyday. Now, it housed the Croppers – the cook and the butler; Eric Pugsley, the odd-job-man-cum-farmhand (who also ran the eyesore of a scrapyard next to Mum's carriage house); and the new housekeeper, Delia Evans, who seemed to love red geraniums.

Speak of the devil: just as I slowed down to navigate a particularly large crater, a stout woman of around my mother's age was leaning her bicycle against the wall of number 3. When she heard my car, she turned around and gave a friendly wave before disappearing inside carrying a canvas tote bag.

Lavinia was right. The colour of Delia's hair *was* aubergine. Not only that, it was unnaturally shiny and cut in a perfect chin-length bob.

It had been almost a year since a housekeeper had actually lived on the estate. Up until a month ago, Edith had relied heavily on a handful of local women from the nearby village of Little Dipperton to help out at the Hall. I hoped Delia would like it here.

Fifty yards further on, the road split, with the left branch circling back to the kitchen and the servants' quarters, and the right continuing up to the top of the hill to Jane's Cottage – my home – a converted summer house that had been built on the foundation of a former hunting lodge in the 1800s. Since it was a good half-mile from civilisation, I initially thought the isolation would bother me, but instead I loved the solitude, and the views were spectacular.

Just as I was parking my car, my mobile rang. The caller ID told me it was Piers.

'Hello, gorgeous,' he said. 'What are you wearing?'

'Actually, I'm wearing wet jodhpurs and I smell of horse.'

'Hmm. My favourite scent, especially when it's worn by you.'

I groaned. 'God. You are so predictable!'

Piers always came up with the corniest of lines. It was all part of his charm. He knew it exasperated me, but he liked to tease.

'I am seventy-five per cent sure that I will be cooking you dinner tonight,' he said.

'Seventy-five? That's hopeful.'

'I'll have a better idea in a few hours.'

'Well, I don't want a late night,' I said. 'I've got a big day tomorrow.'

'Don't worry,' he said. 'I'll be gone before the clock strikes midnight so that you can get your beauty sleep.'

'Speaking of beauty, I met Cassandra today.'

'Who?' Piers said.

'Cassandra? Your … your friend?'

'Oh! You mean *Kitten*.'

'Yes. Kitten.' For some reason the nickname bothered me.

'Father gave her that nickname,' said Piers, as if he were reading my thoughts.

'She told me you had a lisp and that *you* gave her the nickname.'

'Did I? Maybe I did. I can't remember. She's rather lovely, isn't she?'

I hesitated before saying, 'Yes.'

He laughed. 'You don't like her!'

'I do!' I protested. 'I hardly know her. I met her for five minutes.'

'You're not going to go all jealous on me, are you?'

'Of course not! Why would I?' But Cassandra's comment about Piers's preference for lingerie from Agent Provocateur hit me afresh. Maybe I *was* jealous.

'Don't worry. You won't be the first. Most women feel threatened by her.'

'Well, not me.' I'd made it quite clear to Piers that I wasn't looking for a serious relationship, but I had to admit that I quite enjoyed being the object of his ardour. Cassandra's reappearance was unsettling.

'Kitten spent most of the school holidays with us,' Piers continued. 'Her parents lived out in Saudi Arabia and only came back for Christmas. Her brother Hugo died when she was twelve, then her mother had a fatal car crash five years after that.'

'Oh, I'm sorry.' I felt terrible. 'I didn't realise. What about her father?'

'He lives in New York with his second wife,' said Piers. 'She never sees them. We're really all the family she has. You'll grow to like her. Just you see.'

Twenty minutes later, I'd showered, donned black jeans, a dark maroon cashmere sweater and leather ankle boots, and grabbed my raincoat. For the past week, the weather had been atrocious. Gusty wind and rain one moment, then watery sunshine the next. There wasn't time to wash my hair, so I just pulled it up into a messy topknot, but there *was* time to deliver the Ann Summers lingerie to my mother.

I was always struck by how pretty the Carriage House looked now. Thanks to Mum's vast royalty cheques, which came in regularly only to be squirrelled away in an offshore account in Jersey, the details of which I really did not want to know about, she had enlisted Alfred to help smarten it up.

When I'd first seen the property, I'd been horrified. Although the two-storey red-brick building had been covered in swathes of wisteria and Virginia creeper, it couldn't hide the crumbling brickwork, the cracked and broken windows and a slate roof full of gaping holes.

Knee-high weeds dotted with buttercups, thistles and ragwort had been replaced by window boxes full of red, pink and white geraniums. In the summer, roses filled the wooden planters that sat on the steps of the stone mounting block, and wild honeysuckle wrapped itself around the wishing well.

Today, however, a large orange skip stood in the middle of the courtyard like a beached whale, next to a grapple truck with the name *Crown Haulage & Clearance* above a mobile phone number. Mum had mentioned her plan to clear out the semi-derelict outbuildings that ranged around the cobbled courtyard. They were full of rusting farming equipment, useless bits of wood, old henhouses and metal feed bins. I was pleased to see that she had decided to rent a skip to haul it all away.

Just as I was wondering where the driver could be, a man in orange overalls and a pork pie hat emerged from the carriageway entrance.

I pulled up alongside him and opened my window. 'Can I help you?'

Chapter Five

'Troy King,' he said with a smile. 'Mrs Stanford?' The man was in his late twenties, with sandy-coloured hair and a rather sad-looking 'mouche' – a small patch of facial hair that was barely visible under his lower lip.

'I'm her daughter,' I said. 'Is she not home?' I could see inside the carriageway, where we now parked our cars. There was no sign of my mother's red Mini. I checked my watch. One thirty. Mum was a stickler for routine and always stopped for lunch between one and two.

'Doesn't look like it,' Troy said. 'I tried both the front and the back doors. Just need a signature.' He brandished a yellow delivery slip. Two signatures in one day!

I got out of the car and obliged.

'Just tell her to call when she wants the skip taken away.'

'Do I need to pay you anything right now?'

'Not until we pick it up. We charge by the day.' He glanced at my signature. 'Are you *the* Katherine Stanford from the telly? The antique dealer?'

'That's me.'

'Your photograph is all over the countryside for that bear festival tomorrow.' He smiled, showing a pair of boyish dimples. 'My mum's a great fan of yours. She'll be there tomorrow. Someone left her a fancy bear that she wants valued.'

'What's your mother's name?'

'Elsie. Elsie King.'

'Tell her to mention that we met.'

He nodded to the Carriage House. 'Pretty cool in there.'

'It is.'

'Nice to see it's being kept as it used to be rather than pulled down or converted into flats.'

'Yes,' I agreed. 'My mother wanted to keep all the original fixtures.' Alfred had worked hard on renovating and repairing the skylight that ran the length of the arch-braced roof. He'd also spruced up the rows of stalls that stood on either side of the carriageway, accessed through red-brick arches bearing the Honeychurch family coat of arms and motto. 'There used to be room for four carriages in here.'

'Cool,' he said again.

I decided I liked Troy.

We said our goodbyes just as Alfred appeared. I noticed he was wearing an EcoChamp badge.

'I see Cassandra has recruited you,' I said as Troy drove away.

He grunted an answer. 'Who was that?'

'Mum got a skip delivered,' I said. 'Looks like you're going to be busy.'

'She's still not back yet?' He checked his watch. 'Do you know where she is?'

'No.'

'She wasn't here this morning either – or she'd left early to do God knows what. I had to make my own breakfast,' he grumbled.

'What time did you come by this morning?'

'Eight thirty. I get up at six to see to the horses and then drop in for bacon and eggs. I don't think she came home last night either. The kettle was cold.'

'What do you mean?' My stomach did a strange flip-flop. It was so unlike my mother to disappear. Not only that, she had told me she was on a roll writing *Betrayed*, her latest novel, and that was why she had had to cancel our Thursday-night ritual of pizza and a rom-com DVD.

'She stopped by my flat last night to tell me that she had to go out urgently and wouldn't be able to play Snap.' It was another of my mother's evening rituals that I generally tried to avoid. There are only so many games of Snap a woman can play in a lifetime.

'But … go out *where*?' I demanded.

'Dressed up like a dog's dinner she was,' said Alfred in a tone of disgust. 'Lipstick and rather too much rouge for my liking.'

'Are you *sure*?' I had a thought. 'You don't think she decided to make an overnight trip to the Channel Islands?'

'She'd be a fool if she tried to do that,' said Alfred. 'That's my job.'

I couldn't have agreed more. My mother's secret offshore account with the National Bank in Jersey was a constant worry for me. Her reason for having it – *Why should the British*

government tax my hard-earned money? – was all the more iron-
ic given the fact that Dad had been an inspector with HM
Revenue & Customs. Unfortunately, Mum had gone too far
now to come clean, and her fear of being incarcerated for
evasion of taxes was well founded. Consequently, if ever she
needed access to a large sum of money – which had happened
many times with all the Carriage House renovations – Alfred
(whose idea it had been in the first place) had to go and get it
via the ferry from Weymouth. He would return with £9,999
because that was the maximum amount he could legally bring
into the UK without declaring it. Mum kept all this cash in a
suitcase in the attic.

All I knew about Alfred's past was that he had spent a
number of years in and out of various prisons at Her Majesty's
pleasure for assorted crimes ranging from forgery to robbing
banks. As far as I knew, he had not committed murder. Even
now I didn't know if he was on parole.

My mother was devoted to Alfred and had persuaded
Edith to take him on as the stable manager at the Hall – a job
that included a nice flat. The story Mum told was that Alfred
had been working with retired circus horses in Spain, which,
naturally, was a complete lie.

'And of course we can't call her because she refuses to
use a mobile phone.' I was exasperated. 'I'm relying on your
Romany intuition, Alfred. Should we be worried?'

'Not yet,' he said darkly. 'But I know she's up to something.'
He checked his watch again. 'I'll have to get back – unless you
can make me a sandwich?'

'Sorry,' I said. 'You'll just have to starve.'

Alfred scowled, turned on his heel and hurried off in the direction of the gate, from where a path through the pine forest provided a short cut to the stable yard.

I retrieved the package from the front passenger seat of my car and went into the Carriage House. Mum always left the door unlocked, which concerned me, but she was adamant, claiming this was the way people did it in the country. She had a habit of leaving her car keys in the ignition as well, but in the end I gave up nagging her.

I suppose I could easily have left the package on the kitchen table, but my mother's disappearance had aroused my curiosity. I headed upstairs to her office.

A grey metal filing cabinet five drawers high stood in one corner. In another was the standard lamp from the sitting room in Tooting, Dad's leather wingback chair, and a hexagonal table stacked with *Country Life* and *The Lady* magazines.

Set against one wall was our old dining room table, on which stood Dad's Olivetti typewriter and a stack of neatly arranged typewritten pages. The top page had *Storm/Betrayed* typed in the top left-hand corner. I read:

Ada knew she could never tell anyone about her late-night visitor, but oh, how she longed to. She felt her face burn with shame as she remembered his touch on her naked breasts and how she had begged him to take her right there on the cold stone floor. Ever since Ada had arrived at the Hall, she had been violently attracted to the duke's youngest son. Even Millie, the parlourmaid, had warned her of Gerald's weakness for pretty girls with long red hair, but Ada believed she was different. Why else would he have given her such luxurious silk underdrawers?

I set the package on top of the pile of pages and hoped that my mother would appreciate her twenty-first-century silk underdrawers. And again I couldn't help thinking: who was this 'ardent admirer'? It was driving me crazy.

As I left Mum's office, I peeped into her bedroom. A variety of dresses had been tossed on to the bed; shoes had been pulled out of their boxes and lay scattered on the floor. It was so unlike my mother not to put her things away. Used tissues lay balled up on the kidney-shaped dressing table, and a palette of blusher – or rouge, as my mother insisted on calling it – lay open along with a jar of translucent face powder.

Even though Mum's personal life was her own, I'd actually believed that apart from her writing, she didn't really have one. But now it was clear that she did.

There was no mystery to this at all.

My mother had been meeting a man.

Chapter Six

My mind was spinning. I ran through the available men I could think of, but drew a blank. There was Eric Pugsley, who ran the scrapyard next door, but my mother made no secret of the fact that she barely tolerated him. There was the vet, but he had to be at least twenty years her junior.

As I pulled out of the tradesmen's entrance, however, and into Cavalier Lane, I forgot all about my mother.

The black Citroën I had seen earlier was parked in front of a five-bar gate just a little way up the hill. And yet again, the man was looking through his binoculars.

Without another thought, I turned left instead of right. He saw me. Leapt off the gate. Wrenched his car door open and floored it.

There was only one direction to go in this time – mine.

The Citroën roared past me, clipping my wing mirror. I caught a glimpse of a man in his fifties wearing heavy-rimmed glasses and with a full head of thick grey hair.

I thought of Edith's remark about his being a birdwatcher

– it was possible. It was also possible that he was a journalist for a foreign magazine, but if so, wouldn't he have wanted to bombard me with questions? Then I had a horrible thought. What if he was some kind of stalker?

I'd had one before, years ago. It had been very upsetting – a young man was convinced he was in love with me and took to camping outside my house for hours on end. The day I walked in and found him asleep in my bed was one I would never forget. In the end, the case went to court. I never wanted to go through that again.

I hoped Edith had reported him to the police, but it wouldn't hurt for me to report him too. With any luck, I would get Malcolm the desk sergeant at the local nick, and not Detective Inspector Shawn Cropper. Things between us had grown strained ever since Shawn learned that I had spent a weekend in Paris with Piers. Nothing physical had happened between us other than a few kisses. True to his word, Piers had been the perfect gentleman. I'd had my own room, with not so much as an interconnecting door.

Unfortunately, fate had other ideas. As I drew close to the hawk-topped granite pillars that marked the main entrance to Honeychurch Hall, I saw a police panda car parked outside the West Gatehouse beyond. Shawn emerged from the driver's seat and waved me down. He was wearing an EcoChamp badge.

I opened my window, surprised that I felt a twinge of nerves. 'Are you looking for me?'

'I'm afraid so.'

'Am I in trouble?' I teased.

He did not smile. 'Possibly. Please would you step out of your car?'

'I'm on the way to an appointment,' I said. 'Will this take long?'

'It depends.'

Perplexed, I pulled in behind his panda and got out.

Shawn retrieved a pair of disposable gloves from the trench coat he always wore, rain or shine, and endeavoured to get them on. The fingers were all stuck together, but he was determined.

Lanky, with a mop of curly brown hair and striking dark brown eyes with specks of gold, Shawn had a penchant for unusual ties that he blamed his twin boys for choosing. Today he sported a turquoise one covered in red and black dinosaurs. It really was hideous, but I refrained from making a comment. He was obviously not in a joking mood.

Finally, the gloves were on.

'What have I done?' I said.

'This way please, Ms Stanford.' He gestured for me to follow him to the boot of his car. So, I *was* in trouble. He never addressed me as 'Ms' unless it was police business.

He opened the boot. Inside was a very large thick plastic bag containing what looked like a torn black dustbin liner. Household waste pooled in the bottom. It looked disgusting. He lifted it out and upended the contents on to the ground.

'What are you doing?' I exclaimed.

Returning to the boot, he retrieved a long litter picker tool with a sharp spike and started poking around the debris.

Food waste mingled with a box that had once held gran-ny knickers, with the words *Reinforced Gusset* stamped on the side, a bottle of breath mints bearing the slogan *Kills Halitosis Instantly!* and a tube of paste to wax that *unsightly upper lip*, along with several Tena Lady incontinence pads still in their cellophane wrappings.

Puzzled, I watched as Shawn nudged a crumpled pink box revealing five half-eaten doughnuts. I stared at them in rising horror. Surely those weren't the doughnuts I'd bought a few days ago? I'd eaten just half of each before throwing them away, determined to start yet another new diet.

He spiked a wad of sodden envelopes and offered them to me. 'Yours, I presume?'

I was stunned. He was right. The envelopes had my name and address on them. There was even a subscription reminder from the *Antiques Trade Gazette*.

'The doughnuts are mine too,' I said slowly. 'But absolute-ly nothing else ... Oh, wait.' I'd spied a blue-and-white-striped sock. It was the mate to Mr Chips's treasure. No wonder it had looked familiar. 'And yes, the sock.' I couldn't help it. I actually laughed. 'Seriously? I would never use ... well ... those prod-ucts are—'

'Fly-tipping is a criminal offence,' Shawn said coldly. 'It can cause serious pollution of the environment, risk human health and harm wildlife and farm animals.'

'I know that—'

'Fines, especially for repeat offenders, can be as much as fifty thousand pounds, along with a possible prison sentence of up to five years.'

'Yes. I am fully aware of those facts, but none of that rubbish belongs to me. Except for the doughnuts and the envelopes,' I said again. 'I know the South Hams County Council recycling rules off by heart. Let me see, blue sacks for newspapers and cardboard; clear sacks for plastic bottles, tins and aerosol cans; brown bins for food and garden waste and grey bins for everything else.' I had a thought. 'Where did you find that bin bag?'

'The dowager countess called the station this morning to report it,' said Shawn.

'What!' I couldn't believe it. 'Don't tell me ... it was found blocking the entrance to a bridleway on Barton's Ridge?'

'Yes!' Shawn seemed surprised. 'How did you know?'

'Because I was there when she found it.' How infuriating! 'I can't believe you went through it all. What a horrible job.'

'Not exactly pleasant, no,' said Shawn. 'In cases like these, one of the first things we do is sift through the rubbish to see who it belongs to.'

'That's rather time-consuming.'

'But effective – as you can see.'

'Did Edith happen to mention a man in a black Citroën acting suspiciously?'

'Yes,' said Shawn. 'She mentioned it was a left-hand drive and that she couldn't see the number plate.'

'There was one of those blue European Union flag stickers,' I said. 'If that helps.'

'She mentioned that too. But unfortunately, since he was not trespassing on private land, there isn't much we can do until he steps out of line. Meanwhile, let's talk about your rubbish.'

I started to walk away.

'Where are you going?'

'I want to show you something.'

I took the path around the side of the East Gatehouse to the old potting shed where I kept all the bins and bags neatly organised.

The first thing I saw when I opened the door was a fly-tipping sign – presumably the very one that Rupert had declared stolen from Bridge Cottage.

No fly-tipping!
Flycapture installed here!
Maximum penalty: £50,000
Hotline: 803 555 111

'Oh!' I exclaimed.

'Ah,' said Shawn.

I was seething. 'OK. Someone is trying to frame me.'

'Hmm.'

'Come on, Shawn,' I said, exasperated. 'You know I would never steal a sign, and as you can see, all my recycling bags are perfectly organised – obsessively so.' I looked at him and fancied I saw the beginnings of a tiny smile.

'I was worried when I saw the box for the granny pants,' he said. 'But yes, I believe you're right. This is someone's idea of a practical joke.'

'It's not funny,' I said.

'Perhaps a fan with a warped sense of humour?'

'I suppose it's possible.'

Once I'd agreed to headline the BearFest, the organiser, Fiona Reynolds, had used her contacts from her corporate special events days to pull out all the stops. True, I had been getting a lot of exposure, but would someone really go to all this trouble to try to embarrass me? It wouldn't be the first time that I'd received what amounted to hate mail. My assistant used to handle all that. She'd shield me from the nasty letters and just pass along the nice ones.

'Do you think it is someone you know?' Shawn went on. 'The mystery man in the Citroën?'

I shrugged. 'I have no idea.'

I thought of Cassandra. Was this the kind of thing she would do? But according to Lavinia, Cassandra had only arrived by train the night before. Besides, given her zeal as Aubrey's EcoChamp campaign manager, I thought it highly unlikely.

'Are you worried about this man, Kat?' Shawn seemed concerned.

'A little.'

'You might want to put a padlock on that storage shed.'

'Yes. I shall.'

'And at Jane's Cottage as well,' he said.

'I have to bring my rubbish here because the dustmen can't get their lorry up there – it's too narrow.'

'If you see that man again, call my mobile,' he said. 'Call me any time at all.'

'Will you answer it?'

'If it rings, yes.' Shawn smiled. 'Or the police station, but only between nine and five Monday to Friday … but probably my home number is better. Do you have it?'

'Yes.'

'Good.'

An uncomfortable silence fell between us.

'Are you bringing the twins to the BearFest tomorrow?' I asked for something to say.

'Wouldn't miss it for the world.' He picked up the fly-tipping sign. 'I'm sure his lordship will be happy to have this back.'

I had an awful thought. 'Did you have to file an official report?'

'Unfortunately, yes,' said Shawn. 'Malcolm took the call from the dowager countess.'

'I suppose there isn't much I can do now.'

'That's how they caught the ice-skater woman,' he went on. When he realised I hadn't any idea what he was talking about, he said, 'Tonya Harding? That's how the FBI found out about the hit. The plan was found on a scrap of paper left in a dumpster outside a bar in Portland, Oregon.'

'Oh.'

'You can tell a lot about a person from their rubbish.'

'Except for mine,' I reminded him. 'Can't you *un*file the report?'

'I'm sorry, but no.' Shawn had the grace to look uncomfortable. 'All fly-tipping incidents are sent directly to the Earl of Denby.'

'Oh dear.' This was bad news.

'The offender is put on his watch list,' he went on. 'As you know, he's the presiding magistrate and a bit tough when it comes to this sort of thing.' He touched his EcoChamp badge. 'In fact, he's merciless.'

'Yes, I know.'

'You could always ask your boyfriend to put in a good word,' said Shawn with ill-disguised sarcasm.

'Piers is—'

'Save your breath,' he said somewhat rudely. At the mention of Piers, it was as if a switch had been flipped.

'I was just—'

'You need to clear that up.' He gestured to the rubbish on the ground.

'Oh.' I was annoyed. 'In that case, can I borrow some disposable gloves?'

'Sorry, those were my last pair.' And without another word, he left.

It took me half an hour of tidying up before I could set off for the committee meeting in Dartmouth. I was going to be late.

It was pure luck that I didn't hit my mother's Mini as she turned into Cavalier Lane, hogging the middle of the road. We both slammed on the brakes. Mum's car stalled. I drove up alongside.

At first I didn't think she was going to open her window, but when she did, I caught the strains of Elton John's 'Rocket Man' from her CD player.

'I thought you hated Elton John!' I said.

'You drive too fast for these narrow lanes,' said Mum.

'Where on earth have you been?

Chapter Seven

'Do I have to tell you everything I do?' Mum retorted.

'You told me you had a deadline.'

She looked defiant. 'I went to see a friend.'

'Who?' I demanded. 'Which friend?'

I took in her usual Marks & Spencer outfit – a cream jumper under a dark green puffa jacket. A pretty scarf in autumnal rust, gold and amber was tied at her throat, only partially hiding an EcoChamp badge. Her make-up was immaculate, although I did detect dark circles under her eyes. I thought back to the bed strewn with discarded clothes and tried to see if there was an overnight case in the back of her car, but I couldn't tell.

'Alfred told me he's not eaten since yesterday,' I went on.

'I'm getting fed up with feeding Alfred,' my mother grumbled. 'It's like having a husband all over again. He's come to expect two, sometimes three meals a day, and it's got to stop.'

'Were you out all night?'

'No,' Mum snapped. 'And if I were, it's none of your business.'

'It is if I have to call the police and report a missing person.'

My mother's eyes widened. 'You wouldn't!'

'I might have done. Come on, Mum. I tell you everything. Why the secrecy?'

'There is no secrecy. Delia and I went out last night for a meal.'

'The new housekeeper?'

'Yes. She started at the Hall a month ago and we've rather hit it off.'

'So you *did* come home last night.'

'Of course I came home,' Mum exclaimed. 'What are you implying exactly? I'm not chained to my desk, you know. And this morning I got up early to go shopping in Exeter.'

'Where is your shopping?'

'Really, Katherine! Who do you think you are? The Spanish Inquisition?'

'No. A concerned daughter who was worried you could end up in a ditch somewhere, and since you refuse to use a mobile, it could be weeks before your body was found.'

'You're so dramatic.'

'Anyway, a rather interesting package arrived for you,' I said.

'Interesting?'

'Don't worry, I didn't open it.' Now it was my turn to lie. 'I left it in your office. Also, that haulage company dropped off the skip. I signed for it.'

'Thank you, dear. Is that it? Is that the end of all the questions?'

'For now,' I said darkly. 'Oh – just one more thing …'

'*What?*'

'Where did you get that EcoChamp badge?'

'This? This old thing … I can't remember. Oh, wait, yes. I got it at the post office. That dreadful Aubrey Carew is forcing everyone to wear one. What happened to your wing mirror?'

'I got side-swiped by a black Citroën,' I said. 'The driver had binoculars and a camera with a telephoto lens.'

Mum's demeanour changed in a flash. 'Oh darling, I do hope you haven't got another stalker.'

'I had thought of that too,' I said. 'But Edith thinks it could be a birdwatcher.'

'Or perhaps a journalist?' Mum suggested. 'Let's try to be optimistic. That would be nice, wouldn't it? Back in the spotlight again.'

'Let's hope so.'

'Come by for supper and we'll talk about it.'

'I can't this evening.'

'Why?' she said. 'What are you doing? Do you have a date?'

'I'm busy.'

'Who with?'

'It's none of your business!' I exclaimed.

'Now see how you like all those questions.' There was a hint of smugness in her voice. 'Is it Shawn? Has he come to his senses at last? Or is it that lunatic Piers?'

'I'll stop in on my way home. Goodbye, Mother.'

Dartmouth was one of my favourite fishing ports. Steeped in history that could be traced back to the Celts and the Saxons, the town had attracted all manner of traders, dealers, cutpurses and thieves. One of my favourite stories involved the capture by Sir Francis Drake of the *Nuestra Señora del Rosario*, the 'pay ship' from the infamous Spanish Armada. It was reportedly anchored in the River Dart for more than a year, and the crew used as labourers on the nearby Greenway estate, Agatha Christie's former summer home, which was now owned by the National Trust.

I had a sudden thought. My mother had just recently applied to volunteer as a guide at the property. Perhaps she had met her admirer there?

I pulled into the Dartmouth Antique Emporium car park, which was just a few minutes outside the centre of town. Bunting and coloured flags hung from the eaves of the newly converted barns, and a massive billboard poster of a heavily airbrushed me was positioned by the front entrance with the promise of an exceptional day out.

Meet Kat Stanford
Former host of *Fakes and Treasures*
Celebrating 116 years of teddy bears 1902–2018
Valuations, auction, raffles and more!
Special guest: Paddington Bear
Tickets: Adults £25, children free

For me, a lot was riding on the success of this first ever bear festival in Dartmouth. I desperately needed more business and the exposure it would bring – even if that meant being tailed by the paparazzi. Perhaps I hadn't been completely forgotten by the media if an international magazine was sending one of their journalists out to rural Devon.

Initially I'd rented a space at the Emporium just for the summer, but I found I enjoyed the company of kindred spirits. Even though I was happy with my antique shop at the West Gatehouse, foot traffic was wishful thinking. I had decided to implement an appointment-only system, otherwise I could easily have sat there all day and not seen a soul.

Inside the Emporium were twenty-five spaces individually rented by a variety of dealers. Not every dealer was there every day, and the general idea was that we would all help each other out. A roster showed who was working that day and who was not. Some spaces were just small booths that specialised in one field, like mine; others had larger areas to accommodate furniture and display cases. It was an emporium in the true sense of the word. Mahogany long-case clocks brushed shoulders with vintage gramophone players; old leather-bound books and maps, oriental carpets and tapestries jostled with china figurines, model animals and ceramics.

I parked my car and headed for the front entrance, where gales of laughter were coming from a trio of women clustered around a dapper man in his mid sixties sitting in a wheelchair. One woman cuffed him lightly on the shoulder and said, 'You are a rogue, Major!'

The major saw me coming and shouted, 'Look who it is, ladies! It's tomorrow's star attraction!'

I waved a greeting.

'Come and say hello, my lovely – oh, don't go, ladies!' The women were making their excuses, seemingly glad of the opportunity to escape. As they passed me, I overheard, 'What a terrible flirt! He's a dirty old man!' and 'He's lonely, Val, that's all,' and 'A doctor should look at that sting before it gets infected.'

'Ah, come and talk to an old soldier,' the man said. 'I'm Major Timothy Gordon, but everyone calls me Major.'

'Hello,' I said, taking his outstretched hand. 'Kat Stanford.'

Bright blue eyes sparkled behind wire-rimmed spectacles above a neat pencil moustache, but it was hard to miss the nasty red bump on his cheekbone.

The major wore a flat tweed cap, a herringbone blazer adorned with medals and the distinctive yellow regimental badge of the Parachute 2 Club. A red tartan blanket covered his legs. At the base of his chair was a pewter tankard filled with coins, and a hand-written sign saying:

Goal today

Supper – with a nice nip of whisky!

I pulled out my purse and put in a five-pound note. 'I can't have a man live without his whisky.'

'Laphroaig is my poison,' he said. 'Speaking of poison ...' He gestured to the unsightly bump on his face. 'Got stung by a wasp. Of course I couldn't get away from the little bugger. Someone told me that if you want to escape from a wasp, you run in a straight line. If you zigzag and wave your arms around, it sees a big target and ... well, the little bugger saw me.'

'It looks painful.'

'Not as painful as this.' He tapped the tartan blanket. 'Falklands. Parachute Regiment.'

'I'm so sorry.'

'Stepped on a landmine,' said the major. 'Lost my lower leg.'

'I'm so sorry,' I said again. 'I really have to go. I'm already late for a meeting.'

'No, wait!' He gave a sheepish grin. 'Full disclosure. I've actually been waiting for you to arrive.'

My heart sank. He must have seen it in my face, because he seemed hurt. 'Oh, never mind. I know you're busy.'

'No ... I mean, yes, I am busy but—'

'It's a big favour,' said the major. 'I hope you'll say yes.'

'Why don't you tell me what this favour is, and then we'll see?'

Chapter Eight

'What would you say if I told you that I had in my possession some extremely valuable merchandise?'

'I would say I'm intrigued,' I said carefully. 'But I feel I must tell you that military memorabilia is not my strong suit.'

'Who said anything about military memorabilia? I'm talking about bears. Rare bears.'

'OK: I'm intrigued. Go on.'

'I want you to come to my humble abode today and take a look at what I've got.' He wiggled his eyebrows and gave me a blatant leer. 'Don't worry. You're quite safe. I can't invite you upstairs to come and see my etchings. Couldn't even get upstairs if I tried.'

'Why don't you bring the bears to the BearFest tomorrow?' I said. 'The valuation is free for ticket holders. I would have to charge you if I came to your house.'

'I know, but I'd rather pay you. The thing is ...' He paused for a moment. 'I don't want to make a spectacle of myself. Bears aren't exactly manly, are they?'

'It depends on what kind of bear you mean.'

'Not a grizzly, that's for sure.' He laughed. 'No, tiny little chaps about so high.' He opened his thumb and finger to demonstrate. 'Maybe three to four inches?'

'They could be mascot bears.' During the war years, J. K. Farnell – the company that manufactured the first teddy bear in 1906 – produced these bears in their thousands. Sold for just a shilling, they were given to the men fighting at the Front as a reminder of home. 'Go on.'

'My grandfather fought on the Somme. He was killed but the bears came back with all his personal effects.'

'You have mascot bears that survived the *Somme*?' Finding a mascot bear that had actually been to battle was a collector's dream. They were unbelievably rare. In fact, the last such bear was sold for £4,230 back in 2002. His name was Edwin and he had belonged to Second Lieutenant Percy Kinnersley Baddesley, one of 420,000 British casualties in a battle that symbolised the horrors of World War I. When Percy died, Edwin was sent back to his wife, Verna, who cherished the bear for the rest of her life.

The major cleared his throat. 'I want to say … would they be … *Campbell* bears?'

My heart skipped a beat. Campbell bears were hard to find. Brothers David and Guy Campbell had amassed an incredible collection of 398 mascot bears of varying colours over a period of years. Their collection was sold at auction in May of 1999 to Leandra Harwood at Sotheby's, who then split them up into red, white and blue sets. The bears were given swing tags and put inside little leather suitcases along with booklets telling the Campbells' astonishing story.

'You're right about having some valuable merchandise,' I said. 'I definitely want to see them.' I thought for a moment. 'You did say *bears*, as in plural. How many do you have?'

'Three,' said the major.

I thought for a moment. 'I would much prefer it if you brought them tomorrow. We'll have media coverage and I suspect the kids would love to see them close up.'

He shook his head. 'No. It could tarnish my macho image. I'm more of a guns-and-daggers kind of man.'

I laughed. 'OK. I'll come by later. Where do you live?'

'Riverview retirement village. It's a village that does not have a view of the river. In fact, it's behind a rather ugly storage facility off the A381. Here's the address.' He handed me a scrap of paper.

'You came prepared,' I said.

'That's me. *Utrinque Paratus!* Ready for Anything! I'll expect you at seventeen hundred hours.'

'Make it closer to six p.m.,' I said. 'I have a busy afternoon – oh, and Major, this valuation is with my compliments. I wouldn't want to deprive a man of his whisky money.'

'Then I won't keep you any longer.' He pointed to his mobility vehicle, which was parked in a disabled parking space. 'I'll be off home.'

'Do you need help?'

'I can manage. I've been doing this for years.'

Bidding him goodbye, I headed into the Emporium.

Fiona and her marketing guru husband, Reggie, had moved to Dartmouth from London ten years ago. They had bought the barn and surrounding outhouses and transformed them into a bustling antique market. A gourmet coffee shop had recently been added, along with outside seating in the interior courtyard. But today, a Clearspan tent structure had been erected over it at great expense. It was here that the main events would take place.

I found Fiona in the vestibule, arguing with a scruffy young woman in a fluorescent green sweatshirt and jeans. The sweatshirt bore the EcoChamp logo.

'No, Sandra,' Fiona scolded. 'People are here for the BearFest. They don't want to see that when they walk in.'

A large board was covered in graphic photographs of fly-tipping dumpsites. One showed a cow eating part of a plastic tarpaulin.

Save our countryside!
Protect our livestock!
Become an EcoChamp!
JOIN TODAY!

Sandra dug her heels in. 'The Earl of Denby says it's the visual material that attracts supporters. This is the perfect place. Right near the entrance.'

'I highly doubt the earl will come,' said Fiona. 'So he'll never know. You can set up outside the loos – now run along.'

Sandra was about to protest, but Fiona was adamant. 'Shoo! Off you go.' Then she turned to me and smiled. 'Ah. I thought you weren't coming.'

'I got held up,' I said.

'We're short of volunteers. Have you seen Cassandra

Bowden-Forbes? She gave me her assurance that she was going to pitch in today.'

Cassandra had said nothing of the sort to me.

Fiona gave a heavy sigh. 'This really is too bad. We didn't see her all summer either.'

I didn't know what to say.

'Aren't you a friend of hers?'

I assumed it was because Cassandra and I both specialised in antique bears and toys that Fiona would think so. 'Not really. I only met her briefly for the first time today.'

'*Today?* You saw her today?'

'Briefly,' I said again, wishing I had thought to keep my mouth shut.

'Well? What did she say? Did she say she was coming or not? It's for her benefit as well, you know.'

'It was very brief,' I said for the third time, but Fiona didn't seem to hear. It wasn't often I saw her frazzled. Usually she wore a neat navy suit, but this afternoon she was dressed in jeans and a black sweater.

'As you know, here at the Emporium we all pull together and help each other out,' she went on. 'But clearly Ms Bowden-Forbes thinks she is the exception. That's the problem with these socialites.'

I smiled politely and changed the subject. 'Tell me what you'd like me to do.'

Fiona sighed again. 'We really needed her to run through the timing of the programme.'

'Am I missing something? Why would we need Cassandra to run through the timing of the programme?'

'Because she is in it now.'

'Cassandra is in the *programme*?' This was a surprise to me. She hadn't mentioned that either.

Fiona must have sensed my confusion because she added, 'She'll be doing a few valuations, too. Her father is an old friend of Reggie's and one of the main sponsors for this event, and asked a favour.'

I felt my jaw drop. I only just managed to keep my misgivings to myself. Not for a minute had I assumed that Cassandra was a serious antique dealer, but clearly I was wrong.

'She'll take over from you at noon,' said Fiona. 'I thought you'd probably be ready for a break before you do your presentation. She was so determined to be part of the programme. Of course, she's a celebrity in her own right and will prove quite a draw. Did you see her on that awful reality show, *Made in Monte Carlo*?'

'No.'

'She ran an antique shop on the show.'

To my dismay, I felt weird about this revelation. The antique bears and dolls world was my special domain. It had taken me decades to learn my craft.

'Between you and me,' Fiona went on, 'I would have thought there were plenty of places far more glamorous than Dartmouth to set up shop.'

'I would have thought so too.' I forced a smile.

'But apparently her fiancé lives nearby and she expects to be here more often.'

My stomach turned over. '*Fiancé?*'

'Viscount Chawley? You know, the Earl of Denby's son?

Quite the playboy, I hear. Well, enough of all this gossiping. Shall we go into my office?'

Fiona's comment about Piers had me floored. I knew it wasn't true *now*, but had it been true before? It made me feel off balance and I didn't like it one bit.

The committee meeting went by in a blur and I was determined not to think about Cassandra again.

Tomorrow promised to be an exciting event. I was especially looking forward to giving my presentation, since it ended with the audience voting on the top ten most loved bears of all time.

As well as the valuations that would go on throughout the day, there was a mobile bear hospital offering procedures such as eye transplants, paw pad restoration, new noses and of course the very popular growlectomies. A lot of people had already signed up for the bear-making workshop, where fans could purchase everything necessary – mohair fabrics, stuffing, eyes, nose threads and felt – and make their own bears on the spot. Other attractions included a local artist on hand to sketch portraits of favourite bears and their owners, and an adoption centre for bears – orphaned and unwanted – that needed new homes. The finale would be a spectacular raffle, with the grand prize being a 1900s humpback Steiff bear called Alexander, donated by me.

It was gone six by the time I left the Emporium and set off to see the major.

Riverview retirement village was easy to find. At one time the location would have had a lovely view of the River Dart. Now, an ugly range of self-storage buildings was in the way.

One had a banner reading *Crown Haulage & Clearance* – the same company that had delivered a skip to Mum's carriage house earlier this morning.

An effort had been made to make the retirement village attractive. Accessed down a paved path lined with low box hedges and neatly pruned rose trees, twelve red-brick bungalows with tiny dormer windows and matching red doors were set around a perfectly manicured bowling green. White-painted wooden seats were dotted around the perimeter.

A grey-haired woman in her early fifties with enormous red-framed glasses emerged from one of the bungalows holding a birdcage. Inside was a canary. She wore an EcoChamp badge pinned to her beige raincoat.

I was beginning to feel as if I was the only person on the planet who wasn't wearing one.

'Can I help you?' she said.

'I think I know where I'm going. Number four? Major Gordon?'

The woman stared at me and then broke into a smile. 'You're Kat Stanford, aren't you?'

'Yes.'

'I'd recognise you anywhere. It's your hair. No wonder they call you Rapunzel.'

'I haven't been called Rapunzel in quite a while,' I said.

'So pleased to meet you,' she beamed. 'I'm your biggest supporter. I never missed an episode of *Fakes and Treasures* when you were the host. I don't like the new person much. Sorry – I'm Elsie King,' she ran on. 'I'm the warden here.'

A man with a grey beard, dressed in a sports jacket and

slacks, came out of the bungalow. He was carrying a black leather bag. 'All done, Elsie.'

'I'll take it from here, thanks, Dr Smeaton,' said Elsie. 'This is Kat Stanford. She used to be on the telly.'

'Ah yes,' said the doctor. 'My wife was a big fan.' He turned to Elsie. 'You're sure you'll take the canary?'

'I told Miss Philpot I'd look after him.'

'You're a saint. See you next time.'

Elsie turned back to me. 'I can never say no. I've got quite the menagerie now.'

'How many animals do you have?'

'Five cats and now one bird,' she said. 'You'd be surprised at how much we have to handle when there's a death if there's no family involved.'

'Oh, I see.'

'Orphaned pets, piles of personal papers and photographs … but that's all part of the job. Now the major, he's got a daughter in New Zealand.'

'Ah.'

'Yes. I know everything about my residents,' Elsie continued. 'He was quite the war hero. His wife died years ago. Pity about his leg. Blown clean off at the knee at some famous battle or other. And now he's got that infection on his face.' She tut-tutted. 'I told him Dr Smeaton would give him some antibiotics, but he said no. Didn't want to appear soft.'

'Ah,' I said again.

'I'm walking that way. He keeps his door unlocked, so just go on in …' She frowned. 'Are you valuing something for the major?'

'Possibly.'

'I'm coming to the festival tomorrow,' said Elsie. 'I've got a fancy bear and a Lalique vase I want valued as soon as possible.'

'I'm only valuing bears tomorrow. Sorry about that.'

'Troy said I was to tell you I was coming.'

'Of course!' I said. 'You're Troy's mother. Yes, he did.'

'So can't you make an exception?'

'If I make an exception with you, then I would have to do that with everyone,' I said. 'But I could come back on Monday.'

'I'd have to pay for that, though, wouldn't I?' Elsie frowned. 'What about popping into my house now and having a quick look? It would only take a minute.'

'I'm really sorry, but I can't,' I said firmly. I wanted to add that I did have a business to run, but bit my tongue.

Elsie's jaw hardened. 'I could put more business your way, you know. The turnover here at Riverview is quite fast, especially during the flu season. I'm always asked if I know of anyone who can do valuations. Call it quid pro quo. You scratch my back and I'll scratch yours.'

I didn't reply. I was beginning to dislike Elsie.

We stopped outside number 4. A wheelchair ramp extended from the pavement up to the front door.

I withdrew my business card from my tote bag. 'It was good to meet you, Elsie,' I said. 'Here's my card – just in case you want to make an appointment.'

She took it, albeit reluctantly, then turned on her heel and walked off without another word, swinging the birdcage.

I felt that I had just made an enemy.

Chapter Nine

'I'd rather given up on you.' The major was waiting in the hallway when I pushed open his front door. Elsie was right. It wasn't locked.

'It was a busy afternoon. I am sorry.'

'Punctuality is the politeness of kings.'

I wanted to point out that I had come as a favour, but the truth was that I really wanted a look at the mascot bears.

The major had removed his jacket and was wearing an olive-green military jumper along with his regimental tie.

'Follow me.' He deftly reversed down the hall and swivelled the wheelchair into the kitchen. I took in the dozens of framed photographs of his military endeavours that lined both walls.

A narrow staircase led to upstairs. 'Spare bedroom,' he said. 'Elsie makes it up for when my daughter comes to visit. She lives in New Zealand.'

The kitchen was spotlessly clean and rather sterile. It had been adapted for his disability with low counters and plenty of room to manoeuvre his wheelchair. With a thrill, I spotted a little tan leather suitcase with the initials F. H. B. embossed on a brass tag on the counter above the fridge.

The major bypassed the suitcase. 'Tea?'

The suspense was killing me, but I said, 'Lovely. Do you want a hand?'

'No. I have two of those,' he said with a grin. 'Been fending for myself for decades. Never been able to persuade a woman to have me, not since my wife died. I'm not much of a catch.'

'Of course you are,' I said, all politeness.

'Do you know of a good woman willing to take on a dazzling ex-army major?'

'I'll give it some thought.'

The major bustled about setting bone-china cups and saucers on a tea tray along with a bowl of sugar and an open packet of McVitie's chocolate digestives.

As I watched him, I thought that Elsie was right about the wasp sting. It looked horrible. He wheeled over to the fridge and my heart gave a leap of excitement. But he ignored the little suitcase, instead fetching a small jug of milk and returning to the table.

'All in good time. All in good time,' he said, as if reading my mind. 'Can I tell you a story?'

I glanced at the clock on the wall. It was almost seven. 'Perhaps a quick one.'

One quick story turned into almost an hour of reminiscing. The floodgates had opened, and because I sensed he was lonely, I just let him ramble on as the little suitcase sat there tantalisingly out of reach.

'Goose Green,' he said. 'Now that was some show. So Maggie ... that's Margaret Thatcher to you – you probably weren't even born—'

'Actually, I was,' I said.

'The twenty-eighth of May 1982 is a day I'll never forget – Argentinians, fifty-five dead, one hundred wounded and fifteen hundred taken prisoner. The Paras – fifteen dead and thirty-seven wounded. Miracle there weren't more ... but then came Wireless Ridge ...' He shook his head and struggled to compose himself. 'Still haunts me to this day. We lost forty good men. Ninety-three were wounded.' He pulled a handkerchief from his trouser pocket, lifted his glasses and wiped a tear from his eye. 'I'd give up all my medals if I could just have my men back.'

'It must have been awful,' I said.

'Military Cross, Conspicuous Gallantry Cross and Distinguished Service Cross to name just a few.'

'You're a true hero.'

'I don't know about that,' he said quietly. 'My injury is nothing compared to those poor buggers who served in the trenches in the Great War.'

'Yes!' I said, almost too eagerly. 'And that's why I am here.' My eyes drifted over to the little suitcase again. 'You mentioned your grandfather was killed on the Somme.'

'That's right.'

'He had *three* mascot bears?' I exclaimed. 'Were they all sent back from the Front?'

'That's right.'

'Can I look at them now? I don't think I can wait another minute.'

'Be my guest.'

I leapt up and grabbed the case.

The major pushed his wheelchair back from the kitchen table. 'If you'll excuse me, I need to use the little boy's room.' He disappeared, leaving me to open the case alone.

And I was glad I did.

The minute I saw them, I knew they were fake. My heart sank. What a disappointment. How could the major believe they were authentic? Thank heavens he had left the room. Even though these bears were beautifully made – exquisite, in fact, with individual expressions and an astonishing attention to detail – they were definitely copies. I took out the jeweller's loupe I always carried in my bag.

Bona fide bears had wires stretching from arm to arm and leg to leg. That was not the case with these. There were also tiny remnants of stitching on the inside right leg that looked as if a label had been snipped out.

They were excellent copies, with patchy fur and grubby paws intended to simulate the effect of standing in a soldier's breast pocket. The placement of the glass eyes was correct, sewn high on the head supposedly so that the bear could gaze up at its owner. And, like the original bears, these too were nose-less. It was extremely rare to find an authentic bear with an original nose – perhaps a small disc of felt or some simple stitches. I always felt that minus their noses they had a charming, mole-like appearance.

The originals were made of mohair stuffed with folded wood wool rather than kapok. An authentic bear's ears would have been made out of a pipe cleaner pushed into holes on the head. After more than one hundred years, these pipe cleaner hoops were nearly always visible – not so here.

I was in a real dilemma. This was the bit I always hated – telling someone that their treasure was actually a fake.

'Lovely chaps, aren't they?' I hadn't heard the major return. 'Belonged to three brothers.'

'*Brothers?*' I said. 'I thought they belonged to your grandfather?'

The major reddened. 'No. Three brothers. That's what my father told me.'

'So *not* your grandfather?' I was confused.

'What are you going to offer?'

'And you say they have been in your family all this time?'

'Why? Is there a problem?'

'I'm afraid there is.' I took a deep breath. 'Although these are really very charming, I'm afraid they are copies.'

'Copies?' The major's jaw dropped. '*Copies?* What? You mean they're *fakes?*'

'I'm sorry, but yes.'

The major seemed stricken. He bowed his head. 'All these years … all this time … my father lied.'

'I'm sure it was unintentional.' I was surprised at his reaction. Even if the bears had been authentic, they would have fetched a few thousand pounds at best.

'They are still very beautiful bears,' I said.

'I don't want them,' he said harshly. 'Give me whatever you think they're worth and take them out of my sight.'

This was awkward. I didn't buy copies of anything, regardless of how good a copy it might be.

'Make me an offer,' he said. '*Please!*'

Cursing myself for being such a soft touch, I said, 'I'll give you seventy-five pounds.'

'Seventy-five *pounds*?' The major seemed insulted. 'Good grief. Actually, I think I'm going to get a second opinion.'

'Of course. You absolutely should.' I was surprised but relieved. It let me off the hook. 'Can I just take a quick photograph of them?'

'Why?'

'I always take photographs of items I value.'

'But they're fake,' he said quickly. 'So I don't see the point.' He swept the bears back into the little suitcase and closed the lid. 'I'm sorry you had a wasted journey.'

'Not wasted at all,' I said. 'I enjoyed hearing about your adventures very much. I am truly sorry I didn't have better news for you.' And I realised that I really was sorry.

I walked back to my car feeling baffled. For a man who had boasted about his heroics in the Falklands, the major's reaction to the mascot bears being fakes seemed completely out of proportion. I was glad that he hadn't brought them to the BearFest. It would have been embarrassing for him.

I remembered how I had felt when I first learned that my mother had been lying to me for most of my life. For decades she had regularly pleaded a migraine and taken to her bedroom, when in fact she had been writing racy romance novels. Neither my father nor I ever suspected what she was up to.

Even though I was happy that Mum had made a major success of writing, I still felt sad that she had thought to lie to me about it.

Before I drove away, I checked my mobile, disappointed to find that there was still nothing from Piers. I assumed our date was off.

It had been such a strange day. At least I knew I could count on my lovely mum to make me feel welcome.

Chapter Ten

'**The major was very upset,**' I said to Mum as I sat at the kitchen table nursing a gin and tonic.

'He probably thought he was on to a good thing,' she replied. 'Everyone thinks they have a bargain in the attic these days.' She glanced at the clock. 'Goodness. Is that the time! Are you planning on staying long tonight?'

'I thought we could watch a DVD or something.'

'You told me you had plans this evening.'

'They changed.'

'Oh. Well I've got plans now.'

The lingerie and fluffy mules flashed into my mind. 'Who with?'

'None of your business!'

'Are you going out?'

'Why?'

I was actually disappointed. I got up from the table. 'I'll leave you to your mysterious evening.'

'Oh for heaven's sake,' said Mum. 'You don't have to go

yet. I'm just struggling with *Betrayed* at the moment. You know how I am when I'm in the middle of a book. I've got plot droop.'

'Perhaps when you finish building your writing house, you'll be able to focus,' I said.

'Why do you think I'm not focusing?'

'I didn't say I didn't think you weren't focusing.' I frowned. 'Is that even a proper sentence?'

Mum forced a smile. 'I just have a lot on my mind.'

'Like what?'

'It's stressful having to clear the outbuildings.'

'But you're not doing that. Alfred is.' I regarded her with suspicion. 'And how can it be stressful?'

She shrugged. 'I have to make decisions, such as …' she frowned, 'do I want to keep that old henhouse?'

I laughed. 'OK. Don't tell me if you don't want to.'

'I had quite a lecture from the earl the other day making sure I'd hired a skip,' Mum said. 'Asking if – I quote – it "complied with the Environmental Agency regulations for the efficient disposal of waste". Some don't, you know.'

I was surprised. 'Rupert actually said that?'

Mum blushed. 'I meant the other earl – Aubrey Carew. He's very knowledgeable about things like that.'

'I'm sure your conversation must have been fascinating,' I said drily.

'Yes. It was.' She'd obviously missed my sarcasm. 'Did you know that it costs local authorities alone around forty-four million pounds each year to deal with all that fly-tipping. It's a major problem for over three quarters of landowners and affects sixty-seven per cent of farmers. The Environmental Protection Act of 1990—'

'OK, I get the picture,' I said. 'I had no idea you were such a supporter.'

'Of course. We must all do our bit for the environment.' She touched her EcoChamp badge.

'Well, he's definitely rubbing Rupert up the wrong way.' I went on to tell her about the argument between the two earls at Bridge Cottage. 'It's not fair that Rupert should have to bear the brunt of it all and pay for rubbish to be taken away when it isn't his fault.'

'Exactly,' said Mum. 'But the law is the law and we should all follow it.'

'Says someone who has millions secretly stashed away in an offshore bank account,' I remarked.

'Not millions, darling. Just thousands.'

'Well I had my own fly-tipping incident today. Someone dumped a bag of rubbish containing stuff that actually belonged to me.'

'What are you talking about?'

'Actually, only the half-eaten doughnuts were mine, along with some junk mail with my address on it and a pair of socks.'

'Obviously it must be some kind of joke.'

'Shawn didn't think so.'

'*Shawn?*'

I gave a heavy sigh. 'Edith reported it.'

'What? *No!*'

'I was out riding with her when we found it blocking the path.'

'Ah, I see.'

'Shawn personally delivered it to the gatehouse and tipped it out on the drive. You should have seen what else was in there!'

'Like what?'

'Promise you won't laugh?'

'I promise.'

I listed the items, realising how ridiculous they sounded, and so obviously not mine.

Mum tried to keep her composure, but it got too much for her. 'Tena Lady?' she shrieked. 'Isn't that for *incontinence*?'

'Yes. Apparently.'

'Shawn will never ask you out now, will he?' she sniggered. 'Far too risky.'

'Quite,' I said. 'But what I don't like is the fact that someone has been snooping around the gatehouse.'

'Oh dear.'

'And there's something else. The warning sign from Bridge Cottage was stolen only to magically reappear in my storage shed – and of course Shawn found it. That's far too close for comfort, but what really concerns me is that the report goes straight to the Earl of Denby.'

'That's right, it does.' Mum nodded. 'He's a bit of a tyrant, but you might only get a warning since it's your first offence.'

'Offence! I was framed!'

'Hard to prove, I fear – unless you can find out who did it. It's obvious that someone picked those items out deliberately to embarrass you.'

'I actually thought of Cassandra,' I said. 'But she only arrived late last night.'

'Cassandra? Who is Cassandra?'

'Cassandra Bowden-Forbes—'

'*The* Cassandra Bowden-Forbes, with the pink streak in her hair?' Mum exclaimed. 'The one from *Hello!* magazine? The one who was in that reality TV show, *Made in Monte Carlo*?'

'I thought you didn't watch reality TV.'

'Euro-trash, I know, but it's a guilty pleasure.'

'They call her Kitten.'

'Kitten?'

'It's a nickname that was given to her when she was in the womb.' I knew I sounded sulky, but I couldn't help it.

'You're jealous!' Mum teased.

'Of course I'm not.'

'What's she really like?'

'Impossibly beautiful. Impossibly slim. Like a fashion model,' I said gloomily. 'And it's quite obvious that Aubrey thinks the world of her. She's overseeing his EcoChamp campaign.'

'Oh, who cares what that cantankerous old man with his silly obsession with fly-tipping thinks!'

'I thought you were in awe of the earl and his title.'

'Whatever gave you that idea?'

'Your knowledge of household waste?'

'Now you're being silly,' said Mum. 'Cassandra did come across as quite a sex kitten – no pun intended – on the telly.'

'She's fun,' I said. 'And charming.'

'You think she'll seduce *your* Prince Charming?'

'I think she already has. Piers and *Kitten* – such a stupid nickname – go back years … but speaking of seduction, did you find the package I left in your office this morning?'

Mum looked me straight in the eye. 'Why did you think of *seduction* and *package* in the same sentence?'

'No reason.'

'I knew you were snooping.'

'Not intentionally,' I admitted. 'It was addressed to Stanford. I assumed it was for me.'

'It *was* for you,' Mum said. 'I knew you'd snooped! You haven't changed a bit. You could never resist opening your Christmas stocking and pretending that Father Christmas's elves hadn't bothered to wrap up your gifts.'

'Mum, that happened once. I was seven! And what do you mean, the lingerie was for me?'

'Well, I thought the fluffy mules would go well with your incontinence pads.'

We both exploded with laughter.

When I'd managed to recover, I said, 'And the card inside? "To Iris, from your most ardent admirer"?'

'That's a standard greeting card with a typo.' Mum was struggling to keep a straight face. 'Can't I admire my own daughter?'

'With lingerie and fluffy mules?'

'You'll look irresistible in … fluffy mules.' She burst out laughing again. 'Good grief, I think I'm going to need one of your Tena Ladies.'

By now we were in convulsions, and only stopped when we became aware of Delia standing in the kitchen holding a red Le Creuset casserole dish. She had a canvas tote bag over her shoulder and she did not look amused.

'Shall I come back another time?'

'Don't be daft,' Mum said. 'Come on in. I've already put the oven on.'

Chapter Eleven

'Kat was just leaving,' said Mum.

'Yes, that's right, I am.'

'Don't go on my account.' Up close, Delia's aubergine hair looked just a little bit too perfect. I wondered if it was a wig. I also wondered how long this new friendship between them had been going on for – something else my mother hadn't thought to tell me. But I was glad to see she had made a new friend.

'Can I take that dish, Delia?' I asked. 'It looks heavy.'

'You can put it straight in the oven,' said Mum. So I did. 'Then mix Delia a gin and tonic.'

'I'll make my own,' said Delia. 'I know how I like it.'

She took off her coat and hung it behind the door. An attractive woman in her mid sixties, she was dressed in a Marks & Spencer geometric-print A-line flock skirt with a pale grey jumper. I knew it was from Marks because my mother had an identical outfit. A love of gin and tonic *and* Marks & Spencer – that was definitely a match made in heaven.

'I hope you didn't cycle over here carrying that casserole.' Mum turned to me, adding, 'Delia doesn't drive.'

'I never bothered to learn,' said Delia. 'But no, I walked over. I like the exercise. Can't afford to let myself go.'

'It smells good,' said Mum. 'What did you make?'

'Not me. It's a venison casserole made by a house guest who has completely taken over the kitchen.' Delia marched to the kitchen counter, where Mum had set a bottle of Bombay Sapphire gin, a bucket of ice, slices of lemon and a bottle of tonic water. 'Oh, fancy. Bombay Sapphire. Personally, I prefer Gordon's.'

'I bet Peggy Cropper hated her kitchen being taken over,' Mum said with glee. Her personal feud with the cook had been raging for months over some slight from the distant past when she used to spend summers in Honeychurch Park with Bushman's Fair and Travelling Boxing Emporium.

'Oh no,' Delia declared. 'Peggy loves her. They all do. Calls herself Kitten.'

Mum and I exchanged pained looks. 'Speaking of Kitten, I'd like to formally introduce you to my daughter, Kat.'

'Hello,' I said.

'Are those hair extensions?' Delia demanded.

I was thrown off guard by her bluntness. 'Excuse me?'

'Your hair,' said Delia. 'You can't tell me it's all your own.'

'Of course it's all her own,' Mum declared. 'Katherine's hair is her crowning glory. Take it down from that awful messy up-do, dear. Show Delia it's real.'

I rarely wore it down any more. 'Another time, Mum.' I was beginning to feel embarrassed. 'It gets in the way.'

Delia's scrutiny continued. 'And you don't even dye it?'

'No,' I said. 'All natural. But I have noticed a few grey hairs recently.'

Delia gave me a look that I could not fathom – a mixture of contempt and fascination, perhaps?

'Cheers!' Mum said. 'To new friends!'

We raised our glasses in a toast. Delia drained hers in one go, then got up from the table – somewhat unsteadily. I didn't think for one minute that she was drinking her first gin and tonic of the evening. 'Anyone else?'

'I'm fine, thanks,' I said.

'I've got to pace myself,' Mum put in.

'How are you settling in, Delia?' I asked.

'I've never been in service before, but what else can you do when you're alone and money is tight?'

'I'm sorry to hear that,' I said.

'That's why I was happy to meet Iris,' Delia went on. 'Two peas in a pod, aren't we?'

'Delia's a widow too,' said Mum. 'Not even six months, is it?'

'You miss them every day, don't you, Iris?'

Mum nodded. 'It's like a knife in my heart.'

'A knife.' Delia nodded too.

'Still, we've got our children to keep us company,' said Mum.

'I never see Linda any more,' Delia grumbled. 'She lives in Scotland with her husband, Hamish. Don't you think that's selfish? I hardly ever see my granddaughter.'

'Show Kat the photos.'

Delia retrieved her canvas tote bag from the floor and

plonked it on the kitchen table. The exterior of the bag had four photo pockets. Each one showed an enchanting little girl of six with a head of blonde curls.

'She's adorable,' I said, and she was.

'You're lucky, Delia,' Mum said. 'I despair of ever becoming a grandmother.'

'Thanks, Mum.'

Mum mouthed, *Sorry*. She knew it was a sore point for me.

'You shouldn't wait much longer,' Delia declared. 'Linda was thirty-five, and even she had problems conceiving. You're going to be hard pushed—'

'And you have a son called Guy,' Mum interrupted.

'He's a helicopter pilot at the Royal Naval Air Station in Yeovilton,' said Delia.

'Is he single?'

'Mum!' I protested.

'He is now. He only got posted back to the UK three weeks ago,' said Delia. 'He's been in Germany for years.'

'How exciting.' Mum gave me a knowing look that I pointedly ignored. 'You must be thrilled. Yeovilton is only a couple of hours up the road. When is he coming to visit?'

'Oh, I don't know.' Delia seemed uncomfortable. 'Do you think the casserole is ready yet?'

'Is there enough for Kat?'

'I'm not staying,' I said. 'Just finishing up this drink and then I'll be out of your hair.'

Delia self-consciously adjusted her own, confirming my suspicions. Then she took a pair of knitting needles and a ball of wool from her tote bag.

'Delia's knitting some outfits for the bear boutique,' said Mum.

'Yes, I love to knit.' And as if to prove a point, she proceeded to do so at breakneck speed, brow furrowed in concentration.

'You are a fast knitter,' Mum observed.

Delia paused. 'I've been meaning to ask you about the earl, Iris.'

'Which one? The Earl of Grenville or the Earl of Denby?'

'The one who wears that hideous orange tweed newsboy cap,' said Delia. 'He looks like he's wearing a traffic cone on his head.'

'You mean Aubrey Carew?' Mum said. 'What about him?'

'I just wondered how often he was at the Hall.'

'Why?'

'I've just seen him hanging around a lot. Ever since I started really.'

Mum shrugged. 'I can't say I've noticed.'

'Oh yes,' Delia said. 'When I cycle back to my cottage for lunch, I always see his car parked in the service road. Sometimes I see him on horseback.'

'He's obsessed with catching the fly-tippers,' said Mum. 'They've started dumping at Bridge Cottage now. They'd better watch out. The earl takes no prisoners.'

'They call him the hanging judge in the village,' said Delia.

'That wouldn't surprise me,' Mum agreed.

'And the other earl – Lord Rupert – is just as bad. Do you know, he goes through all the rubbish at the Hall to make sure it's in the correct recycling bag. I never had this problem when I lived in Cornwall.'

'Well, the South Hams are a bit strict,' said Mum.

'Strict? It's ridiculous. I was told in no uncertain terms at my interview that one false step and I'd be fired.'

'It could be because Rupert has had a few run-ins with Aubrey,' I ventured.

'So I heard,' said Delia. 'They've fallen out in quite a big way.'

'His lordship can be difficult,' Mum put in.

'Which one?' Delia and I chorused.

'I don't like anyone going through my rubbish bins.' Delia was determined not to let it go. 'It's embarrassing.'

'Someone went through Kat's—'

'Mum,' I said sharply. 'Let's not go there.'

'I'd like to go there,' said Delia. 'What happened?'

'Honestly, Mum. Please …'

'Kat's not had a good day,' said Mum. 'She's in a bad mood.'

'Oh, my daughter is always in a bad mood,' said Delia. 'Daughters can be so difficult. Sons are much easier.'

'I am not being difficult!' I protested.

'She's in a bad mood because she thought she'd found a bargain in an old soldier's attic but it turned out to be fake.'

'There was more to it than that,' I said.

'A military man?' Delia perked up. 'I always love a man in uniform.'

Mum tittered.

'Can't stay a widow forever, right, Iris?' Delia winked. 'Is he single?'

'He was injured in the Falklands,' I said. 'He's in a wheelchair.'

'Wasn't your Lenny out in the Falklands?' Mum demanded.

'That's right,' said Delia. 'What's this man's name?'

'Major Timothy Gordon,' I said. 'I think he served in the Parachute Regiment.'

'Your Lenny was in the Parachute Regiment, wasn't he?' Mum exclaimed. 'They must have known each other. You should meet this Major Gordon.'

'No!' Delia exclaimed. 'I mean … I don't like looking back, Iris. I'm very much a "now" person … now. Can we change the subject?'

I finished the rest of my drink and put the glass down on the table. 'I'll leave you two friends together.'

'Off you go,' said Mum. 'But watch out for the paparazzi.'

Delia frowned. 'Paparazzi?'

'Kat's back in the limelight again,' Mum went on. 'Man driving a black Citroën.'

'He might be a birdwatcher,' I reminded her.

'Not with a foreign car,' said Mum. 'I've been thinking. I bet he's from *Hello!* magazine.'

'*Hello!* magazine is actually British,' I pointed out. 'You're thinking of ¡*Hola!* – the Spanish version.'

'Well, who cares which magazine he works for,' Mum declared. 'He's got a camera with a telephoto lens, and to me that means paparazzi.'

I was glad that my mother hadn't mentioned the possibility that he could be a stalker, but Delia didn't seem to be listening anyway. She'd gone very still. In fact, she had even stopped knitting.

'Where have you seen this car?' she said.

'All over the place,' Mum replied.

'Sometimes parked along the service road, but always tucked out of sight.'

'And along Cavalier Lane,' Mum put in. 'You must have seen it, Delia.'

'No. Never.'

'But you're always cycling around the estate,' Mum persisted.

'You should report him to the police,' Delia said.

'They already know,' I said.

'Well, I suppose that's the price you pay for fame.' And off she went again, her needles clattering away. Almost immediately, though, she stopped again. 'Anyway, how do you know he's following you? Maybe he's following Cassandra? No offence, but you've been off the air for a long time, and *Made in Monte Carlo* is very popular on the telly.'

'Kat's popular off *and* on the telly,' Mum said.

'Yes, but you say it's a foreign car, and Cassandra's show was filmed in Monte Carlo.'

I got up to go. 'It was nice to meet you, Delia. Are you both going out again tonight?'

Delia looked blank. 'Out? Are we?'

'You are funny, Delia,' Mum said with a hearty laugh. 'What a hopeless memory you have. We had a great night out last night, didn't we?'

'We did?' Delia clapped her hand dramatically over her mouth. 'Oops. Senior moment. Yes we did. It was a very good film.'

'And a very good meal,' Mum reminded her quickly.

'That's right. Mustn't forget the very good meal.'

I regarded them with suspicion. Delia was right when she said they were like two peas in a pod. They also seemed to share a mutual love of fibbing.

As I got into my car, I checked my mobile again. *Still* nothing from Piers! So much for his seventy-five per cent certainty for being available tonight! I couldn't ignore a niggling feeling that Cassandra's arrival at Honeychurch Hall could have something to do with it.

It was only as I drove out of the courtyard and turned into the service road that I saw the black Citroën *again*! It was pulled in tightly against the hedge, but it was empty. He must be skulking in the shadows. What if he was a stalker after all?

This upsetting thought stayed with me all the way up the hill, and when I reached Jane's Cottage and parked my Golf, I immediately sensed that something was wrong. The cottage was lit up like a Christmas tree. I was certain I hadn't left any of the lights on.

I sat in my car in an agony of indecision. I knew I couldn't reach Piers, so that left Shawn.

I dialled his mobile.

Of course it went straight to voicemail and, at the beep, asked me to leave a message. I changed my mind and disconnected the call, then changed it back and redialled, only to hang up yet again.

Suddenly the front door was flung open and Piers, in a white chef's hat, stood there holding two glasses of champagne. 'Where have you been?' he exclaimed. 'I thought I'd have to send out a search party!'

Chapter Twelve

'**Where is your car?**' **I demanded as I followed him inside.**

'There is a reason for that.' He handed me a glass. 'You should find somewhere other than the plant pot to put your front door key – or better still, give me one of my own.'

I ignored him. 'And why didn't you call me?'

'There is a reason for that too.' We clinked glasses and toasted each other. 'Cheers!'

I made a mental note that I'd already had a large gin and tonic and needed to be careful. I didn't want to start tomorrow's big day with a hangover. 'It had better be a good reason.'

'It is, *chica*.' He gently kissed my forehead.

I felt myself relax. 'I've had a really weird day.'

'Then it's just as well I am here.'

A few weeks ago, Piers had cut his shoulder-length dirty-blonde hair and now he no longer resembled an eighteenth-century Casanova. He told me that it was in the hope I'd take his romantic intentions towards me more seriously – the logic of which I couldn't quite figure out. I still wasn't sure how I felt about him. When I was away from him, I honestly didn't think there could be any future. But when we were together, he just won me over every time because he made me laugh.

Mum was desperate for me to give him a chance. He was rumoured to be the most eligible bachelor in the entire western hemisphere.

The Carew clan were as old as the neighbouring Honeychurches and had fought on the winning side during the English Civil War. Unlike the Honeychurches, they had kept their fortune intact. When Aubrey Carew died, Piers would inherit everything, including the title.

He had been running the twelve-square-mile family estate for years and was making extensive renovations to Carew Court. He made no secret of the fact that he was ready to settle down. Of course I was attracted to him, but a part of me couldn't help but wonder if he regarded me solely as a challenge.

Now he took my hand and led me over to the sofa. 'We'll start the evening by taking off your boots ...'

'That's all that's coming off,' I said as I allowed him to do just that. A delicious smell drifted from the kitchen. 'Something smells good.'

'I think it's your feet.'

'No!' I laughed. 'You've got something cooking.'

'Let's go and find out.' He pulled me up, catching me around the waist and kissing me again. 'Follow me.'

Jane's Cottage was cosy. It was essentially a one-storey house with a loft room that I had converted into a bedroom under the eaves. It was accessed by a spiral staircase. The ground floor comprised a large living room with a second bedroom and a small study leading off, a galley kitchen, and beyond that, a bathroom that I had completely renovated to include a power shower.

Piers had set the breakfast island with cutlery, linen napkins and a jug holding a few cornflowers. He'd lit candles, too. Sultry Cuban music played quietly in the background from his iPod in my docking station. It was very romantic.

He pulled out a stool. 'Sit.' I did, and he topped up my glass.

'Dom Pérignon!' I said. 'I feel spoiled.'

'And you should be. Always.'

'Are we celebrating something?'

'Just being together.'

I groaned. 'You are the master of corny lines. What's on the menu?'

'Venison casserole.'

'What?' I exclaimed. 'No! You're joking! Don't tell me. Cassandra made it.'

'Guilty as charged,' Piers said sheepishly. 'She made gallons of the stuff. How did you guess?'

I told him that the housekeeper had delivered some to my mother earlier that evening. 'And now we're having it here.' Suddenly I felt as if Cassandra was sitting in my kitchen, too.

'Kitten is an excellent cook.' Piers took a casserole dish out of the oven. 'She used to be a chalet girl at Klosters.'

'So I've heard,' I said. 'She seems to be good at everything.'

'Yes, she is,' said Piers with ill-disguised admiration. 'Although she's never settled at anything. A woman of fads, but when she's determined to do something, she has to be the best. She was a model for Ford for two years before she got bored. Then she started a clothing line and spent months out in Bali. Soon tired of that. Let me see, what else has she tried? Professional horsewoman, restaurateur, croupier – that was a laugh. I went on a few cruise ships when she was dealing, to surprise her, but ended up losing quite a lot of money at black-jack. Oh, and then she was in that terrible reality TV show. I didn't approve of that.'

'Didn't approve?' I said sharply.

'Kitten runs everything by me first,' said Piers.

'And now she's an antique dealer,' I said.

'And let's not forget EcoChamp. Father would be lost without her. She's very good at social media and marketing. She's amazing.'

'I'm sure she is.' I was growing weary of the wonderful Cassandra. 'So what happened between you two?'

He shrugged. 'We know each other too well. She's more like a sister to me.'

I remembered Fiona Reynolds's comment about Cassandra's fiancé. 'I don't think she thinks of you as a brother.'

Piers regarded me with curiosity. 'Kitten has been part of my life for as long as I can remember. Her brother died in a horrible accident when he was fourteen and she was twelve. She's family. What is it?' he said gently. 'Do you need to be reassured of my feelings for you?'

'Of course not,' I said – though did I? 'I just thought you should know that people believe you and Cassandra are engaged.'

'Oh *that*.' He rolled his eyes. 'We've been betrothed since before birth. I don't take any notice and I can assure you

Kitten doesn't either.' He took my champagne glass and set it down on the counter, then helped me off the bar stool and positioned me between his jeans-clad legs. Taking both of my hands in his, he looked into my eyes. 'Kat, I want to be with you,' he said. 'Only you.'

I felt flattered. 'You do?'

'Yes! You keep my feet on the ground. With Kitten … it was just one wild adventure after another.'

This was not the reassurance that I had been hoping for, despite pretending I didn't care. I pushed him away. 'Lavinia has already told me that you and Cassandra were a couple up until just a few months ago.'

Piers laughed. 'My sister doesn't know what she's talking about. Poor old Vinnie. She's not very bright. Kitten went off to Europe for the summer and had a wild fling with a Greek shipping magnate. Sure, we were spending time together before that, but just as friends.'

I didn't like this conversation. The last thing I wanted was another love triangle. I'd had to compete with my former boyfriend's estranged wife for years, and I wasn't going to start doing that again.

'Really, *chica*, you have nothing to worry about. Ever.'

'Let's eat,' I said firmly. 'I'd like to see just how good a cook she is.'

To my annoyance, the venison casserole was delicious.

'So … you were going to tell me why you didn't return my phone calls today.'

'Because I left my mobile in my car and I lent my car to Kitten this afternoon,' said Piers. 'Rupert refuses to let her drive any of theirs because he says they always come back scratched or dented.'

It explained why Piers's Mercedes had not been outside.

'She dropped me off,' said Piers as if reading my mind. 'So you see, I'm stranded here for the night.'

'Oh. I see.' I felt my face redden. 'Well, as long as—'

'Don't worry,' he said. 'She's going to come and pick me up later. I told her carriages at ten thirty. I know you need an early night.'

'Oh.' I felt distinctly put out. Was he delusional? Didn't he see what was going on here? Cassandra was elbowing her way into our relationship. There! I'd said it. I *was* in a relationship with Piers.

He poured the remaining champagne into our glasses.

'At least you don't have to worry about drinking and driving,' I said.

I could sense his eyes on me. I glanced up and smiled, but I felt unsettled. I scrambled for something to talk about that didn't involve *her*, and ended up telling him all about the black Citroën and its mysterious driver.

'Now I'm going to worry about you,' he said grimly.

'I'll be fine.'

'No.' Piers shook his head. 'We're going to get you a dog. Since you won't allow me to protect you – at least for the moment ...'

'Really, I'm fine,' I said again, but then went on to tell him about the black bin-bag incident. 'So someone has been going through my rubbish.'

'Right! That does it. I'm *not* leaving you here alone tonight,' he said. 'I'm staying here, on the sofa.'

'The police know—'

'The police are less than useless,' he said.

'And if your father doesn't know yet, he soon will.'

'Ah, Father could be a problem. He has become increasingly fanatical about fly-tipping, to the point of obsession. Is there anything that could prove the rubbish wasn't yours?'

When I told him the embarrassing contents, he laughed. 'Granny pants! How unbelievably sexy!'

'Shut up,' I said, and cuffed him on the shoulder.

'I love a challenge. They are almost impossible to get off with one hand.'

'I think that's all I am,' I said. 'A challenge.'

'Don't be silly.' He kissed me very gently again.

Over the past few months, Piers's pursuit of me had turned from being ardent to tender. He told me it was the only way to train a young wild horse, and of course I found that intensely flattering. I'd never regarded myself as such and liked it.

Suddenly he reached up and freed my hair from its pins. It cascaded down my back. He picked up a lock and lifted it to his nose, inhaling deeply. 'I love the smell of your hair.'

'Horse, you mean.'

'Stop talking,' he whispered.

It was a very sensuous gesture. For the first time, I felt tempted. Was this really what I wanted? Was it because I felt threatened by Cassandra? I couldn't be sure. I felt so confused.

Piers turned me away from him, then slipped his arms around my waist, lifted my hair and kissed my neck. I didn't move away until we were caught by a blinding light.

'Police! Freeze!'

Chapter Thirteen

Startled, we sprang apart to find Shawn standing in the kitchen doorway looking horrified. His expression was thunderous, then disgusted. I realised that not only was my hair all dishevelled, but the top button of my shirt had come undone, exposing my lace bra. I covered myself up. My face burned with embarrassment. I didn't know what to say.

'What the hell is going on?' Piers demanded angrily.

Shawn's jaw hardened. 'Ms Stanford called for my assistance.'

Piers was furious. 'Somehow I doubt that.'

'Actually, it's—'

'Ms Stanford,' Shawn interjected. 'Did you or did you not call my mobile phone twice this evening?'

'Yes,' I said.

'What?' Piers exclaimed. '*Why?*'

'But I didn't leave a message.'

'Why on earth would you call *him* and not me?' said Piers.

'Because I couldn't get hold of you.' I found I was gabbling.

'I was worried about that Citroën – the stalker – and the fly-tipping. But I'm sorry, Shawn. I should have left you a message. I didn't want to waste your time.'

'Given your track record of courting danger, I regard calling my mobile at night and failing to leave a message as a cry for help. Clearly I was mistaken.'

'I appreciate you coming out—'

'Yes, you were mistaken,' Piers said harshly. 'And since you are not in uniform, I am asking you respectfully – man to man – to leave Kat alone. I am here now.'

'This is a police matter.'

'I don't see how,' said Piers.

I felt as if I was starring in one of my mother's romance novels and that at any moment they would both draw swords. I knew the two men couldn't stand each other before I came on the scene. I'd heard it was some childhood disagreement – the sort that tended to be quite prevalent in rural communities.

'Is the officer bothering you, darling?' Piers winked at me. 'If anyone is going to take you away in handcuffs, it has to be me.'

'Piers!' I protested.

Shawn's expression darkened. 'Perhaps one day I'll have the pleasure of putting *you* in handcuffs. It's been a long time coming and you can't hide behind Daddy forever.'

'Oh come on, Shawn, we all know you've got the hots for Kat, but I'm sorry to say, she's just not interested in you.'

'Piers!' I protested again.

'Running all the way up here on the off chance that she'd be alone tonight.'

'Piers, stop,' I said. 'Shawn, I am *so* sorry—'

'Were you spying on us?'

I didn't think Shawn could get any redder, but he did.

'How long were you standing there in the doorway watching us?' Piers demanded.

I looked from one man to the other in dismay. If the situation hadn't been so awkward, it would have been funny.

'I think you should both leave,' I said.

'I think that's a good idea,' said Shawn. 'I see you don't have any transportation, sir. I'm sure I can run you home …'

'Don't worry,' came a female voice. 'I'll take him.'

Cassandra stepped into the kitchen. I couldn't believe it. She looked stunning in a tightly belted Burberry trench coat.

'The door was open.' She slipped her arm through Shawn's. 'Oh goodness,' she said with a hint of mischief. 'Have we caught them in flagrante delicto?'

'Stay out of this,' Piers snapped.

'I assume you are wearing your Ann Summers lingerie?' Cassandra scoffed. 'How tantalising!'

I ignored her.

'We haven't been officially introduced. You must be the Croppers' grandson, Detective Inspector,' said Cassandra smoothly. 'I'm Cassandra Bowden-Forbes, but all my close friends call me Kitten.'

I watched Piers. A vein had begun to throb in his temple. I could tell he was furious.

'Have you been misbehaving, darling?' she asked him.

'*Cassandra!* Stay out of this,' he said again.

Not Kitten now, I thought.

Cassandra went white. The intended slight was brutal. 'Why, how grumpy you are,' she said gaily. 'Not only am I your chauffeur this evening, I came to return your mobile.' She delved into her pocket, retrieved Piers's iPhone and handed it to him. 'You left it in your car. It's been ringing off the hook.'

Piers took it without a word.

'You're always losing it,' Cassandra continued. 'You need that find-my-phone thingy on your laptop – that way you always know where it is. Don't you agree, Officer?'

'Excuse me.' Shawn turned on his heel and strode out of the room. I heard the front door slam.

'Well, darling?' said Cassandra. 'Are you staying here, or do you want me to take you home?'

'Tomorrow is a big day,' I found myself saying. 'I think I need an early night.'

'Right,' said Piers coldly. 'Yes, of course. In that case, Cassandra, I'll drive myself home in *my* car and drop *you* at the Hall.'

'See you tomorrow at the BearFest, Kat – oh, and Mrs Cropper will want that dish back. I hope you enjoyed the casserole. Coming, Piers?'

Piers stormed out of the kitchen with Cassandra in hot pursuit. I heard her laughing outside but couldn't tell if he was laughing too. Then came the sound of the Mercedes starting and driving away.

I wasn't stupid, nor was I blind. As far as Cassandra was concerned, Piers was still very much her property.

I felt depressed. My ex-boyfriend's estranged wife had always haunted our relationship – and with good reason, as it turned out, given their ultimate reconciliation. I wasn't going to tread on another woman's toes.

I resolved to speak to Piers tomorrow and tell him that it would be better if we remained just friends.

Chapter Fourteen

Both car parks were full when I arrived the next morning, an hour before the doors opened for the BearFest.

Fiona had persuaded a neighbouring farmer to allow us to use his field as an overflow car park – perhaps not so smart given the amount of rainfall that we'd had recently.

I followed the signs for *Reserved Parking and Press*. Next to a West Country ITV news van were four more cars bearing press placards on their dashboards – the *Daily Post*, the *Western Times*, the *Dipperton Deal* and the *Dartmouth Packet*.

I realised I was nervous. It had been a long time since I'd stood in front of the cameras.

A line of adults and children clutching bears snaked around the building. Many were sporting EcoChamp badges. I was glad I'd remembered to put mine on but puzzled when I overheard a woman say to her companion, 'Kat Stanford's wearing a badge! What a joke!' to which he replied in a very loud voice, 'Because the rules don't apply to people like her.'

The pair were dressed in scruffy jeans and sweatshirts emblazoned with an image of a teddy bear above the logo *Give Us a Cuddle*. Both clutched carrier bags in which I glimpsed the top of furry heads and ears.

I slipped through the entrance and into the vestibule, where two long trestle tables held alphabetised boxes for pre-purchased tickets and wristbands. It looked like Sandra had got her way after all. The EcoChamp campaign table had been set up by the wall next to the walkway that led out to the courtyard.

'Kat!' Fiona called out. 'Quickly, in my office, now.'

I did as I was told.

She closed the door and turned to me, her expression grave.

'Is everything all right?' I asked.

She gestured to a stack of today's edition of the weekly *Dipperton Deal*. 'Not great publicity for our debut, Kat.'

'I'm sorry,' I said. 'I don't understand.'

She handed me a copy from her desk. 'Take a look at that.'

My heart sank. There on the front page was a photo of me superimposed against the backdrop of Bridge Cottage and surrounded by a sea of rubbish, with the caption: *Fly-Trapped: Caught Red-Handed!*

The piece went on to say that a large bag of household waste belonging to me had been dumped on a public bridleway. Even worse, the report announced that I would be headlining the BearFest in Dartmouth today, and made some snide recommendation that I should hide from the 'EcoChamp earl'.

I was livid. 'Anyone can see that this has been Photoshopped!'

'Of course it's been Photoshopped,' Fiona snapped. 'But that's irrelevant. The damage has been done.'

'It makes no sense,' I said half to myself, whilst Fiona continued to make noises of disgust.

The *Dipperton Deal* was still printed in the dark ages. Whoever had done this to me must have planned it at least a week ago to coincide with my appearance at the BearFest and so cause maximum embarrassment. I instantly thought of the journalist and his wretched telephoto lens. But why would he do something like that? Even at the height of my so-called fame, when I'd often be humiliated in the trashy tabloid *Star Stalkers*, the exposés had had some basis in truth. This had been blatantly made up.

I had a sudden thought. 'There'll be a reporter here from the *Dipperton Deal*,' I said. 'I'll talk to him.'

'What good is that now?' Fiona exclaimed. 'A retraction is far too late.'

'Not a retraction. I want to find out who submitted that photograph. The newspaper pays ten pounds for photos of people caught fly-tipping. Only four people work there. Someone must know who submitted it.'

'Personally, I think you're wasting your time,' Fiona said. 'I'm inclined to keep all the newspapers back here, although I fear the locals will have already read it.'

'But not those coming from further afield,' I pointed out.

'Well, never mind. There's nothing we can do about it now.'

The Dipperton Brass Band suddenly burst into a rousing rendition of 'The Teddy Bears' Picnic'.

Fiona cracked a smile. 'Doesn't this song just take you back to your childhood?'

'Yes,' I said. 'When life seemed so much simpler.'

I knew all the words.

> If you go down to the woods today
> You're sure of a big surprise.
> If you go down to the woods today
> You'd better go in disguise.
> For every bear that ever there was
> Will gather there for certain
> Because today's the day
> The teddy bears have their picnic.

The first Dartmouth BearFest had officially begun!

As we headed to the interior courtyard, I spied Shawn's six-year-old twins Ned and Jasper, who were clutching the hands of a very attractive woman in her mid sixties. In their free hands they were holding pale brown bears.

'Boys! How lovely to see you and your bears.' I smiled at their chaperone. 'Hello, I'm Kat Stanford.'

'I know,' she said. 'I'm Helen's mother, Lizzie Parker.'

'Oh. Hello.' For a moment, I was lost for words. I knew that Helen's mother helped Shawn take care of the twins, but I hadn't expected her to be so un-grandmotherly. With her shoulder-length highlighted blonde hair swept off her face, she was a picture of elegance. It made me wonder what Helen had looked like. I'd always imagined her slightly dowdy.

'I've heard so much about you from my son-in-law.' Lizzie extended a hand in greeting, and I took it.

'It's lovely to meet you at last,' I managed to say. 'You don't want to believe everything Shawn says about me.'

'I can assure you he is very complimentary, and I can quite see why.' She smiled. I detected genuine warmth.

'That's very kind.' I struggled for something to say. 'Shawn is a very good father.'

'Devoted,' Lizzie agreed. 'It's been five years since my daughter died, and it's time for him to have his life back. Of course, no one will ever take Helen's place. She was his whole world. Her shoes are big shoes to fill, but I suspect you are up to the job.'

'Oh. Thank you.' This was already horribly awkward, and then I looked up and saw Piers walking in with Harry and Fliss and wished the floor would swallow me up. 'Boys!' I said quickly. 'Let's go to the bear hospital.' Swiftly I steered them away from Piers, who fortunately, hadn't seen me. Lizzie seemed surprised, but followed me all the same.

Behind the safety of a potted plant, I said, 'What are your bears' names?'

'Teddy,' said Ned, thrusting his bear in my face.

Jasper hugged his. 'This is Mr Ted.'

'They put a lot of thought into naming those bears,' said Lizzie.

'I see that poor Mr Ted has a bit of stuffing coming out from under his armpit,' I said. 'A quick stitch and he'll be as right as rain.'

Jasper looked worried. 'I had to have stitches once and they really hurt.'

'The nurses have a magic cream that they use so the bears don't feel a thing,' I said.

'Why can't they give that to humans?' Ned wondered. 'It seems silly that you can give it to bears and they're not real, and humans are.'

'It *is* silly.' Lizzie ruffled the boys' heads affectionately. 'I hear you are going to do a talk about where teddy bears came from. The boys are very excited about that.'

'I know where mine came from,' said Ned. 'Toys R Us.'

Lizzie and I laughed.

'Yes, we're going to vote on the top ten bears of all time,' I said. 'So I hope you know your bear history.'

'Ooh! It has to be Paddington Bear!' Jasper cried.

'Of course it has to be Paddington,' said Lizzie. 'We'd better let you go, Kat.'

As they moved into the crowd, I wondered where Shawn was. Unexpectedly, my face grew warm as I remembered his look of horror when he caught me in Piers's arms. *Don't think about it, Kat!* Instead, I made my way over to the area where I would be conducting the valuations, surprised at the length of the queue.

Fiona and I had set up the space like a cosy living room, furnished with items from the Emporium – a beautiful oriental rug, a wingback leather armchair, bookshelves lined with bears from my own collection, as well as antiquarian books. In the centre stood a small gateleg table that I would use for the bear valuations. There was a giant headshot of myself propped on a stand.

I'd selected as broad a variety of bears as I could lay my

hands on, as well as some unusual dogs and cats. I added Jazzbo Jenkins and Ella Fitzgerald, my two vintage Merrythought Jerry Mice to the group.

Edith had offered to loan me the family's Steiff *Titanic* Mourning Bear, but I'd had to tactfully refuse. As one of only 655 black mohair bears that were made to commemorate the loss of so many souls when the *Titanic* went down on 15 April 1912, it would have been a fantastic addition. Unfortunately, this particular bear had been reported as stolen decades ago in an insurance scam that had been hushed up by Edith's husband, the 14th Earl of Grenville.

I'll never forget the moment I first saw Edward Bear, crammed into a pine chest of Harry's toys. To begin with, I thought it was a copy, but it wasn't. Persuading Harry to part with his precious bear had been surprisingly difficult. In the end, Lavinia and I had hatched a plan. Whilst Harry was away at boarding school – fortunately, Rupert had insisted that taking a bear to school would be too childish – I took Edward to Jean Grogan, who runs a wonderful soft-toy-making business called Little Scruffs.

Among other stuffed animals, Jean crafts mohair bears – originals and copies – by hand. Apart from the fact that she was legally unable to add the trademark Steiff ear button, the mourning bear was an excellent copy of Edward, complete with the distinctive red-felt-backed shoe-button eyes and black hand-embroidered nose. She'd done an excellent job. Harry never guessed.

For a moment, I was reminded of the major and his mascot bears. Even though they were copies, I wished I had asked him if I could borrow them for the day. Since I would be talking about the history of the teddy bear, these little chaps would have fitted right in.

'Kat?' called out one of the journalists from West Country News. 'Mark Wells.'

We shook hands.

'Take no notice of me,' he said. 'I'll be doing on-the-spot interviews with people, kids, that kind of thing. Nothing formal. We'll be airing on Sunday night's arts and entertainment segment on *West Country Round-Up*. I'll want a few quotes from you, but we can do that a little later.'

Thanking Mark and making sure he had everything he needed, I stepped up on to the dais, ready for the day.

The morning flew by and was a lot of fun. I didn't think about the mascot bears again until I saw Elsie pushing the major in his wheelchair through the crowd. I was surprised to see the little tan suitcase in his lap. Perhaps I would be able to ask him if I could borrow the bears after all.

Elsie left him holding court to a handful of women, who were laughing at his jokes, and took her place in the queue. She was soon standing in front of me, sporting an EcoChamp badge. 'Saw you at Bridge Cottage on the front page of the *Dipperton Deal*,' she said. 'Terrible Photoshop job. What a joke!'

It would seem I'd been forgiven.

'Good. I'm glad you thought so.' I was pleased. If Elsie had spotted the obvious, perhaps other people would too. 'What have you got for me?'

She pulled out a rare Eduard Cramer bear with an open felt-lined mouth. Dating from the 1920s, he was made of light brown mohair and had orange glass eyes. As I talked a little bit about the bear's features and distinctive markings, Mark Wells and his camera zoomed in on Elsie's reaction.

'How much is it worth?' she demanded.

'I would value this bear between a thousand and fifteen hundred pounds.'

Elsie was ecstatic. 'I had no idea! I've got three more like this! Some have funny buttons in their ears.'

'They could be Steiff bears,' I said.

'I bet they're just as valuable!' she enthused. 'I'm going to sell them *all*! Do you want to buy them?'

'Why don't I call you and we can discuss it?' I said. 'Where did you get the Cramer bear?'

'Miss Philpot from number two. Before she passed, she gave me a box full of stuff in exchange for looking after her canary. Blimey!' Shock was making Elsie garrulous. 'And to think I was going to throw it out!'

'Oh!' I was appalled. 'Never throw bears out! At the very least you should find them a new home. Children's hospitals especially love to have bears donated, and today we have a bear orphanage for that very reason.' All bears that were not adopted by the end of the day would automatically be given to the South Hams Children's Centre.

'Troy!' Elsie screamed as she waved at a young man in the crowd dressed in orange overalls and wearing an American baseball cap back-to-front. 'There's my son. I must go and tell him. He'll be gobsmacked.'

Suddenly there was an explosion of cheers and loud applause. All heads turned to see a life-size Paddington Bear walking into the courtyard as the Dipperton Brass Band struck up the *Paddington* theme tune. Children and adults alike soon swallowed him up, leaving me all alone with the major.

I took my chance and darted over to see him.

'I'm glad you're here,' I said. 'Can I borrow your bears?'

Chapter Fifteen

'Why?' The major seemed horrified. He clutched the case close to his chest, as if I was going to snatch it away. 'Why do you want to borrow them?'

'To show the children,' I said, before adding, 'I'll be talking about the history of the bear, and since yours featured in World War I, they'd be a great addition to my presentation.'

'Where is the other girl?' he demanded. 'The one who starred in *Made in Monte Carlo*?'

'Cassandra Bowden-Forbes?' I was puzzled. 'Why? Is she valuing' – I pointed to the little suitcase – 'your bears?'

'That's right. She's an expert.'

I wanted to say, *So am I*, but I kept quiet. He'd find out soon enough.

'Kat!' came a familiar shout. It was Mum, and she had Delia in tow. I was grateful for the interruption. 'Will you excuse me a moment, Major?'

The two women were dressed alike in matching grey single-button wool coats from Marks & Spencer with EcoChamp badges on their lapels. Both were holding plastic glasses full of a clear liquid. Somehow I didn't think it was water.

'You look like twins,' I said.

'It wasn't planned.' Mum laughed.

'Great minds think alike,' Delia put in. 'We love Marks, don't we, Iris?'

'We love to get our fix,' Mum agreed.

'Have you both been drinking?'

'There's a bar!' Mum cried.

'You sound like my Linda,' said Delia. 'Nag, nag, nag.'

I didn't want to sound like Delia's Linda. 'I was just thinking about driving, Mum.'

'I'm only having one,' said Mum. 'Delia's knitted some adorable outfits for the bear boutique. She's been up half the night finishing them. Look! Show her.'

Delia opened her tote bag and brought out three little knitted coats and scarves in a rainbow of colours.

'They're lovely,' I said, and they were.

'I'm a great knitter and I love to sew,' said Delia. 'Lady Edith says I am the neatest seamstress she's ever known.'

At this comment, I saw Mum bristle. My mother fancied herself as the neatest seamstress at Honeychurch Hall, and had made the most exquisite costumes for last May's English Civil War re-enactment. She flapped her programme at me. 'It says here that Cassandra is a valuation expert in antique bears and toys. I thought you said it was just a hobby of hers.'

'Clearly not,' I said.

'She ran an antique shop in *Made in Monte Carlo*,' Delia put in.

'But we know that was staged, Delia,' said Mum.

'It's unscripted, Iris,' Delia insisted. 'That's why reality TV is called reality TV, because it's real.'

'No, Delia,' Mum declared. 'You are completely wrong.'

I sensed an argument brewing and seized the perfect distraction.

'Major!' I said. 'Come over here and say hello.'

He didn't need a second invitation. 'I was hoping you were going to introduce me to these lovely ladies.'

'This is my mother, Iris Stanford, and her friend Delia Evans. This is Major Timothy Gordon—'

'Call me Major,' said the major with a leer.

'Ah yes, I know all about *you*,' Mum said.

'I must say, it's a pleasure to be surrounded by such beauty. Now, don't be put off by my wasp sting.' He pointed to his cheek, which still looked horribly infected. 'I can tell you it's more painful than it looks.'

'It does look painful.' Delia leaned down and studied the swollen lump. 'You need a good woman to rub some salve into that.'

'Are you offering?'

The two of them shared a conspiratorial laugh.

'Delia, this is the major Kat was telling us about,' Mum interrupted. 'The one who might have known your Lenny.'

Delia froze. 'I'm not sure what you mean.'

'Don't you remember? We talked about it yesterday.' Mum rolled her eyes at me.

'Did we?' said Delia. 'I don't recall.'

'The major fought in the Falklands too,' I said.

'That's right, I did,' said the major. 'Lost my leg.'

'Which regiment was it?' I asked him.

'Two Para.'

'Delia! Fancy that!' Mum exclaimed. 'They *must* have known each other.'

'A lot of men fought in the Falklands, Iris,' said Delia quickly.

'That's right,' the major hastily agreed. 'A lot of men.'

I was surprised. Mum was too. 'But surely wouldn't everyone have known everyone else?'

'Not necessarily,' the major and Delia chorused.

A flicker of something I couldn't quite describe raced across Delia's face. 'I must take these outfits to the bear boutique. Excuse me.'

And with that, she plunged into the crowd and promptly collided with Aubrey Carew, who was heading our way. It was impossible to miss him – he was a good six inches taller than everyone around him. Delia was right. His orange tweed flat cap really did stand out in a crowd.

As we watched, the most peculiar thing happened. Delia did a little curtsey. Aubrey asked her something – we were too far away to hear exactly what – then leaned in close and, to our astonishment, roughly grabbed her arm before steering her out of sight.

'I thought they didn't know each other,' I said.

'So did I!' Mum's expression was thunderous.

'Why would she lie about that?'

'Well, she can find her own way home. I'm not a taxi service.'

I regarded my mother with surprise. 'I thought you didn't like Aubrey.'

'I don't,' said Mum. 'But ... but ... I didn't like the way she insisted that reality TV was scripted.'

'Excuse me,' said one of Fiona's minions, who was holding a poster of Cassandra's headshot. 'Got to swap this over.'

'Isn't she here yet?' the major asked.

Mum and I had forgotten that he was still there and must have been listening to our exchange.

'Ah! There she is at last!' he cried.

Cassandra was strolling towards us in a beautiful tailored pearl-grey suit that accented her tiny waist. Her long blonde hair had been swept up in a chignon, with the pink streak falling perfectly over one eye. Even her EcoChamp badge seemed to be more elegant than that of anyone else in the room. A swarm of fans accompanied her, begging for autographs.

'Did anyone ask for *your* autograph today, darling?' Mum said in a low voice. I ignored her.

'Ah, Kat – Iris – glad to see you're supporting the cause for a cleaner environment.' Cassandra turned to the major. 'I am so sorry to keep you waiting, Major Gordon.'

'No apology necessary,' he said.

'Well? Where is the fabulous merchandise?' she asked. 'In that little suitcase?'

'All in good time, my dear,' said the major.

Despite the fact that I should be prepping for my talk, I really wanted to see Cassandra in action.

'Don't you have to do your presentation now, Kat?' she

said. 'You should get over there. It took for ever to cross the room – autograph hunters everywhere.'

For a moment I hesitated, wondering if I should warn her that the bears were copies. 'I wanted to point out—'

'Kat's always swamped by fans,' Mum declared.

Of course this rarely happened any more, but I loved my mother for saying so.

'Hang on a moment.' I knelt down beside the major and said in a low voice, 'Are you sure you want your bears valued in public?'

He nodded.

'Don't you trust my judgement?' said Cassandra with a laugh. 'Don't worry about a thing here. I'll hold the fort for as long as you like. Bye!'

Once out of earshot, I expected my mother to say something about Cassandra, but instead she was searching the crowd. 'Where do you suppose Delia went?'

'Probably the bar.'

'I know I'm fond of my gin, but I definitely don't drink as much as she does.'

'I agree,' I said.

Mum suddenly stopped. 'I've just had a thought. Delia could have a point about the paparazzi. I bet they *are* following Cassandra and not you at all.'

'Let's hope so,' I said. 'You are going to stay for my talk, aren't you?'

'Yes, of course, darling, though … have I heard it before?'

'Some of it,' I said with a sigh. 'Don't worry. You don't have to stay.'

'Would you mind terribly if I didn't? I have to run Delia back to the Hall.' Mum searched the crowd again. 'She's on her lunch break.'

'I thought you said she could find her own way home,' I reminded her.

'I want to know what she and Aubrey were talking about.'

'Why?'

'No reason … Oh, there's Piers,' said Mum.

Piers was making his way to the rows of chairs that had been set up in front of the podium where I would be speaking shortly. I saw Harry and Fliss too. All three – including Piers – had bears. It was rather sweet.

I soon forgot all about Cassandra, the major and my mother's mini spat with her new best friend as I focused on my presentation. Luckily, it went far better than I expected, with a lot of audience participation in naming the top ten most loved bears of all time.

We couldn't quite narrow the list down to ten. But we ended up with Michael Bond's Paddington Bear; A. A. Milne's Winnie-the-Pooh; Bungle from the TV show *Rainbow*; Rudyard Kipling's Baloo from *Jungle Book*; Rupert the Bear, created by artist Mary Tourtel; the Hanna-Barbera cartoon characters Yogi Bear and his sidekick Boo Boo from Jellystone Park; Grumpy Bear, one of the Care Bears, who were originally created by artist Claire Russell for American Greetings; Maw and Paw Rugg from the Hillbilly Bears – another popular Hanna-Barbera cartoon – and lastly, Fozzie, Kermit's best friend from *The Muppets*.

The kids loved it. My ears were still ringing from the

screaming after the result was announced for the number one favourite, who – no surprise – was Paddington Bear.

When the noise had died down, Fiona asked for questions from the floor. She darted around with the cordless microphone, closely followed by Mark Wells and his ever-present camera.

I saw Piers whisper something into Harry's ear. Harry stuck up his hand.

Fiona gave him the microphone.

Harry cleared his throat and shouted, 'Do you sleep alone or with a teddy bear?'

There was a ripple of amusement from the adults.

I glowered at Piers, who just shrugged.

'As a matter of fact, I sleep with a bear.' I'd had the foresight to bring my battered old teddy and leave him on the shelf under the podium. 'And here he is!'

Having valued so many wonderful bears so far, I felt a bit sorry for mine, who was definitely no pedigree. Underneath his cotton dress and yellow cardigan was a pale blue knitted body. His arms and legs were stuffed with cotton wool and most of his fur had worn away. He only had one eye.

'Allow me to introduce Old Teddy,' I said, and held him up to be admired. 'My mother made him and all his clothes. She gave him to me when I was born.'

Piers grabbed the microphone from Harry. 'Did you say *him*?'

'Yes.'

There was more laughter from the adults.

'Then why is he wearing a dress?'

This was a question I had puzzled over myself. I had always thought of my teddy bear as a boy and yet he had always worn dresses. 'He's a very modern-thinking bear.'

I noticed Harry whispering to Piers, and then the three of them got up and left. Piers waved and mouthed, *Sorry!*

'Speaking of clothing,' I went on. 'Don't forget to take your bears clothes shopping at the bear boutique. If you show your entrance ticket or wristband, you get a ten per cent discount.'

'Any more questions?' Fiona noticed that the major's hand was up. 'Ah, yes – sir?'

'I have a question,' he boomed.

Fiona hurried to his side and handed him the microphone.

'Ask Kat Stanford why she would tell a combat veteran that his bears are fake when in fact they are worth thousands and thousands of pounds. She's a crook!'

Chapter Sixteen

There was a deathly hush. Everyone turned to stare at the major. Fiona made a bold attempt at taking the microphone away from him, but he was too fast and sped backwards into the crowd.

'Granny-farming,' he roared. 'That's what you're doing, Ms Stanford. You should be ashamed of yourself. Trying to take advantage of an old soldier with nothing but his disability pension. It's disgraceful.'

I was so stunned I couldn't speak.

There were murmurs of disapproval running through the courtyard. It was obvious that Cassandra did not know what she was talking about. The whole thing was horribly awkward.

'Perhaps we can invite Cassandra Bowden-Forbes up to tell us all about your bears?' I scanned the room but couldn't see her, but I did see my mother with Delia. Mum looked horrified, but Delia wore a grin as wide as that of a Cheshire cat. She seemed to be enjoying my embarrassment.

'Isn't that the antique dealer from *Made in Monte Carlo*?' I heard someone from the audience say.

'Yes. That's her!' Delia shouted out.

'She's gone,' said someone else. 'Left with the Earl of Denby about five minutes ago.'

Lovely, I thought. Cassandra had bolted, leaving me to sort out her mistake.

'Anyone seen today's papers?' came another voice, waving a copy of the *Dipperton Deal*. 'Our Ms Stanford has been fly-tipping. Disgusting.' There were more murmurs of disapproval and a few insults too. To my dismay, I saw Sandra passing out copies of the newspaper.

'Settle down, please, settle down!' Fiona yelled above the noise.

'Granny-farming!' yelled the major into the microphone again. 'Crook! Crook! Crook!'

Suddenly Paddington Bear crept up behind him and snatched the microphone away with a large paw. 'That's enough of this nonsense now. Calm down, everyone. Calm down.'

It was Shawn. I couldn't believe it. Shawn was dressed as Paddington Bear!

'Does anyone have a marmalade sandwich?' he said calmly.

'Will you have jam instead?' his son Ned shouted from the audience.

Everyone burst out laughing. There was a round of applause. Good grief, I'd just been saved by Paddington Bear!

'There is obviously a misunderstanding here,' Shawn went on from the depths of his costume. 'So let's all carry on with the day and allow the professionals to sort it out.' There were a few ragged cheers, and he handed the microphone back to Fiona.

'Thank you … Paddington,' said Fiona. 'Ladies and gentlemen, boys and girls, if your bears are in need of a check-up, now is the time to take advantage of the lunchtime lull and get your furry friends in to see the doctor. And a reminder, that the auction and raffle will be starting here at two thirty p.m. sharp.'

She turned to me. 'In my office. Ten minutes.' Then she grabbed the handles of the major's wheelchair, ignoring his protests, and sped off.

As I hurried after them, Mum and Delia materialised.

'What a disaster!' Mum exclaimed.

'Yes, I know,' I said.

'Rather sweet of Shawn to come to the rescue,' she went on. 'And so dashing as Paddington Bear.'

'I need to sort this out, Mum,' I said grimly.

'You made a mistake.' I could hear the slur in Delia's voice. 'Never mind. It happens to the best of us.'

'Kat doesn't make those kind of mistakes,' Mum snapped. 'She's the top expert on bears in the country.'

'No one is perfect, Iris,' Delia retorted.

Mum bristled. '*Your* daughter may not be perfect, but mine is.'

'She's perfect to me too.' Piers stepped up and kissed my cheek.

'Thanks,' I said.

'And also, it would seem, to Paddington Bear,' he added. 'Maybe I should wear fur.'

'Where are Harry and Fliss?' I asked.

'At the hospital. Fliss's bear is getting new paw pads. Harry stayed with her for moral support … Kat, what happened up there?'

'I honestly don't know.'

'Granny-farming to go with your granny pants?'

'It's not funny.'

Piers scanned the room. 'Where's Kitten?'

'She left with the Earl of Denby,' Delia said. 'And I must go too. Iris? Are you ready?'

'Kat valued three mascot bears for the major,' said Mum, pointedly ignoring Delia's question. 'She offered to take them off his hands—'

'The bears were fake,' I said. 'But Cassandra has obviously declared them to be originals, and the major believes her.'

'What are you talking about?' Piers said sharply.

I repeated the story.

His jaw hardened. 'Well, I'm sure there is a simple explanation.'

'Yes. I'm sure there is. The copies were good. It's an easy mistake. I'm going to sort it out now with Fiona and the major.'

'Will you excuse me?' said Piers, and without another word, he turned on his heel and walked off.

'Well I never!' Mum exclaimed. 'What's wrong with *him*?'

'This will be all over the Internet tomorrow,' Delia said somewhat gleefully. 'Mark my words.'

'How would you know? You don't have the Internet,' Mum pointed out.

'Iris, I really must leave. Do you want to get me in trouble with her ladyship?'

'Get a taxi,' said Mum rudely. 'I'm staying here with my daughter. She needs me.'

'Fine!' Delia stormed off.

'Nick Bond with the *Dipperton Deal*.' A tiny tape recorder was shoved under my nose.

'Actually, I want to ask you about—'

A giant paw pushed the recorder aside. 'No questions. No questions.' Shawn put his furry body between the reporter and myself. 'Fiona is waiting for you in her office. I'll escort you there.'

'Oh, Paddington to the rescue again,' said Mum. 'No wonder you got voted number one.'

Shawn offered me his arm and we wove through the crowds, garnering more than our fair share of comments – most, thankfully, light-hearted.

'I thought you'd left,' Fiona said as I stepped into her office.

The major was holding the little suitcase on his lap. He seemed extremely uncomfortable. 'I'm sorry, my dear.'

'Where is Cassandra?' Fiona demanded.

'She was last seen leaving with the Earl of Denby,' I said wearily.

'I see.' Fiona's eyes flashed with annoyance, but somehow she managed to switch on the charm. 'The major told me about your visit yesterday evening to his home.'

'That's right. The bears are copies – good copies, but copies all the same.'

'He has agreed that you can take another look,' she said.

'I'm sorry,' the major said again, and handed me the suitcase. I put it on Fiona's desk and snapped up the locks.

My stomach turned over.

'I don't understand.' I looked to the major in confusion. 'These are not the same bears that I saw in your house yesterday.'

'What do you mean?' Fiona exclaimed.

'These are *definitely* not the bears I valued yesterday.'

'Are you accusing me of lying?' the major cried. 'First you try to deceive me and now you insult my character. This is *unacceptable*!' His fleeting sympathy for my predicament had gone as quickly as it had arrived. If anything, he was even more indignant.

'Lying is a very serious accusation, Major,' Fiona put in. 'I'm sure Katherine meant no such thing.'

'I don't understand.' I was truly baffled.

'Are they or are they not authentic?' she asked.

'Yes. Yes they are.' And they were – right down to the exposed pipe cleaner ears. 'I must have made a mistake.' But even as I said it, I knew that I hadn't.

'Katherine has admitted that she was wrong,' said Fiona smoothly. 'I think an apology is all we need today.'

The major shook his head. 'She was deliberately trying to trick me, and the public need to be warned.'

I was horrified.

'You offered to take these bears off my hands,' he went on. 'Why would you do that if you thought they were fake?'

Fiona raised a questioning eyebrow.

I didn't have the heart to say that I had felt sorry for him and had wanted to save him more embarrassment. The bears I had seen yesterday weren't even worth seventy-five pounds. So I said nothing.

'You see! That's a sign of guilt right there.' The major was triumphant. '*That's* why I wanted a second opinion.'

There was a tap on the door and Fiona's husband Reggie poked his head in. 'We've got reporters outside wanting interviews.'

'Reporters?' The major sounded alarmed.

'Absolutely not,' said Fiona.

'They're insistent,' Reggie said. 'You know the saying, "there's no such thing as bad publicity".'

'Well stall them!' Fiona cried.

'I'm not talking to any reporters,' said the major. 'I think this has gone far enough.'

I looked at Fiona and saw the relief in her eyes that I knew was mirrored in my own. 'I'm so glad we agree on that score, Major,' she said. 'Would you like a cup of tea?'

I thought for a moment. 'The bears are worth a great deal of money. Would you like me to sell them for you on consignment?'

Fiona beamed. 'What a good idea.'

'No! They're not for sale. I want to go home.' The major gestured for me to return the bears, which I did.

'But … don't go out there yet,' exclaimed Fiona. 'Wait! The reporters …'

But the major had already yanked open the door, where Paddington Bear was holding back the reporters.

'Allow me, Major,' he said as the pair were swallowed up in the crowd.

Fiona turned to me. 'I think the less said about this the better. What a disaster!'

'I disagree,' I said. 'The event has been very successful.'

'For us, yes, but for you – your reputation?'

'Time will tell, I suppose.'

'And what with the fly-tipping incident as well,' Fiona went on. 'I am so angry with Sandra for distributing the *Dipperton Deal* despite me giving her specific instructions to keep the copies in my office.'

'I'm sure she just forgot.'

'We'd better get back for the auction,' said Fiona.

The rest of the afternoon went by without a hitch, and I even forgot the major as I put all my energy into being the auctioneer. Mum stayed until the raffle, but I didn't see Shawn or Piers again.

Dismantling the stands and clearing up the courtyard took a long time, but I was glad of the distraction. It was almost eight o'clock by the time Fiona and I and her handful of volunteers were finished.

I managed to corner Sandra in the car park.

'I'm so sorry,' she said before I even had a chance to speak. 'Fiona has already yelled at me; please don't yell at me too. I just didn't think – the kids were so cute.'

I thought of Shawn's boys. 'Were they twins?'

'No, a boy and a girl. The little boy – I think he's Lord Honeychurch's son – said the order came from the top. Something about conducting an undercover operation and that the earl's son wanted the newspapers given out immediately.'

My heart jolted. 'His son? You mean Viscount Chawley – Piers Carew?'

'I think so.'

After thanking Sandra and reassuring her that she wasn't in trouble with me, I headed for home feeling utterly depressed. Why would Piers have done that? He'd always derided the local newspaper.

It was only when I stopped for petrol that I realised I had missed three phone calls from a number I didn't recognise. I had turned off the ringer at the beginning of the day and forgotten to turn it back on.

But the caller had left a voicemail.

To my astonishment, it was the major.

'I'm sorry for today. You're a kind woman. There is something I need to—' The message ended abruptly.

I played it again. Then I tried to call him, but the phone went straight to answerphone.

I started for home, but something felt off. I thought back to the major's discomfort and then his outrage – mood swings that could be the result of PTSD. Regardless, I was desperate to see those mascot bears again.

I turned around and headed for Riverview retirement village.

Chapter Seventeen

The major's bungalow was in darkness, with the curtains drawn. Since I'd parked my Golf next to his mobility vehicle, however, I knew he had to be home.

The front door was locked, which – if I were to believe Elsie's comment that he always left it open – struck me as a little odd. And after repeated knocking and with no response, I began to grow concerned.

I went to fetch Elsie.

Troy answered the door hatless.

'Oh, it's you again!'

'Is Elsie home? The major isn't answering his door.'

'Come on in.' He stepped aside. 'Mum's in the dining room. Door on the left.'

I navigated my way along the narrow corridor, which was crammed with mismatched furniture. The living room was even worse. Valuable antiques stood side by side with cheap mid-century tables and chairs. It was chaotic to say the least, with a plethora of bookshelves crammed with china, stuffed toys and all kinds of junk.

The canary's cage hung from a hook in the ceiling, which was just as well given the number of cats snoozing in various parts of the room.

Elsie was so engrossed in what she was doing at the dining room table that when she leapt up, she knocked a stack of newspapers on to the floor. As I helped her pick them up, I noticed they seemed to be local papers, all turned to the Classifieds section. Some items were circled in red pen.

'Thank you,' she said, snatching them away. 'Did you forget something?'

'The major—'

'If this is about him calling you a crook, I don't want to get involved.'

'Oh!' I was stung for a moment. 'He left me a message saying he needed to talk to me.'

Elsie just stood there. Troy entered the room. 'What's going on? Everything all right, Mum?'

'I don't know,' said Elsie.

I was perplexed. 'Look, all I know is that he left a message on my mobile wanting to talk to me and now he's not answering the door – and it's locked.'

'Probably because he *doesn't* want to talk to you,' Elsie put in.

'No offence, but you should leave the old bugger alone,' said Troy. 'He seemed pretty upset after today's scene – all those reporters asking him questions. Just leave him be.'

'Yes, leave him be,' Elsie echoed. 'Don't keep bothering him.'

For a moment, I wondered if I should take their advice.

But I couldn't shake off this horrible feeling that something was wrong. 'OK. Fine. But if anything has happened to him, this is on you.'

'I didn't say that I wasn't going to check on him,' Elsie declared. 'I care deeply for my residents, if you don't mind, and I resent your tone.'

'I didn't mean it like that ...'

'Troy will see you out,' said Elsie with a sniff.

At the door, Troy withdrew a business card from his top pocket, all smiles once more. 'For Lord Honeychurch,' he said. 'Heard he's been battling with fly-tippers. We'll give him a special deal to haul it all away. You can tell him we're licensed and bonded.'

'I'll let him know.' I took the card and left.

I had to pass the major's bungalow on my way back to my car. It was still in total darkness. Even if he hadn't wanted to see me, why would he have turned all the lights off?

I went to his front door again and peered through the letter box. My iPhone flashlight cast a pencil beam in the small hallway, catching the metal of his wheelchair. My heart turned over. Yes, something was definitely wrong.

'Major? Major!' I called out. 'Are you all right?'

'What are you doing?' I heard Elsie say sharply behind me.

'Elsie, thank heavens you're here,' I said. 'I think something has happened. I'm sorry, but—'

'Stand back, please.' She produced an enormous bunch of keys and selected one. Unlocking the door she added, 'Stay behind me. I'm used to this sort of thing.'

She flipped on the hall light and promptly threw her arm

protectively across my body, but it didn't prevent me from seeing the major sprawled on the floor at the bottom of the staircase. His head rested awkwardly on the lower step.

'Stay here.' Elsie darted forward and knelt down beside him to check his vital signs, whilst I hovered nearby feeling sick.

'Is he OK?' I said.

'He's dead,' she declared. 'It's the angle of the neck, you see. Happens a lot with falls. I am surprised, though. Usually I have a feeling in my water when one of them is going to go.'

Something didn't seem right. Although the major had fallen, the tartan blanket still covered his legs. Not only that, his wheelchair was pushed against the far wall.

'What do you think happened?' I said. 'Do you think he tried to get out of his wheelchair to ...' I thought desperately, 'use the bathroom perhaps?'

'Looks like it,' Elsie mused. 'But I can't think why. All our bathrooms here are adapted for wheelchair use. Maybe he tried to hop there.' She nodded. 'Yes, that's probably what happened. He must have hopped, overbalanced and hit his head.'

'I'll call 999.'

'Don't bother. I'll ring Dr Smeaton.' She stepped over the major's body, marched to the telephone on the hall table and dialled. I just stood there feeling useless and upset.

'Ambulance will be fifteen minutes,' she said. 'Dr Smeaton will be longer since he's on his way to deliver a baby, but I told him not to rush.'

'OK.'

'I'm sorry for what I said earlier, dear,' she went on. 'It's

just that I'm very protective of my residents, and ... well ...
with what happened at the BearFest ...'

'I understand.'

'I should go home if I were you,' she said. 'I'll take it from
here.'

'I will, thank you.' I was about to leave when I had a sudden
thought. This could be my only opportunity to see if he had
the fake bears *and* the real ones, but at the same time, I was
reluctant to even suggest it.

'Actually,' I said, 'do you mind if I have a quick look for
something?'

'Look for what?' Elsie regarded me with suspicion.

'I just wanted to have another peek at those bears,' I said. 'I
know it's inappropriate, but—'

'Yes. It is inappropriate.' She seemed shocked.

'You can come with me if you like,' I said.

'I don't like to snoop ...' she said. 'But all right.'

For someone who didn't like to snoop, Elsie quickly
seemed to get into the spirit of it. She was opening and closing
cupboards, dragging out drawers and rummaging around in
every available nook and cranny. There was no sign of the little
tan suitcase.

'What about in here?' She flung open the bedroom door,
but we only found an austere, drab room with a military bunk.

'Perhaps they're upstairs?' I suggested.

'Well, I haven't been up there before.'

'I thought you helped the major set up the spare room for
when his daughter came to visit.'

'No.' Elsie shook her head. 'And she's never visited. He

tells me she's coming but then she always cancels. He used to get very disappointed.'

The stairs were narrow, steep and had no handrail. At the top was a tiny landing area with an archway that led into a small room under the eaves.

Elsie gasped. 'Blimey! Fancy that!'

I was astonished.

It was an office complete with a computer station under the dormer window. A large Union Jack flag covered one wall and a glass display case of memorabilia stretched along a second.

Neatly arranged and meticulously labelled was an impressive array of World War II memorabilia, ranging from a Japanese engraved silver cigarette case to an RAF Irvin sheepskin flying jacket.

A second display cabinet held a variety of bayonets, knives and daggers belonging to the Allies and the Germans. A third was devoted to handguns – Lugers, Mausers, Brownings and Colts, to name just a few.

This was a valuable collection.

I stared at the placement of the handguns and noticed there was an empty space. It wouldn't have caught my attention had the other display cases not been so perfectly laid out.

'Will you look at this German helmet?' Elsie broke into my thoughts. 'The label says "World War II German Waffen SS M42 Single Decal Helmet" – ooh, and a … what does that say? A gorget? What's a gorget?'

'It's an article that was worn around the throat,' I said.

'Sounds horrible to me.'

I wandered over to the computer station. Next to a telephone was a large notebook opened to a page full of notations and scribbles. I recognised familiar websites – LiveAuctioneers.com, Invaluable.com and UKAuctioneers.com.

'Where does he get all this from?' Elsie marvelled. 'I mean, how?'

'Online auctions, eBay,' I said. 'It looks like the major was running a little business up here.'

'He was always getting deliveries,' she said. 'I didn't even know he had the Internet.'

We heard knocking on the door downstairs. 'That'll be the ambulance.' She hesitated. 'I'm afraid I can't leave you up here.'

'The suitcase isn't here,' I said. 'Thank you anyway.'

Elsie welcomed John and Tony Cruickshank, identical twins and paramedics. Both had ruddy faces and curly brown hair. I could never tell them apart.

One was carrying a collapsible gurney. 'Here we are again,' he said cheerfully. 'Got any more of your lemon drizzle cake, Elsie?'

'Just a couple of slices left, Tony,' she said. 'But I think you've had more than enough, judging by your waistline.'

He laughed. I felt uncomfortable given the circumstances – talking trivia whilst the major lay at our feet with a broken neck.

John set up the gurney. 'Poor old sod,' he said. 'Looks like he fell down the stairs.'

'He's only got one leg,' Elsie put in helpfully. 'And that wasp sting on his face got all infected.'

'That *does* look painful.'

'He refused to see the doctor, you know.'

John donned a pair of disposable gloves, removed the tartan blanket and gasped. 'Well I'll be buggered.'

'What's the matter?' Elsie exclaimed.

'You said he had *one* leg?'

Elsie stepped forward and gasped too. 'Oh, good heavens!'

I joined her and my jaw dropped.

'If I'm not mistaken,' said John, 'the major here has not got one leg, he's got two. Someone had better call the police.'

Chapter Eighteen

Shawn scratched his chin and stared down at the major's two naked feet. John Cruickshank had removed the soldier's carpet slippers and socks to confirm the deception. 'And you're certain he told you he only had one leg, Mrs King?'

'Got it blown off – or maybe it was shot off.' Elsie was practically hyperventilating with excitement. 'Does it matter? He *lied*!'

'It does matter,' said Shawn. 'He could just have had difficulty walking. There is no crime in that.'

'Do you think he was working undercover?' Elsie's imagination was in overdrive. 'There's a German helmet upstairs. And a lot of guns and knives.'

'I would assume it was more to do with claiming disability and housing allowance than imagining he was James Bond,' said Shawn mildly.

Tony emerged from the major's kitchen sipping a mug of tea. 'Anyone else want a cup? We could be waiting a long time for Dr Smeaton. He's delivering a baby out at Rattery.'

No one answered.

'Perhaps someone was after his collection,' I said.

'A robbery gone wrong, you mean?' Shawn turned to a fresh page in his notebook. 'There were no signs of forced entry. Why would you say that?'

'The major was very neat and tidy, but one of the display cabinets seemed disturbed.'

'Did he have anything worth stealing?'

'To a collector, yes,' I said. 'His military memorabilia look pretty valuable.'

'And what about those little bears?' Elsie gave me a pointed look. 'The ones you came looking for?'

'Yes. Those. I couldn't find them.'

Shawn looked at me too. 'Is that why you're here?'

'The major left a message on my phone.' I handed it to him. 'You can listen to it if you like. Elsie let me into the house.' I felt myself blushing. 'She was with me all the time.' Was I really explaining myself? Why did Shawn always make me feel guilty!

'Actually, Officer,' said Elsie, 'can I have a word with you in private?'

'Certainly,' said Shawn. 'If you can just give me five minutes, I'd like to listen to the major's message.' Once he had done so, he handed my mobile back. 'Thank you. If I need to listen to it again, I'll let you know. You're free to go, Kat – are you feeling all right? You look rather pale.'

'I'm fine, thank you.'

I said my goodbyes and headed for home. I'd lied. I wasn't fine at all.

Finding the major had upset me deeply. It wasn't the first time I'd seen a dead body, but I prayed it would be the last. All I wanted now was my mum.

Unfortunately, when I stopped by the Carriage House, she wasn't home. Seeing the empty carriageway made me realise just how shaken up I really was. And then, to make matters worse, I spotted the black Citroën parked under a bank of overhanging trees halfway along the service road. Now he *was* officially trespassing.

I pulled up alongside, but the car was empty. Where was he? What on earth was he doing? What was he *waiting* for exactly? I hadn't noticed if he had been at the BearFest today, but if he had been looking for a story to humiliate me, he'd have got a good one there. Why bother to keep hanging around?

Call it madness, but I had finally had enough. I was determined to confront this wretched man and demand to know what the hell he was up to.

Grabbing a torch and my pocket Mace defence spray, I got out and marched over to the car shouting, 'This has gone far enough! Whoever you are, come out now!' Then added, 'The police are on their way.' But the only response I got was the sound of the wind whistling through the trees.

Tentatively I approached the car and switched on the torch. The interior was strewn with fast-food wrappers, polystyrene cups and water bottles. A pillow and a duvet were laid out on the back seat. In the rear footwell was a duffel bag.

It brought back the horror of the stalker who had set up camp outside my house all those years ago.

I raced for home, where, to my relief, Mum's Mini was parked outside Jane's Cottage.

I found her in the galley kitchen, perched on a bar stool at the counter. She was sipping a gin and tonic.

I gave her a hug. 'I'm so happy you're here.'

'Where have you been?' She sounded irritated. 'It's almost ten!'

'Wait until I tell you.' I poured myself a gin and tonic. 'I had the most horrible shock, Mum.'

'Well, I'm not surprised. They have history, you know.'

'What are you talking about?'

'Piers and Cassandra,' said Mum. 'I passed them in the car over an hour ago.'

'Passed them? Where?'

'You know how narrow these roads are,' she went on. 'His Mercedes was parked in a gateway on the back road to Totnes. I had to slow right down to squeeze by. The windows were pretty steamed up, but I got a glimpse of a passionate embrace.'

My stomach turned over. 'What are you trying to tell me?'

'Put it this way, they looked very cosy in the front seat. Those Carews are bad news,' she declared. 'Every single one of them.'

'Oh.' I felt sick.

My mother must have seen the distress on my face because she added, 'You can't blame him, dear. Look at Mr Collins in *Pride and Prejudice*! Elizabeth Bennet wouldn't have him despite his protestations of love, so he married Charlotte Lucas instead.'

'This isn't a Jane Austen novel.'

Mum reached out and squeezed my hand. 'I thought you weren't that bothered. In fact, I thought you found him rather annoying.'

'Really? I don't remember saying that … Oh, I'm so confused! I thought I wasn't bothered, but that was before I saw *her*.'

'You don't want him but you don't want her to have him either,' Mum said.

'I don't know what I want.' Then a thought struck me. 'What were *you* doing on the back road to Totnes? I thought you were on a deadline.'

It was only then that I took in my mother's attire. She was wearing a dress that she wore for special occasions – a dark burgundy knee-length cocktail number with a plunging neckline. Wrapped around her shoulders was a cream pashmina, and tucked into her extremely revealing cleavage was a beautiful gold pendant. It was very pretty and it looked expensive.

'Where did you get that necklace?' I said. 'Why are you dressed like that?'

Mum grabbed the gin bottle and topped up her glass. 'I've got no gin left at the Carriage House.'

'And don't change the subject.'

'Seriously,' she grumbled. 'Delia drinks me out of house and home.'

'Have you had a falling-out with your new best friend?'

'She's just so pushy,' Mum moaned. 'Besides, I don't like the way she talks about you.'

'She seems friendly enough.'

'Delia doesn't get along with her daughter,' Mum went on. 'They fight all the time.'

'So I'm not *that* bad a daughter.'

'You're a *wonderful* daughter.' Mum swallowed hard. I could have sworn that she wiped away a stray tear. 'Delia is jealous of what we have.'

'Aw, that's a lovely thing to say.' I stepped up to give her a hug and was practically asphyxiated by a waft of Chanel No. 5. 'Are you wearing … *perfume?*'

Mum gave a dismissive wave.

'I can see why you decided to take the back road,' I said. 'How much *have* you had to drink?'

'Delia's daughter – I can't even remember her name now – she never amounted to much,' Mum continued, ignoring my question. 'She's on her third marriage. Doesn't work. I think she's on benefits. Delia said she was a real disappointment to Lenny.'

The mention of Lenny brought back the horror of the major's death. 'Mum, I have to tell you something really awful – please let me talk—'

'She was very proud of Lenny,' Mum garbled on. 'Just like I was proud of your father – both of them fighting for their country. You know, Dad may not have fought in the war but he was fighting on behalf of Her Majesty's government, keeping the tax evaders exactly where they belonged. In prison.'

'Mum! Please let me speak!'

'I'm not stopping you!'

'The major is dead.'

Mum's jaw dropped. 'Who?'

'The major!' I said impatiently. 'The man in the wheelchair. I found his body tonight.'

'Good grief! What happened?'

'A fall, apparently. Hit his head.'

'Did you call the police?'

'Shawn is with him now.'

'Ah, Shawn,' said Mum. 'A true knight in shining armour. The way he came to your rescue today as Paddington ... Wait – what do you mean, a *fall*? Out of his wheelchair?'

When I told Mum what was beneath the tartan blanket, she couldn't hide her surprise.

'Well I'll be *blowed*! *Two* legs, you say!' she exclaimed. 'He accuses you of granny-farming and all the time he's on the fiddle. It never ceases to amaze me the lengths people will go to dupe the government.'

'Did you seriously just say that?'

Mum blushed. 'Well, my situation is a little different.' She started playing with a bracelet that had been hidden under her pashmina. I hadn't seen that piece of jewellery before either.

I regarded her with suspicion. 'Speaking of fiddling – where did you get that bracelet?'

'Why do you always question me?'

'So you have a new pendant and a new bracelet ... and Ann Summers lingerie. Mum, what is really going on?'

'Oh Kat,' Mum wailed. 'I didn't want to tell you, but ... I have never been so humiliated in all my life.'

'Whatever's happened?'

'I've been stood up!'

Chapter Nineteen

'Stood up?' I said slowly. 'What do you mean ... *stood up?*'

'Promise you won't judge – no ...' Mum put her head in her hands and groaned. 'It's no good. I know you will.'

'I promise I won't judge.'

'It doesn't take away anything I felt for your father. I mean, it's not as if I'm dead from the waist down.'

I was shocked. 'Are you telling me ... have you *met* someone? Have you ... have you actually – no, don't tell me. I don't want to know.'

'Good heavens, nothing like that, although it could have been quite a different story tomorrow morning if—'

'Oh, that's disgusting!' Somehow I never expected my mother to ever have feelings for someone else. 'Who is it? Please don't tell me it's Eric.' I gave a shudder of revulsion as I imagined him picking out the lingerie for my mother. 'Ugh.'

'With those eyebrows?' Mum declared. 'Do you think I'm blind?'

'I can't think who else is available.'

'You can't guess?'

'You know I hate playing guessing games ... Oh! Wait! Is it the driver of the black Citroën?'

Mum pulled a face. 'What? No. Why would you think that? No,' she said again, then, taking a deep breath, 'It's Aubrey.'

'Excuse me?'

'Aubrey – the Earl of Denby? Our local magistrate? The man I thought I loved!'

My jaw dropped. 'But ... you've only ever had one conversation with him ...'

'In your presence, yes, but – oh, I know he had that disastrous second marriage but it only lasted a few months,' Mum went on airily. 'He freely admits it was a mid-life crisis.'

'Isn't he your age? Does that qualify as mid-life?' I was still trying to take it all in. 'Does Piers know that his father—'

'Good heavens, no!'

'And Lavinia? Alfred?'

'Good heavens, *no*!' she said again. 'Alfred can never find out! I've been avoiding him in case he's able to use his Romany telepathic abilities to read my mind. No, he'd kill me. Or maybe he'd kill *him*.' She shook her head. 'It was our secret. We didn't want anyone to know because ...' she shrugged. 'It's only been a few months since his second wife—'

'Jess? The one he sent to prison?'

'I knew you would judge!'

'Mum! She tried to kill me.'

'She was influenced by her brother,' said Mum dismissively. 'And that's no reflection on Aubrey, although I must admit sentencing his own wife seems a little unusual. Still, he was only doing his job.'

'He's a magistrate! Of course it's his job!' I was upset. 'You lied to me. You told me you were writing your book, but instead … you were *living* it!'

Mum looked shamefaced. 'I suppose so.' She gave a heavy sigh. 'But as I said, he didn't turn up. No message. Nothing.'

'What about asking Delia?'

'*Delia?* Why would I ask Delia?'

'She was speaking to him at the BearFest, remember? You were going to find out what they were talking about.'

'I tried, but she denied it and said I needed my eyes tested – the cheek of it! Oh, wait.' Mum's eyes widened. 'Do you think … do you think there is something going on between Aubrey and Delia? I mean, why else would she deny knowing him? In fact, she was very rude about him.'

'Just like you were,' I pointed out. 'Trying to throw me off the scent.'

'Good grief!' Mum sounded hysterical. 'You think Aubrey and Delia are having a fling!'

'No!' I was beginning to get exasperated. 'I didn't say that.'

'Yes. Yes … it's possible.' She frowned. 'Do you remember when she sat in my kitchen and asked me point blank how often the earl came to the Hall?'

'Now you're overthinking things. Why don't you just call Aubrey and ask him outright? You are both adults – at least I like to think you are.'

'No.' Mum stared gloomily into her empty glass. 'But why didn't he call me?'

'You don't have a mobile phone,' I pointed out.

'I sat in that restaurant like a pathetic old woman—'

'Mum, stop! Something must have happened and he couldn't reach you. Maybe he called the restaurant and they forgot to give you the message.'

'Maybe.'

'Which restaurant?'

'A discreet little place,' said Mum. 'The Sea Trout Inn in Staverton.'

I didn't want to tell her that I had met Aubrey Carew there myself when I'd been valuing a doll of his earlier in the year. It was the place people went to when they didn't want to risk being seen by anyone they knew.

'Are you sure you didn't get the wrong day?' I said.

'I sat there like an idiot for a whole hour!' Mum exclaimed. 'The special table. The corner table.'

'So he *had* made a reservation.'

'I suppose so,' she said again.

'You didn't try to call him?'

'Why should I? I don't care. As far as I'm concerned, he's dead to me.'

'Oh Mum.' I looked at my mother and my heart contracted with love. She seemed so vulnerable – and so impossibly naïve.

'I put myself out on a limb,' she went on. 'I took a chance. I should never have agreed to any of it – all the snatched meetings in ridiculous locations … and now I'm being punished. Frank is punishing me from beyond the grave.'

'Now you're being dramatic,' I said. 'And for the record, of course I don't judge you. I want you to meet someone eventually, but maybe not Aubrey.'

'Why not?' Mum demanded. 'You don't think I'm good enough for him?'

'You hardly know him,' I said, adding, 'Are you in love with him?'

'I don't know,' Mum wailed. 'But for the first time in decades I felt a stirring … a stirring of – how can I put it – a frisson of something or other.'

'I told you! No details!' I cried. 'But you should at least wait for an explanation before you do something drastic. What if he's had an accident?'

'I suppose you're right,' said Mum grudgingly. 'It's just that with Frank, when I met him, we fell so passionately in love. We eloped—'

'Yes. I know.' In fact, I still hadn't completely forgiven her for hiding the true story of their elopement from me – and everything else that followed.

'There was none of this baggage,' Mum said.

'Baggage?'

'Ex-wives. Children. Especially the children. What if they don't accept me?'

'Children? As in … Piers and Lavinia?'

Mum nodded. 'Although I must say that Lavinia is as thick as mud and Piers should still be in short trousers – or any trousers judging by what I saw in that car tonight.'

I felt as if I had been punched in the stomach. Mum must have realised her lack of tact because she reached over and squeezed my hand. 'Not that I could see much through the steamed-up windows.' She gave a nervous laugh. 'Oh dear. Am I making it worse?'

'It doesn't matter.' But of course, it did.

I could see from my mother's strangled-cow expression that she was searching for something comforting to say. 'I always seem to put my foot in it, don't I? I am so sorry.'

'I know you don't mean to,' I said – and I knew she didn't.

'Well, when I met Aubrey in Newton Abbot this morning – there's a little coffee shop that no one goes to because the coffee is disgusting – anyway, I gave him an ultimatum.'

'Why?' I groaned. 'Why would you do that? That's the number one no-no of any relationship.'

'I don't have that kind of time!' she said. 'I'm not forty like you! I'm seventy – all right, I could easily pass for sixty-five – and if there is a future for us, I need to know right now otherwise I'm just not interested.'

'Real life isn't a romance novel, Mum,' I said wearily. 'And Aubrey got really burned by his second wife. Why would he want to marry a third time?'

'He told me that he'd never met anyone like me.'

'Well that's definitely true,' I said drily.

'He told me that Jess seduced him with flattery and that she was the first woman he'd looked at since his wife died eighteen years ago. That is, until he met me.'

'That's very sweet of him.'

'I told him I'm not shacking up with him. Why should I be a glorified housekeeper?'

'Just think, if I marry Piers and you marry Aubrey … that would make you my mother-in-law as well as my mother.'

'I'll always be your mother.' She cracked a smile. 'And Piers would be my son-in-law *and* my stepson.' She sighed. 'All right. I'll give Aubrey another chance. I quite fancy being a countess. I might even meet the Queen.' She got up and handed me her empty glass, then kissed me on the cheek. 'Now I know what it feels like to be young again. I must say, I don't think I like it very much.'

'Sweet dreams, Mother.'

'Oh, I meant to tell you, I saw that black Citroën again today, parked near the Emporium.'

'It was in *Dartmouth* today?'

I told her that I thought the man was sleeping in his car.

'Well, regardless of whether he is a stalker or the paparazzi or wanting to steal eggs from birds' nests, I think Delia is right. Perhaps he is after Cassandra. Without putting too fine a point on it, reality stars are de rigueur these days when it comes to the media.'

'Oh – I'm not sure whether I should be relieved or disappointed.'

'If he was dangerous, we'd all be dead in our beds by now, wouldn't we?'

'I still don't like it.'

'Call Paddington Bear first thing in the morning,' said Mum. 'Tell him to pull his finger out and go and arrest him. I'm going home.'

I walked her to the door just as a crackle of lightning lit up the sky, followed by the boom of distant thunder. 'We're going to have a storm. Will you be OK driving home?'

'Of course!'

Despite the sound of rain pounding on the roof, sleep came quickly until I was violently awoken by my mobile phone ringing. This time I had forgotten to switch it off. The sound jolted me out of one of the most bizarre dreams I had ever had. Paddington Bear was wrestling with Cassandra whilst Piers hit him over the head with his bear, Mortimer.

Dismayed, I saw Piers's name flash on the caller ID.

It was almost three thirty in the morning! What was he thinking? That he could just come around for a chat?

Irritated, I switched off the phone.

Mum was right. We were both much better off without the Carews.

Chapter Twenty

I was woken abruptly by the sound of someone hammering and shouting outside.

'Kat!' yelled Piers. 'Open the damn door!'

I lay there, furious. It wasn't even half past seven!

'Kat! I'll break this door down if you don't open up right now.'

Still I lay there motionless, but then – to my dismay – I heard the jangle of keys and a click as the front door opened. I'd forgotten about the spare key under the plant pot.

I leapt out of bed, dragging on a towelling robe, and paused at the top of the spiral staircase. 'Have you any idea what time it is?'

Piers stopped at the bottom of the steps as I glowered down. 'Kat – please!'

Stubble covered his chin and his hair stuck up on end. I noticed that apart from a Barbour jacket, he was wearing the same clothes as he'd worn yesterday, which seemed unsuitable for such a wet and windy morning. But it was the look of sheer despair that made my anger vanish.

I hurried downstairs.

'What's wrong? What's happened?'

'Why didn't you answer the phone last night?' he demanded. 'No, don't tell me. I suppose *he* was here.'

'Who?'

'Paddington – but it doesn't matter. I don't care.' He seemed distraught.

'What's going on?'

'Father is missing.'

I swear my heart stopped beating. Had my mother met up with Aubrey after all? I was in a dilemma. She had specifically told me she wanted their relationship kept a secret.

'How do you know?'

'Because his horse came home without him on it.'

'He came off?'

'Father is one of the best horsemen in the country. He wouldn't just *come off*.'

'I'm sure he's probably walking home right now.'

'No, you don't understand.' An expression of such agony crossed Piers's face that for a moment I pushed aside my confused feelings for him and my jealousy of Cassandra.

'What do you mean?'

'This was yesterday!' he exclaimed. 'Not this morning.'

'You mean late last night?'

'Why would you say *late* last night?' Piers said sharply. 'Do you know something?'

'I just assumed that … I assumed that since he was at the BearFest, he must have ridden later in the day.'

'Yes, yes!' Piers cried. 'I *know* all that.'

'Have you looked—'

'What do you think I've been doing?' he snapped. 'I've been combing the country lanes for hours. I didn't realise that something was wrong until I went to check on the horses.' He raked his fingers through his hair, making it stick up even more. 'I *always* check on the horses before I go to bed. Cromwell's door was wide open. He was inside and still fully tacked up.'

'Oh. I see.'

'One of the stirrup leathers was missing ...'

'*Oh*, I see,' I said again as the full meaning of a missing stirrup leather began to sink in. It was little wonder that Piers was concerned. If Aubrey's foot had caught in the stirrup iron and the safety catch on the stirrup bar had accidentally been closed or jammed, he could have been dragged until his body weight inevitably forced the safety catch to open. The thought was horrific.

'I drove around all night. He probably would have ridden across country. It was too dark to take the bridleways.' Piers's panic was contagious. 'With both estates to cover ...'

'I'm sorry.' I moved in to hug him, but he stepped away. 'I can't ... I'm ...'

'I'll get dressed.' I retreated upstairs to pull on jodhpurs and a sweatshirt; tied my hair back and cleaned my teeth.

'Kitten is already out on horseback,' Piers shouted from below. 'Lavinia and Rupert too; even Edith and that silly little dog.'

'Mr Chips is a great hunter,' I said as I grabbed a rain jacket and we hurried outside. The weather was atrocious, with high winds and a sky leaden with dark clouds.

'I gave him one of Father's socks,' said Piers. 'Edith thinks he'll pick up the scent.'

Moments later, the Mercedes was careening down the service road at a reckless speed, swerving to miss the potholes. I hung on and kept my eyes down. A Chanel lipstick rolled out from under my seat. I had a quick flash of Cassandra sitting in this very spot last night doing God knows what.

'We should call the police,' I said.

'Not yet,' said Piers. 'No need to alarm everyone. He's probably just fallen. That's it. It wasn't too cold last night – wet, yes but he should be fine.' He continued to talk to himself. 'He's in robust health. Yes. He'll be fine.'

I, however, was not so certain. 'We should tell my mother.'

'Iris?' Piers looked at me, incredulous. 'What on earth for?'

'She would want to know,' I stammered. 'You know how she is.'

'Can she ride a horse?'

'No.'

'Then she's no help,' he said savagely. 'Anyway, Father told me he found her irritating.'

Since neither of them had wanted their respective off-spring to find out about their relationship, it didn't surprise me that both would bad-mouth the other. I desperately wanted to set Piers straight, but now was not the right time, and besides, I had promised my mother.

We turned into the stable yard to find Alfred holding Duchess. She was tacked up and ready to go.

Piers stopped the Mercedes but did not cut the engine. 'Alfred is the point of contact.'

'Aren't we going to look for him together?'

'What would be the point of two people searching the same place?' He must have seen the hurt expression on my face, because he added, 'God, I'm so sorry, Kitten …'

'It's Kat,' I said quietly. 'But I suppose it's an easy mistake.'

He looked embarrassed. 'I'm not myself.'

'So … where do you want me to look?'

He grabbed an Ordnance Survey map from the back seat and handed it to me. 'I divided up the area. I thought you could cover Cavalier Copse and go on through Spitwick Dell.'

'Spitwick Dell? I don't know it,' I said. 'Is that on the Carew estate?'

'It marks the boundary where Honeychurch land ends and ours begins,' said Piers. 'There's a track that eventually leads back to Carew Court.'

'Is it easy to find? Signposted?'

'No, no signpost. Haven't you lived here long enough by now?' I could sense Piers's impatience coming off him in waves. 'You can access the track behind Harry's tree house. You have to look for the entrance because it's pretty overgrown. I assume you *do* know where Harry's tree house is?'

'Of course I do.' I wanted to add that he didn't have to be such a jerk about everything. I was just as worried about Aubrey as he was.

'Edith and Lavinia are using Harry's two-way radio. I can't believe in this day and age it's virtually impossible to use mobile phones around here.'

'It's part of the charm of living in rural England,' I said lightly, but Piers did not smile.

'Have you got your mobile?'

'Yes.'

'You can get a signal from Harry's tree house.'

'Oh. OK.' Did he seriously expect me to do that? I opened my car door. Piers grabbed my arm.

'Kat – wait.' He paused. 'Thank you for this. Really. I want to talk to you and explain what is going on with Kitten, but I just—'

'Don't worry about it.' I didn't want to hear what he had to say. 'Let's just focus on finding your father.'

Piers drove away.

Alfred led Duchess towards me. 'His lordship seems a bit uptight.'

'You're telling me. I take it that Jupiter is unrideable because she cast a shoe?'

'Unfortunately Cassandra insisted on taking her.'

'But she could go lame!'

Alfred shrugged. 'I just follow orders,' he said, barely bothering to hide his dislike. 'She promised there would be no road work.'

Suppressing my irritation, I tried to mount Duchess but she kept sidestepping away.

'It's the weather,' said Alfred. 'There's another storm coming. Horses can sense it.'

'And what can *you* sense, Alfred? Any psychic thoughts?'

'It's a bad business,' he said darkly as he checked then tightened Duchess's girth. 'That's all I can say. A bad business.'

A sudden gust of wind caught an open stable door, slamming it shut. The loud bang spooked the mare and she darted sideways, nearly unseating me. I shortened the reins, sank down in the saddle and gripped her flanks tightly. 'Steady, girl, it's OK.'

'You want to watch her.' Alfred plunged his hand into his pocket and passed up a few cubes of sugar. 'If you run into trouble, just dismount and lead her. She'll be all right if she can see you.'

We set off at a trot. It was one of those blustery autumn days when the wind tore through the trees, rattling the branches. It began to rain.

Leaving the Hall behind us, we turned left along Cavalier Lane.

I knew that the route would take us past my least favourite part of the estate – Bridge Cottage. Since the ruined house backed on to Coffin Mire, the area always seemed full of menace. According to local legend, during the English Civil War, scores of Cromwell's Roundheads were led to their doom in the swamp – hence the sinister name.

It would seem that Duchess felt the same as me. As we drew closer to Bridge Cottage, she stopped and flatly refused to move forward. The bridleway skirted the property and, from this direction, was the only access to Harry's tree house.

I urged her on but she refused to budge.

'Please, Duchess,' I pleaded. 'Come on, girl.' I gave her a sharp kick. With a grunt of protest, she danced sideways, only to stop dead at the sight of a blue tarpaulin flapping in the wind, caught on the corner of a wooden pallet. The snap and crackle terrified her.

I remembered Alfred's advice and dismounted.

With the promise of a sugar cube, Duchess allowed me to lead her through the gate and along the perimeter fence, which was lined with a number of green bottles.

And then I saw it.

Delia's tote bag was caught on a nail. I knew it was hers because I recognised the photographs of her granddaughter in the photo pockets. I grabbed it and, since it was empty, folded it and shoved it inside my raincoat.

Thoughts of Delia were soon gone as Duchess and I reached Harry's tree house.

What had started as a simple wooden platform had evolved into a little hut cradled in the branches of an ancient oak tree. Above the hut, half a dozen struts had been hammered into the trunk, leading up to a second platform.

The hut was painted in tan, beige and sage green to blend in – which it did, perfectly. Falcon's Nest was practically invisible from the bridleway unless you knew exactly where to look.

A few yards beyond, a thick hawthorn hedge marked the boundary line that Piers had mentioned. The entrance to the path was partially hidden by an overgrown blackthorn hedge, but when I paused to take stock, I noticed a series of large dark stains and splodges in the long grass. Even more alarming was the way that sections of the grass lay flattened before the path curved sharply to the right.

I began to suffer a horrible foreboding.

Cautiously I urged Duchess forward. As we reached the bend, my worst fears were realised.

At first I prayed that I was mistaken and that someone had dumped a bag of clothing – but it was Aubrey.

I didn't need to check for a pulse. I already knew.

He was dead.

Chapter Twenty-one

Aubrey's mangled body with his left boot still wedged in the stirrup iron was a hideous sight to see and one I would never forget.

His stirrup had finally broken free, depositing him in the underbrush.

The irony was that the track ended at the road just yards further along. Piers must have driven past his father countless times.

I'd narrowly escaped being dragged myself once; the stirrup's safety catch released me the moment I hit the ground. This had not been the case here. No matter how steady a horse, Cromwell would have been frightened by the weight of a large, heavy object banging along behind him.

I raced back to Harry's tree house, left Duchess to graze, and scaled the rope ladder.

Piers was right. There was a strong signal from the upper platform. I called for help. Of course, the ambulance dispatcher wanted the exact location of the body, but all I knew was that it was in Spitwick Dell.

'A footpath next to a lane isn't helpful, ma'am,' said the dispatcher. 'I will hold the line whilst you find out.'

'I'm calling from a tree,' I said desperately. 'I don't know! There's no one to ask! Somewhere near Bridge Cottage – Honeychurch Hall? Little Dipperton?'

'I will hold the line whilst you find out,' she said again. 'Just keep calm, dear.'

I wanted to scream with frustration, but then I remembered. Harry's maps! He had an Ordnance Survey map – code name Operation Bridge Cottage – tacked to the wall inside his hut.

'Yes, please hold the line!' I exclaimed. 'Don't hang up!'

From the map, I was able to work out exactly where Aubrey was: Redswing Lane – a place I'd never have identified in a million years – less than a mile from Carew Court. He had been close to home all the time.

I informed the dispatcher. And then I called Piers.

I suppose I waited fifteen or twenty minutes before I decided to return to Aubrey's body. I'd been unwilling to leave just in case someone needed to call my mobile.

As I rode up, the Cruickshank twins were already lifting Aubrey on to a gurney. Piers arrived on horseback moments afterwards. He leapt off Fleetwood's back and threw the reins in my direction.

'Piers—'

Clearly distraught, he shook his head, turned on his heel and clambered into the back of the ambulance to be with his father. The twins slammed the rear doors and roared away with the siren blaring.

I just stood there, unsure what to do. But then Cassandra appeared, hauling Jupiter to a stop. Tears were streaming down her face. 'Where is he?'

'The ambulance has been and gone,' I said dully. 'Piers went with them.'

'Oh, this is awful.' She began to sob. 'I can't believe it, oh my God. This will kill Piers. It will just kill him.'

I didn't know what to say. What *was* there to say?

'I told Aubrey to wear a proper safety helmet,' Cassandra went on. 'But he refused. He was so stubborn! He *would* wear that stupid orange cap. We'll never know what really happened, will we?'

'Orange cap?' I realised that I hadn't seen his tweed cap along the bridleway or the footpath. It was such a distinctive colour, it would have been hard to miss. 'Perhaps if we can find that, we might know where he fell off.'

'Does it matter?' Cassandra wailed. 'He's dead! Aubrey was like a father to me.' She touched her EcoChamp badge almost in reverence. 'But I'll carry on his good work. He'd have wanted that.'

'I'm so sorry,' I said lamely.

'Piers told me he was … he was dragged.'

'It looks like it.'

'How can that be possible? He was an excellent rider. Cromwell was bombproof. I just don't understand.'

We both heard the sound of another siren. Over the high hedges, I could see the flashing lights coming our way.

'God, that must be the police,' said Cassandra. 'What good will they do now?'

'I suppose they have to file a report.'

'Whatever for?'

'I have no idea,' I said wearily. I felt tired and emotional.

Cassandra must have realised, because she said, 'Go home. I'll handle them. Honestly. You've had a big enough shock for today.'

'Thanks.'

'Besides, this is a family matter now.'

'Let me know if there's anything I can do,' I said.

'I will.' Cassandra seemed to be rallying. 'But somehow I doubt it.'

I turned Duchess for home. Cassandra was right. There really was nothing more I could do.

I'd only ridden a few hundred yards along Redswing Lane when Shawn drew up alongside in his panda. He opened the window, his face a picture of concern. 'Are you all right?'

'I think so,' I said, and promptly burst into tears. 'It's just … what with … I'm fine. Really.'

'The major, I know.' Shawn got out of the car, retrieved his handkerchief and passed it up.

'Thank you.' I took comfort in the familiar smell of the banana fabric softener that his mother-in-law always used. I blew my nose. 'I don't suppose you want this back.'

'Keep it,' he said kindly. 'Look, I'll come by a little later to check on you. Will you be home?'

I knew I had to tell my mother. 'Try the Carriage House first.'

Alfred was waiting when I got back to the stable yard.

'You all right, lassie?' he said. 'That's two bodies in twenty-four hours. Bit of a record even for you!'

'You know *already*?'

'Bad news travels fast,' he said.

And that meant my mother probably knew too.

'Oh Alfred! Can't you use your magical powers and tell me what happened? Do you know anything? *Feel* anything?'

'It will all come out in the end.'

'What's that supposed to mean?'

'Just what I said. But you need to be careful.'

Fifteen minutes later, I was knocking on my mother's door. There was no answer – and it was uncharacteristically locked.

'Mum!' I shouted. 'I'm going to keep on knocking until you open up!'

Finally: 'Go away!'

'Please, Mum,' I said gently. 'Let me in.'

'Are you alone?'

'Of course I'm alone,' I said.

I heard the key in the lock. A hand pulled me inside. 'Quickly.'

Chapter Twenty-two

'Obviously you've heard,' I said as I took off my muddy riding boots.

'Of course I've heard!' Mum's face was blotchy from crying. 'Delia called me. Mentioned it in passing in the same breath as her recent purchase of a jumper from Marks.'

'She wasn't to know about your feelings for Aubrey,' I reminded her.

'Apparently Lady Lavinia was hysterical and had to be sedated.'

I thought of Piers. I had longed to comfort him but Cassandra had made it clear I wasn't needed.

'My heart is broken,' Mum said. 'Broken.'

'Broken?' I raised an eyebrow.

'Well, I'm upset then,' she amended. 'Really upset.'

Suddenly I found I couldn't move. I just stood in the hallway. 'Oh Mum,' I wailed. 'Seeing him … it was horrible. So horrible.'

'What a mess this is.' We hugged each other tightly.

'I think this calls for a gin and tonic,' I said.

I took off my coat, taking Delia's tote bag into the kitchen and putting it on the dresser. Mum mixed our drinks.

'And to think I believed he had stood me up,' she said. 'When all this time he had been lying dead in the mud.'

'Don't talk about it!'

'What time do you think this happened?' she asked.

'We don't know anything yet,' I said. 'But it must have been after the BearFest and before Piers discovered Cromwell back at the stables late on Saturday night.'

'Poor man,' Mum whispered. 'I know he and I hadn't known each other long, but I enjoyed his company, Kat. He made me laugh. He could be very funny.'

I had never regarded the 'hanging judge' as a comedian, but kept quiet.

Mum dabbed her eyes with a handkerchief. 'Horses are such cruel beasts. Aubrey loved Cromwell. Said he was as steady as a rock. The fact that he was dragged—'

'Dragged?' I hadn't told my mother that Aubrey had been dragged. I'd thought that detail would be far too upsetting.

'That's what Delia said.' Mum pointed to the dresser. 'Wait – is that her tote bag?'

'I found it at Bridge Cottage,' I said. 'Did she mention she'd lost it when she called?'

'No. She was too excited about telling me about Aubrey.' Mum frowned. 'How odd. She and that silly bag were inseparable. In fact I've never seen her without it.'

'Maybe we should tell her we have it.'

'Good idea.' Mum brightened. 'I'll invite her for lunch. Alfred took a sandwich today, so he won't bother us. Apparently

Cropper's put his back out and asked Alfred to help him with the vegetable garden. Bit of a cheek if you ask me. They need to hire a full-time gardener.'

My mother made the call to Delia whilst I looked at the photograph pockets of her tote bag more closely. Her granddaughter really was adorable. I felt a twinge of longing for a family of my own.

'She'll be here in ten minutes,' said Mum, breaking into my thoughts. 'Hide the gin bottles, though – and put the kettle on.'

I did as I was told, then took a moment to brush my hair. Mum dashed upstairs to fix her face. When she returned, she looked as if she hadn't been crying at all.

We rustled up ham sandwiches, found some cherry tomatoes, a jar of mustard and some crisps from Marks & Spencer, and filled tumblers of fresh water.

We heard a call of greeting and Delia strolled into the kitchen. 'Don't you ever lock your door?'

'This is the country,' Mum said. 'We don't need to.'

'I'm glad to get away from that house,' Delia went on as she hung up her coat. 'Such a tragedy. Lady Lavinia is a mess. She idolised her father.'

'You must be upset as well,' I said slyly.

'Me? Why? As I told Iris yesterday, I didn't know the earl. Never met him before in my life.' She reached for a sandwich. 'Are those ham?'

'Yes, they are,' Mum said. 'So you're telling us that the Earl of Denby, Aubrey Carew, our local magistrate, was a complete stranger to you?'

'How many times do I have to tell you?' said Delia. 'Yes.'

'Well don't forget to tell the police that when they come to ask questions,' Mum said. 'Do you want mustard with your ham?'

I shot her a puzzled look. She shrugged.

'Wait – did you say the *police*?' Delia said sharply. 'Why would they want to talk to me? Pass me the jar.'

Mum pushed it towards her. 'It's just the way they do things in Devon. Isn't that right, Kat?'

'Yes, that's right,' I agreed. 'They have to do a thorough investigation …' I racked my brains, 'for the verdict.'

Mum seemed surprised and mouthed, *Verdict?*

'I meant report. They'll want to talk to everyone who ever knew Aubrey Carew.'

'I didn't see anything.' Delia gave me a black look. 'What's wrong with your daughter, Iris? Why is she questioning me?'

'Well, Kat was very fond of Aubrey,' said Mum. 'Very fond.'

'Yes. You can say that again,' Delia said. '*Very* fond.'

'What do you mean, *very fond*?' Mum demanded.

'Nothing.' Delia took a bite of her sandwich.

'You must have meant something,' Mum persisted. 'Otherwise you wouldn't have said it.'

'I was trying to protect you.'

'Protect me? What do you mean, protect *me*? Protect me from what?'

'Well, apparently the earl was … shall we say …' she looked pointedly at me, 'a bit of an attraction for the younger ladies.'

'What's that supposed to mean?' I could tell that my mother was getting upset because two red dots bloomed on her cheeks. Delia had pushed a button.

'*Apparently* he'd been married before, to some young floo-zy,' Delia went on, and again looked directly at me.

Mum bristled. 'His second wife was a con woman. He was tricked.'

'Tricked?' Delia laughed. 'That's what they call it, do they? That's the thing with men. They reach a certain age, divorce their wives, who have stood by them for decades, and run off with younger women.'

'His first wife died, Delia,' I pointed out. 'Aubrey had been a widower for a number of years.'

'And of course *you* should know.'

'Excuse me?' Now it was my turn to bristle. 'What do you mean, *I* should know?'

'He was probably sleeping with the other woman for years and … maybe he got rid of his first wife. Maybe he just decided to knock her off. How did she die?'

'I don't know.' Mum seemed perplexed.

'Exactly!' Delia was triumphant. 'You read about that sort of thing all the time in the papers. It makes it simpler to just get rid of your wife. That way you don't have all the financial hassle of going through a divorce.'

'Have you been *drinking*?' Mum demanded.

'No!' Delia's eyes blazed. 'I'm just saying that young women, especially with all that hair, tits and teeth' – she turned to me *again* and spat – 'they're just *tramps*!'

I couldn't believe what I was hearing. 'How rude!'

'Kat is *not* a tramp,' Mum declared.

Suddenly Delia's eyes began to tear up, and she seemed to shrink in her chair. 'I'd really like a gin and tonic.'

'Kat, make our *guest* a cup of tea – but give her a mug.'

I got up, distinctly annoyed, and switched the kettle on. I'd decided I didn't like my mother's new friend very much.

'Oh good heavens, I am so sorry.' Delia seemed horrified. 'I don't know what came over me. I apologise. Sorry. It's the … it's the shock of it all.'

'The shock of *what*?' Mum said. 'You just told us you didn't know the Earl of Denby, so why should you care?'

'I don't.' Delia stuffed an entire sandwich into her mouth. I plonked a mug of tea on the table – no bone china for our guest today – then fetched a bowl of sugar and a small jug of milk.

'I'd really like a gin and tonic,' said Delia again.

'It's tea or nothing at this hour until you tell us what is really going on,' Mum said, and meant it.

Delia put two heaped teaspoonfuls of sugar into her cup. 'All men cheat.' A tear trickled down her cheek. She brushed it away angrily. 'All men are pigs.'

'Apart from your Lenny, dear,' Mum reminded her. 'You said your marriage was perfect. So was mine. We were lucky to have married good men.'

'You never really know someone, though, do you?' Delia said quietly, and added a third teaspoonful.

Anxious to defuse this strange conversation, I presented Delia with her tote bag. 'Well, I'm sure you'll be happy to know I found this.'

A tide of red raced up her face. She snatched it, thrust it on to her lap, and picked up her mug of tea without saying a word.

I waited for her to ask me where I'd found it, but she didn't, so I told her.

'At the … where? *Bridge Cottage?*' Delia said. 'How extra-ordinary. You mean the rubbish tip on the outskirts of the village?'

'It's not officially a rubbish tip, Delia,' said Mum. 'The tote bag was snagged on the fence.'

'Snagged on the fence, you say,' Delia repeated. 'Well. How extraordinary.'

'Was anything stolen?' Mum asked. 'Kat said the bag was empty.'

'Stolen?' Delia blinked several times. 'Yes. Yes, that's right. The bag *was* stolen. Did I not say it was stolen?'

'No,' Mum and I chorused.

'Well it was,' said Delia. 'Fancy my bag ending up at Bridge Cottage. Are you sure that's where you found it?'

'Positive,' I said.

Mum and I exchanged glances.

'So … where was it stolen from?' Mum asked. 'Whoever stole it must have taken your purse.'

Delia hesitated. 'I must have left it in the taxi yesterday afternoon.' She nodded to herself. 'That's right. After the BearFest, when I had to get home to take care of the dowager countess.'

'I told you I would have driven you home,' Mum said. 'And now look what's happened! A taxi driver stole your purse and then deliberately drove miles out of his way to throw your bag over a fence.'

'Yes!' Delia nodded again. 'I think that's exactly what must have happened.'

'I hope you called the taxi company,' Mum went on.

'I don't remember. Yes. I did. I think.'

'I hope you cancelled your credit cards.'

'I don't remember, Iris!' Delia was becoming hysterical. 'I had the bag in the taxi and the next thing I know, your daughter finds it at the dump site – or so she says.'

'Why would I make that up?' My suspicion that Delia was hiding something was deepening by the minute. 'I saw it, I recognised it – and I knew the bag was special to you.'

'Why were you there anyway?' Delia said. 'Doing a spot of fly-tipping?'

'No,' I said, trying to keep my temper. 'I was helping to look for Aubrey, as a matter of fact.'

'And it was Kat who found him!' Mum seemed to be feeling the same way as I was. 'So it's really good that the police will be here to ask us all questions, isn't it?'

'I told you, I didn't see anything,' Delia said nervously.

'We didn't say you did,' I said.

'But at least you can report the theft of your tote bag to the police, can't you?'

Delia glowered at Mum. 'I thought you were my friend, Iris.'

'I *am* your friend. It's Kat who wants to know why you're lying.'

'Mum!' I was horrified. 'I never said such a thing!'

Delia's complexion had turned an angry red. 'I told you, someone stole my bag.'

'There's been a theft?' came a familiar voice. 'What theft?'

Chapter Twenty-three

'What perfect timing, Officer,' Mum declared. 'Delia was just telling us that she had her tote bag stolen.'

Delia froze. 'But I have it back now,' she said. 'I don't want to trouble anyone. I'm sure the officer has more important things to do …'

'A theft is a theft.' Shawn took out his notebook and pencil.

'I mean, what about the poor earl's accident? Isn't that more important?' Delia gabbled on. 'Besides, I must get back to the Hall. I only have an hour for lunch, and you know the dowager countess, she's a stickler for timekeeping.'

'By the way, my grandmother says that you're doing an excellent job as housekeeper,' said Shawn. 'Everyone is very happy with you being there. I thought you'd like to know that.'

'Oh goodness, really?' Delia turned pink with pleasure, and for a moment, her desperation to escape the kitchen vanished. 'I do like the family, I must say. Everyone has been so kind.'

'And you've settled into your cottage?' Shawn went on. 'I

know my grandfather tends to have the television turned up rather loud.'

'Sometimes I hear it, but it doesn't bother me, and yes, I love the cottage.' Delia smiled. 'Having been an army wife, I never really felt settled. We were always on the move. This is the first time I've ever had something that I can call my own. I want to stay here until they take me out feet first.'

I could see that she really meant that and felt a twinge of guilt. Perhaps we had been too hard on her. Maybe she was just struggling like the rest of us.

'I'm sorry to hear that you lost your husband,' said Shawn. 'Thank you.'

'I know how it feels to lose someone you love,' Shawn went on. 'It's hard to carry on sometimes.'

Mum shot me a sympathetic glance and rolled her eyes, because there she was – the ever-present ghost of Helen Cropper.

'I heard your wife died of cancer,' said Delia. 'So young. So tragic.'

'Delia might be able to help you solve the mystery of the major,' Mum said, deftly changing the subject.

'Oh?' said Shawn. 'How?'

'Her husband served in the same regiment in the Falklands.'

'That would be most helpful, Mrs Evans,' said Shawn.

'A lot of men fought in the Falklands. I don't think I can be of any help. It was so long ago.' Delia stood up, but in her eagerness to leave, she knocked over her chair. 'Oops.'

'Here, let me,' I said, and helped her right it. She seemed nervous.

'Just a few routine questions,' said Shawn. 'We know Major Gordon had a daughter in New Zealand.'

'Had?' Delia paused. 'What do you mean, *had*?'

'He's dead,' Mum said with her usual tact.

'Dead? Dead. You mean, he's really dead?' Delia's face went through an extraordinary transformation. I could have sworn I saw relief. 'Of course I'm always happy to help the police with their enquiries. Ask me anything at all – you know where to find me if you need me. Goodbye!'

'Well, *she* suddenly changed her tune,' said Mum when Delia had left.

Shawn pointed to the last remaining sandwich on the plate. 'Is that ham?'

'Help yourself,' Mum said. 'Tea?'

'Lovely.' He sat down and turned to a fresh page in his notebook. I handed him a mug, realising I knew exactly how he liked to drink it. 'I need to get a firm idea of everyone's movements on Saturday afternoon and evening.'

'Why? Surely you don't think anything suspicious happened to the Earl of Denby?' said Mum.

'I'm afraid I'm not at liberty to say.'

'You never are,' muttered Mum.

'I'll pretend I didn't hear that, but I will say that certain things have come to light.' Shawn took a bite of sandwich. 'As we know, the earl was not a popular man. His environmental activities and zero-tolerance policy on fly-tipping made him a lot of enemies. He was notoriously ruthless as a magistrate and had a habit of following up on those he had convicted to make sure they were toeing the line. A lot of people didn't like that.'

'Well they shouldn't have committed crimes in the beginning, should they?' Mum said somewhat defensively.

Shawn gave a heavy sigh. 'I really don't know where to start. Wherever there is trouble, the pair of you always seem to turn up. Let's start with you, Iris.'

'Me? Why? I was nowhere near anything at all!'

'Iris, Iris, Iris,' said Shawn wearily. 'Where were you last night?'

'*Last* night? Me? You do know I'm an author. I have a very tight deadline. I was writing. Ask Katherine.'

'Since we've already established that Kat was at the major's house last night and actually discovered his body, you'll have to think of another alibi.'

'Oh. Maybe it wasn't last night …'

'It's just to establish a time frame for the accident, Mum.' I hoped she wasn't going to be difficult.

'I'll ask you one more time, Iris,' said Shawn. 'Where were you last night?'

'Writing,' Mum said stubbornly.

Shawn regarded her with disdain. 'The landlord of the Sea Trout Inn in Staverton informed me that you sat at a table in his restaurant for over an hour and a half waiting for the earl to arrive.'

'Landlord?' Mum scoffed. 'I don't know any landlord from the – what was it? The Sea Trout Inn?' She shot me an anguished plea for help that I pretended not to see.

'Iris—'

'Why would you have talked to the landlord at the Sea Trout Inn anyway?' Mum ventured.

'Because *Piers*' – Shawn said the name with a tinge of contempt – 'informed me that his father was going on a date with a mystery woman last night.'

Mum reddened. 'How would he know?'

'Just answer the question, please.'

'Why do you think it was me?' Mum said desperately.

'Because the landlord described you,' said Shawn. 'He also said that you became very belligerent and rude to the staff and started threatening to kill the earl because he'd failed to show up.'

'Oh, all right. I admit it, I was there, but as for the threats, I was just joking,' said Mum. 'I thought I'd been stood up. I was embarrassed. It was a figure of speech. You know, I could strangle Kat sometimes but I never actually would.'

'I'm glad to hear it,' I said.

'I just have to explore every single line of enquiry,' said Shawn in his usual pompous tone. 'Once we get the full report back from the pathologist, we'll have a better idea of timing.'

'So you really *do* believe something suspicious happened?' I just couldn't see how.

'I'm afraid Piers is convinced that there is more to it. He refuses to accept that the horse—'

'Cromwell,' I put in.

'That *Cromwell*, who was trained as a riot horse with the City of London Mounted Branch, would have bolted like that.'

'I don't agree,' I said. 'He would have been panicked by the sense of a large bulky object bouncing along behind him. Have you found Aubrey's cap yet?'

'Cap?'

'He always wore an orange tweed flat cap out riding – like a newsboy cap,' I said. 'He wasn't wearing it when I found him and I didn't see it anywhere along the trail.'

Shawn nodded thoughtfully. 'So ... wherever we find his hat, we could—'

'Find the place where he came off. Perhaps the location of the cap will provide a clue to what really happened. And there is something else.' I went on to tell Shawn to check the entrance to the track behind Harry's tree house. 'I can't be sure if it was blood or not – and the grass was flattened, which could indicate—'

'That he was dragged,' Mum whispered.

'We'll look into that. Thank you,' said Shawn.

Mum's lower lip began to quiver. 'I really liked him,' she whispered. 'Have you no heart, Detective Inspector? *No*. I believe you do not.'

'I'm sorry you feel I am a heartless policeman, but sometimes I have to be,' said Shawn. 'Which brings me to my next question.' He turned to me. 'Ms Stanford—'

'I thought we were dispensing with the official titles – and Mum, don't feel you have to stay,' I said. 'After all, you do have a deadline.'

'I want to,' said Mum. 'I'd like to see what Paddington Bear is about to accuse you of – since we *are* dispensing with the official titles.'

I couldn't be certain, but I was almost sure that I saw a glimmer of a smile flicker across Shawn's features.

'OK, *Kat*, let me see.' He leafed back through his little notebook. 'It seems that you made two visits to the major yesterday.'

'No. Just one.'

'You were seen that afternoon walking around the court-yard.' He consulted his notebook. 'About five thirty.'

'No,' I said. 'I was still in Dartmouth at that time.'

He made a note of it.

'And then you returned around eight, eight thirty?'

'Are you suggesting foul play?' Mum said.

'Possibly.'

'And since you are questioning my daughter, I assume you think the foulness might have something to do with her.'

'Mum, let Shawn finish.'

'We do know that the major fell from the top of the stairs,' said Shawn.

'And we also know that he had two legs,' Mum put in. 'So he obviously tripped. Hardly enough evidence to accuse Katherine of being involved.'

'I might have been inclined to agree with you, Iris, had it not been for the fact that there is evidence to suggest that a gun was taken from one of the glass display cabinets. Of course, that might not be suspicious. Perhaps he had just sold it and hadn't had time to rearrange his collection.'

'And Kat said that the mascot bears were missing.'

'Shawn knows that, Mum.'

'So let's go back to the beginning,' said Shawn, turning to yet another fresh page in his notebook. 'Walk me through your movements after the programme finished yesterday.'

'I was at the Emporium clearing up until around eight.'

'Can someone vouch for you there?'

'Yes. Fiona Reynolds, and Sandra, who manned the

registration table for EcoChamp, and a couple of other volunteers whose names I don't remember but I can find out.'

'What about … your *boyfriend*?' said Shawn. 'Can he vouch for your whereabouts?'

'Viscount Chawley left abruptly with Harry and his little friend well before the programme had finished,' Mum put in. 'And by the way, he's not Katherine's boyfriend. He just likes to think he is.'

'Oh.' Shawn's ears actually turned pink. 'I see.'

'The only reason I went to see the major at all was because of the strange message he left on my mobile,' I reminded him. 'I told you all this last night.'

'He would hardly have called her on the phone if he could see her outside his window,' said Mum.

'But he wouldn't have been expecting to see her, would he?' said Shawn.

'Although …' I said slowly, 'Elsie *did* ask me if I had forgotten something.'

'Implying that you had been there earlier?' Shawn suggested.

'Possibly. But I hadn't.'

Shawn made a note on his pad. 'Well, I think that's about it for today, although' – he took a deep breath – 'I would like to talk to Kat in private.'

Mum got up from the table and winked at me. 'Of course. Don't mind me. I must get back to my book.'

The moment the kitchen door closed behind her, the atmosphere changed. I actually felt nervous.

Shawn cleared his throat. 'I wanted to tell you something,' he said shyly. 'I *do* have a heart …'

'Don't take any notice of my mother,' I said lightly. 'She says things to shock sometimes.'

'I just don't wear it on my sleeve.'

'Oh.'

A moment passed between us that I could only describe as electric. I had to look away.

'Kat …' he cleared his throat again. 'Elsie King's description of you was very clear.'

I stiffened. How stupid of me to misread Shawn's claim to have a heart.

'As I have already told you, I wasn't there until at least eight.'

'I know, I know, but …' He suddenly reached out to move a lock of hair off my face. 'Your beautiful hair is hard to miss. She was most insistent.'

I was confused. Was Shawn flirting or interrogating me?

'Kat,' he went on, 'I know that things have been strange between us, but I would never want to tread on another man's toes, and the other night …' his face reddened, 'at Jane's—'

'Please!' I felt embarrassed. 'It wasn't what you thought.'

'Well – I'd rather put all that behind us now.' Shawn twirled the lock of hair around his finger and looked into my eyes. 'Your mother's comment has made it clear that—'

'Here you are!' Piers burst into the kitchen.

Shawn and I sprang apart. I felt my face flame red. Shawn stood his ground and seemed defiant. 'Don't you ever knock?'

Piers was furious. 'What the hell is going on?'

'Gosh!' Cassandra peered over Piers's shoulder. 'I think we've interrupted a tender moment, don't you, darling?'

Chapter Twenty-four

'**I am surprised that you, of all people, have managed to recover** so quickly from discovering my father's body,' Piers fumed.

I didn't comment. Shawn just stood there smirking.

'Well, it's not her first time. Lavinia tells me she's stumbled on dozens. It makes one wonder.' Cassandra stroked Piers's arm. He threw it off and stepped away.

'I don't care about the others,' he snapped. 'I just care about this one.'

'Then it's just as well you're both here.' Shawn brandished his notebook, pencil poised. He seemed indifferent, but I could see that his hands were trembling. Piers's fury was intimidating. 'I'm trying to establish a timeline for the earl's last movements.'

'Oh? So you are on duty after all,' Piers declared. 'I am surprised.'

'Naturally, there has to be a hearing—'

'I suspect the verdict will be death by misadventure – wouldn't you agree?' Cassandra said.

'No. I don't agree,' said Piers.

'Darling, we've been through this,' Cassandra said gently. 'Aubrey just fell off. It was rotten luck that he got his foot stuck in the stirrup. The safety catch must have jammed.'

'No,' Piers exclaimed. 'That horse was bombproof. He would never take off like that.'

'Perhaps the girth wasn't done up properly,' Cassandra suggested. 'What's the name of the groom at the Hall? You know, the stable chap?'

'Alfred,' I said. 'But he didn't tack up Cromwell. Cromwell isn't stabled at the Hall.'

'You should talk to him,' Cassandra said, pointedly ignoring my comment. 'There's something I don't like about him. Lavinia says he's one of your mother's relatives, Kat. Worked in a circus in Spain or something.'

One day that lie would come back to bite my mother, too.

'Don't be ridiculous,' Piers said roughly. 'I told you, there was nothing wrong with the girth. Cromwell was wearing his saddle when he got back.'

'Did you ever find Aubrey's cap?' Cassandra asked.

Piers frowned. 'What are you talking about?'

'That darling little newsboy cap that you bought him for his birthday – apparently he wasn't wearing it when Kat found him.'

'My thought was that if we find the cap, we might get a better idea of where he actually fell,' I said.

'Kat! Yes!' Piers cracked a smile. 'You are amazing.'

'Do you remember what time the earl went riding on Saturday afternoon?' asked Shawn.

'I can answer that,' said Cassandra. 'Aubrey drove me back to the Hall after lunch – I don't have a car, as you know. We had some campaign business to discuss. He told me he was going to have a nap – he didn't say anything about riding. Piers and I spent the rest of the day and evening together.' She flashed me a triumphant look.

Shawn turned to Piers. 'Sir?'

'Yes. I dropped Harry and Fliss back to the Hall mid-afternoon and then—'

'We went for a lovely walk on the moors.' Cassandra slid her hand through Piers's arm. I felt an unexpected twinge of jealousy that was most infuriating. 'And then went out for supper.'

'Where did you go?' Shawn asked.

'That funny little place on Dartmoor,' she said. 'I can't remember the name of it, can you, darling?'

'No,' said Piers tersely.

'I'm sorry we can't be more specific.'

'So, to be clear,' said Shawn, 'no one knows what time the earl went out for his late-afternoon ride.'

'I'm afraid not, Officer,' said Cassandra. 'I suppose we'll never know exactly what happened, will we?'

'That's not good enough for me,' said Piers. 'I want to know.'

'And that's why we are establishing a timeline,' said Shawn. 'We also may have a witness.'

'A witness?' Cassandra exclaimed. 'Good heavens. Really? Who? Surely not the new housekeeper?'

Shawn seemed surprised. 'I hadn't considered Delia Evans. Why would you mention her?'

Cassandra shrugged. 'She's always creeping about on her bicycle.'

'Not across the fields, though,' I said.

'There's no need to be sarcastic,' said Cassandra. 'I was just trying to help.'

'Kat was trying to help too,' Piers said.

Cassandra shot him a filthy look and pouted.

'I'm speaking to Delia Evans today about Major Gordon,' said Shawn. 'I'll ask her then.'

'Major Gordon?' Cassandra frowned. 'Why does that name mean something to me?' She snapped her fingers. 'Oh! You mean the chap whose bears I valued?'

Shawn caught my eye. I detected a discreet shake of the head that implied I should keep quiet, which was fine by me.

'What has Delia Evans got to do with the major?' Cassandra said. 'Oh, wait, wasn't she married to someone in the army who fought in the Falklands?'

'Yes, I believe so,' I said.

'Every time I see her, she goes on about how wonderful her husband was and how much she misses him. Rather sweet, actually.'

'Can't we just concentrate on what happened to my father?' said Piers. 'I'm sure the whole thing about the major is very interesting, but it's hardly relevant here.'

Cassandra looked stung.

Shawn consulted his notebook. 'Have either of you seen a black Citroën in the vicinity? Foreign car. European bumper sticker.'

'Yes, a couple of times,' replied Cassandra.

'You have?' I was surprised.

'Just parked here and there,' she said. 'I've never seen the driver, but it does look as if someone is living in it. Hardly a credible witness.'

Piers frowned. 'Is this the man you thought might be a stalker, Kat?'

'Or a birdwatcher. Or paparazzi,' I said. 'I really don't know. And he may not be looking for me.'

'True, he's probably looking for me.' Cassandra didn't seem remotely bothered. 'Happened all the time when we were filming *Made in Monte Carlo*.'

'Regardless. The driver needs to be found and questioned,' said Piers. 'He could have seen something important.'

'Allow the police to do their job, please,' said Shawn.

'Your father's death was just an accident, Piers,' said Cassandra.

'Accident or not, I want to know exactly what happened.'

'Which is why we need to start with finding his cap,' I said.

Shawn said his goodbyes and promptly collided with my mother as she entered the kitchen.

'Oh, am I missing a party?'

'We're just leaving too,' said Cassandra. 'Adorable little kitchen.' She gestured to the oak dresser that held my mother's beloved Coronation china. 'And what a darling little collection.'

I caught the condescension in her voice, but my mother did not. As always when she was in the presence of someone she felt socially inferior to, she became tongue-tied and awkward.

'I'm so sorry about your father's accident,' she managed to

say. 'Poor Katherine hadn't quite recovered from finding the major's body yesterday, and now, just hours later, she discovers another one!'

'Mum!' I protested.

'What!' Piers seemed horrified. 'Why on earth didn't you tell me?'

'I thought you had enough to deal with,' I said.

'The major?' said Cassandra slowly. 'As in Major Gordon?'

'And guess what! He was a fraud!' Mum blundered on. 'He had two legs!'

Cassandra actually laughed. 'That's absurd. How on earth do you know?'

A puzzled expression crossed Piers's face. 'But when was this?'

'Saturday evening,' said Mum. 'Kat went to his house.'

'Mum, please—'

'Let your mother talk, Kat,' said Cassandra. 'Gosh. I'm intrigued. You went to the major's *house*.'

'She wanted to have another look at the mascot bears,' said Mum.

'No – well yes, I did, but I actually went there because the major left me a message on my mobile.'

'How extraordinary!' Cassandra said. 'What did he say?'

'That he had something to tell me.'

'So you went to his house …' Cassandra shook her head. 'You didn't trust my valuation?'

'What on earth happened?' Piers demanded.

'It looks like he fell down the stairs,' I said.

'But the police are investigating,' Mum put in.

'Whatever for?' Cassandra demanded. 'Surely they don't suspect the proverbial' – she used air quotes – 'foul play.'

Eventually I caught my mother's attention and she must have realised that she'd said far too much. She shrugged. 'Oh, who knows?'

'Do they think it was a robbery gone wrong?' Cassandra suggested. 'Was anything taken?'

'Shut up, Cassandra,' Piers barked.

Cassandra turned ashen. 'My name is Kitten,' she whispered.

'Can't you see that Kat is upset?'

'I'm sorry. Of course she is – finding two dead bodies in—'

'*Cassandra!* Just … don't talk!'

There was an uncomfortable silence.

'Well … don't you think we should go, darling?' Cassandra said finally.

'You go,' said Piers. 'I'm staying here.'

'But … I don't have a car.'

'Take mine,' he said. 'Kat will run me back.'

'I can wait,' said Cassandra desperately. 'Besides, don't you want me to help you look for Aubrey's cap?'

'No,' said Piers. 'Kat will help me.'

'Oh.' Cassandra nodded and gave a bright smile. 'That does sound a better idea. In fact, I think I might go and treat myself to a spa since you're loaning me the car. I feel so stressed out.'

'Delia and I were thinking about a spa day,' said Mum. 'But we haven't a clue where to go.'

'Try the Dart Marina Hotel and Spa in Dartmouth,' said

Cassandra. 'It's very nice. You should ask for Debra, she's excellent.' She held out her hand to Piers. 'Car keys?'

'They're in the ignition.' Piers pointedly put his arm around my shoulders. 'You've had a really bad time of it, Kat. I am sorry.'

Cassandra just stood there, disappointment written so plainly on her face that I actually felt a pang of compassion. Piers seemed to be unnecessarily unkind.

'Lovely,' she said brightly. 'What time should I pick you up tomorrow, darling? Remember we are driving to London.'

'I'd rather take the train,' said Piers.

'Nonsense. It's so much easier by car. Lavinia is an emotional wreck,' Cassandra rambled on. 'It's better for her if we drive. You know how overwhelmed she gets.' She smiled again. 'We're going to see the solicitor about Aubrey's estate.'

'That's fast,' Mum said. 'I had to wait months and months when Frank died.'

'Well, goodbye.' Cassandra headed to the door, then paused, 'Oh, Kat, I'm such an idiot. I forgot to tell you that Harry wondered if you might pop up to the Hall.' She looked at her watch. 'Right now, actually.'

'Of course,' I said. 'Did he say why?'

'You know Squadron Leader Bigglesworth.' Cassandra smiled. 'I expect he wants to give you some instructions about a mission. He said to meet him in his quarters.'

And with that, she was gone.

Mum turned to Piers. 'Well, she seems to have bounced back.'

'Yes, that's Cassandra,' he said grimly. 'She always does.'

Chapter Twenty-five

'You weren't very kind to Cassandra,' I said as we sped up the drive to the Hall in my Golf. Naturally Piers insisted on driving.

'She knows the score,' said Piers. 'And I know her. Those are crocodile tears. She just has to have every available man fawning over her, and since Paddington was clearly fawning over you, she didn't like it one bit.'

'I don't think that's true,' I said. 'She's really upset about your father.'

'Well, yes, probably that bit is true,' said Piers.

'I hope you didn't ban her from staying at Carew Court because of me,' I said.

'Of course I did!' Piers exclaimed. 'Kitten has a habit of losing her bearings in the middle of the night, if you know what I mean. No, it's about time she didn't have everything her own way.'

'You're putting me in the middle and I don't like it.' The truth was that the more I got to know Piers, the more I knew that he wasn't for me. But in the circumstances, I could hardly tell him that right now.

'Kitten is just upset because I told her how I felt about you.'

This was so at odds with my mother's comment about seeing them together last night, I felt I had to speak up. So I did.

'I was setting her straight,' Piers said. 'And she didn't like it. She threatened to throw herself out of the car, but she's always been one for drama. Don't worry about it.'

But I was worrying about it. 'I hope you told her that we were just good friends.'

'We're more than good friends,' Piers said. 'You're very special to me, Kat. I'm not usually this patient with the women I date.'

'Patient!' I exclaimed. 'What do you mean, *patient*?'

'Do I have to spell it out?'

'No,' I said quickly, because of course I knew exactly what he was implying.

'I must admit, I had high hopes for us in Paris.'

'I always made it clear that nothing physical was going to happen.'

'And I made it clear that I would do exactly what you asked – and I did.'

'I know.' I couldn't fault Piers's manners. He had been the perfect gentleman. It was hard not to be seduced by his charm. But there was a selfish streak I didn't like, and I definitely didn't like how he was treating Cassandra.

'So what's going on with you and Paddington Bear?' he demanded. 'Should I be jealous now?'

'There is nothing going on with anyone,' I said crossly. 'Can we just stop talking about my personal life?'

Piers reached across and squeezed my hand. 'I don't know what's wrong with me.'

'Piers, you've just lost your father,' I said quietly. 'When I lost mine, we knew it was coming. He'd been ill for quite some time. This is completely different. You're still in shock.'

Piers's jaw hardened. 'If you must know ... Father and I had a row before this happened. A fearful row and it ended badly. I ... I didn't have a chance to tell him I was sorry.'

'But I'm sure he knew you loved him.'

He gave a heavy sigh. 'I may as well tell you. Father and I argued because ... because he had started seeing someone.'

'Oh?' My stomach gave a lurch. 'Did he say who it was?'

'He refused to tell me. He said I'd judge him.'

'Ah.' I felt relieved but also protective of my mother. 'And *would* you have judged him?'

'Too right I would.'

'Don't you think he should be able to make his own choices?'

Piers looked at me with amazement. 'That's pretty rich coming from you! You were the one who was nearly killed by his last wife.'

'Yes, that's true, but—'

'*No!*' Piers struck the steering wheel hard. 'It was another gold-digger wanting to be the next Countess of Denby.'

'If you didn't know who it was, why would you think that?'

'I know Father's type,' said Piers. 'He has – I mean, he *had* terrible taste in women.'

'Women as in plural?'

'Oh he was quite the rogue,' said Piers. 'Where do you think I got it from?'

My heart sank. I distinctly remembered my mother telling me how special she felt because other than Aubrey's disastrous marriage to his second wife, he claimed that he had not been involved with anyone else since Piers's mother died. He must have lied.

'I told him that she would never be welcome under my roof,' Piers went on.

'That seems a bit harsh given that you didn't even know who it was.'

'Father was not happy with my decision,' said Piers. 'He told me that if I didn't accept her, our relationship would be over.' He shook his head. 'And now … it is.'

There was so much I could say to that, but I didn't. I knew he was in a lot of pain and perhaps that was why he was being so irrational.

As we approached the Hall, Piers said, 'We're slipping in through the servants' quarters. I'm not up to making small talk with the butler today, and I definitely can't handle my sister. I've had enough of hysterical women.'

'Piers,' I said. 'Does Harry know what's happened?'

'Rupert told me he would tell him when he felt it appropriate.'

Ten minutes later, we were standing on the galleried landing, having crept up the back staircase. Light spilled from the domed atriums above, illuminating a threadbare carpet that bore the imprints of several pieces of heavy furniture that had been sold off, and a handful of picture lights over empty squares. Two beautiful walnut display credenzas contained an assortment of exquisite porcelain snuff boxes – Lady Edith's cherished collection.

'This place is like a morgue. Rupert really should modernise.'

'I don't think he can afford to.'

'That snuff box collection is worth a bit,' Piers went on. 'He should sell it.'

'It's Edith's,' I said.

'You can't get sentimental over things like that. I kept telling Father ...' A look of deep sorrow crossed his handsome features.

I grabbed his hand. 'Come on, let's go and report for duty.'

Piers gave a wry laugh. 'An escape from reality is just what I need.'

Chapter Twenty-six

'Come!' called a voice from behind the door bearing the *Squadron Leader Bigglesworth* nameplate.

Piers and I stepped into a light and sunny bedroom with two casement windows.

'One moment, please.' Harry didn't look up. Dressed in his usual Biggles attire, he was seated at his desk writing in a large notebook.

Piers and I stood to attention and waited. It was at times like this that Piers redeemed himself with me. I could never have imagined my ex-boyfriend playing along. He would have dismissed Harry's act as precocious, and of course, that was true. But as far as I was concerned, childhood these days was so short. Kids grew up so fast. Why not indulge the boy for however long his obsession with the World War I flying ace lasted?

Harry's bedroom reflected that obsession. As Piers and I waited for Biggles to finish his writing, I looked around.

Model aircraft from World War I were suspended from

the ceiling. Harry's Great-Uncle Rupert, a skilled aviator, had built the Sopwith Camels and the Tiger Moths. This had been his bedroom, and his framed photograph still hung in the corner – a handsome pilot in a flying suit, helmet, goggles and white scarf, just like Biggles, Harry's hero.

Harry claimed that his great-uncle visited him all the time, and I believed him. Honeychurch Hall had more than its fair share of ghosts – something I knew from experience.

The furniture was mainly pine – a narrow bed, a free-standing wardrobe and a chest of drawers. There was a pine blanket chest and a matching bookcase filled with comic books and volumes of adventure stories. A workstation stretched the length of one wall, holding pots of paint, brushes, glue and scissors.

In the corner was an ancient navy school trunk with old leather straps. The name *Rupert E. Honeychurch* had been scratched out and *Harry E. Honeychurch* written in black marker pen above it.

Seeing the old trunk reminded me of the little tan suitcase of mascot bears. That had had initials stamped into it too. I wished I'd paid more attention, because I couldn't remember what they were. Spying Edward sitting on Harry's bed gave me the idea to contact Jean Grogan from Little Scruffs. The bear-making business was a small world. Perhaps she had made copies of the major's bears or knew who might have done. It was a long shot, but worth a phone call.

Harry capped his fountain pen and put it down. He looked up. 'At ease.' He gestured to the two wooden chairs in front of his desk. Piers and I sat down. 'To what do I owe this pleasure?'

'Special Agent, er … Kitten told me I was to report for duty, sir,' I said.

Harry frowned. 'Really? I gave no such order.'

'She mentioned a mission.'

'No.' Harry shook his head. 'She must be mistaken. But since you're both here …' He pushed the notebook towards us. 'I've just completed my report on the German ammunition dump, code name Bridge Cottage. Take a look.'

'I wasn't aware of any such mission,' said Piers.

'It was on a need-to-know basis,' said Harry. 'Special orders from the commander-in-chief.'

He rose from his chair and went to stare out of the window, assuming the pose of a man who carried the weight of the world on his shoulders. 'In my report you will see a thorough description of the enemy.'

Piers and I started to leaf through Harry's notebook.

'Take a look at this,' whispered Piers. 'Who needs CCTV when we have Biggles watching from the tree house – I mean Falcon's Nest?'

Harry's detailed sketches were in the form of a diary. Crude illustrations of cars along with the colour and a number plate were listed, with the date and time and the type of item that had been left at the dumpsite. He'd used colouring pencils for the stick figures, carefully drawing their hair and clothing.

'This is amazing, sir,' I enthused. 'How long have you been doing it?'

'Special Agent Ridley and myself started at the end of the school holidays,' said Harry. 'It's mostly weekends. We have an excellent view of the ammo dump from Falcon's Nest.'

Piers pointed to a square white van with a stick figure of a man in a hoodie. 'No number plate, sir?'

'Unfortunately not,' said Harry. 'They delivered a fridge and an old cooker last weekend. Germans drink a lot of beer and cook a lot of sausages.'

I turned the page and my heart lurched. It was a drawing of the black Citroën and a man with grey hair and heavy-rimmed glasses. Harry had even drawn in the European Union bumper sticker.

'Look!' I said to Piers. 'It's him.'

Piers nodded. 'Where did you see the black Citroën, sir?'

Harry turned away from the window. 'Ah! Now he is definitely a spy. Could be one of ours.'

'Why?' I said.

'Not one of ours as in one of *us*,' Harry said. 'But working against the Germans. For a start, he's driving a foreign car. The steering wheel is on the wrong side. Number plate deliberately smeared with mud.'

'Go on,' said Piers.

'And we've seen him with binoculars *and* taking photographs.'

'He was taking photos of Bridge Cottage – I mean the ammo dump?' I was surprised. 'Why do you think our mystery man would be taking photographs there?' I whispered in Piers's ear.

'Perhaps he was involved in the Tena Lady incident,' he whispered back. 'Perhaps he scours the dumpsite for granny pants.'

'Very funny.'

'If you get any more information on this agent, sir,' said Piers, 'we'd really like to hear about it.'

I turned another page and nudged Piers. Harry had drawn a woman with dark purple chin-length hair riding a bicycle. A bag was on the handlebars. 'Delia Evans, I assume.'

'Ah yes, it most certainly is,' Harry agreed. 'She was delivering schnapps to the men.'

'Schnapps?' Piers said.

'That's right. Apple schnapps,' said Harry. 'In green bottles.'

I almost laughed. Had Delia been dumping her empty gin bottles? She'd said many times that she was a Gordon's Gin girl.

Mum and I had joked about Delia's drinking, but maybe it really was a problem. As she'd pointed out, Rupert was a stickler for recycling. Was that what she had been doing at Bridge Cottage? Transporting bottles in her tote bag during her lunch hour? It would explain the location of the tote bag, but not why she had abandoned it.

'I believe she could be a double agent,' said Harry.

'A *double agent*?' Piers and I said in unison.

'I'm afraid so,' said Harry grimly. 'What's more, I've observed some unusual activity in the walled garden.'

'With Delia Evans?' I was puzzled.

Harry beckoned for us to join him at the window. He was holding a pair of binoculars and passed them to me. 'Take a look.'

I could see Alfred digging whilst Cropper sat on a shooting stick watching.

'Maybe she's been helping Cropper out,' I suggested. 'He's got a bad back.'

'That's what I thought at first, but on further inspection …' Harry pointed to a beehive-shaped building partially below ground, tucked into the far corner. It was the old ice house. 'I've seen her coming out of that bunker carrying a suitcase.'

'A *suitcase*!' I said sharply. 'What kind of suitcase?'

'Brown leather. Like the ones we have in the luggage room in the attic,' said Harry. 'We think it contains top-secret documents.'

It had to be the mascot bears! There could be no other explanation.

'Sometimes she's been seen carrying the suitcase into one of the potting sheds,' Harry went on. 'Special Agent Ridley even saw her going into the henhouse. She was in there a very long time, and I can tell you, she wasn't collecting eggs.'

'Let's go there now,' I said to Piers. 'Search the entire garden if we have to.'

'I'm afraid we've already looked,' said Harry. 'She must have moved it elsewhere, probably under cover of darkness.'

Delia *had* to have got both the real and the fake bears from the major. Perhaps it was *she* who had visited him yesterday afternoon. Mum said that Delia had gone home in a taxi, so she could easily have paid him a visit. But according to Harry, he'd seen her with the suitcase for quite some time. The timing was off. It didn't make sense.

It was obvious that Delia and the major had known each other before and both pretended otherwise – rather like my mother claiming to dislike Aubrey. Perhaps that was why Delia had fled the moment Mum had tried to introduce her to him at the BearFest. But why hide the fact that they knew each other? And why would Delia deliberately want to publicly embarrass me with the bear switch?

Piers had been quietly leafing through Harry's notebook. Now he suddenly gasped. 'Oh, Kat, *look*.'

Harry had drawn Aubrey on horseback. Bridge Cottage was in the background. It was dated yesterday at 4.35 p.m. Aubrey was wearing his orange tweed newsboy cap.

'Did you see where our man was riding to or from?' Piers tried to keep his voice steady.

'He was heading to the ammo dump,' said Harry. 'But our commander-in-chief radioed in and ordered us to return to base, so we lost sight of him after that.'

'Well thank you, Squadron Leader Bigglesworth, for sharing this critically important report,' I said smoothly. 'Permission to be dismissed?'

'Permission granted.'

'Now we have an idea of where to look for that cap,' said Piers in a low voice.

Harry followed us out on to the landing. 'There's one more thing – Flying Officer Stanford, can I have a word?'

'Excuse me,' I said to Piers.

Harry looked serious. He drew me aside and said in a low voice, 'I have observed you at the ammo dump three times, but I did not include my sightings in the report.'

'Me?' I was surprised. 'I was there with Edith – your grandmother – on Friday, but—'

'Oh, I can't bear it!' Lavinia materialised on the landing

wearing flannel pyjamas with cat motifs. She had dark circles under her eyes and her face was blotchy from crying. When she saw Piers, she collapsed into his arms.

'Not in front of Harry,' Piers whispered, and gently pushed her away.

Suddenly Squadron Leader Bigglesworth had vanished and in his place was a frightened little boy. 'What's happened?' said Harry. 'Why are you crying?'

'Mummy was reading a sad book,' Lavinia said between her sobs.

Personally I thought it terrible that they still hadn't told Harry that his grandfather had died. He didn't need to know the details.

'Where is Kitten?' Lavinia said.

'She's gone to Dart Marina for a spa treatment,' I said.

'*Again?* That's twice this week.'

'Twice?' I said sharply. 'I thought she didn't arrive until Thursday evening.'

'Oh, she was staying in Dartmouth.'

'Why didn't you tell me?' Piers demanded.

Lavinia clapped her hand over her mouth. 'Oops. Sorry. That just slipped out. The thing is … Kitten didn't want you to know she was in Devon.' She shot me an agonised look. 'She told me that … that you got a bit possessive, brother-o, and that she needed some time on her own. Oh golly! Please don't tell her I told you. She'll kill me.'

'That's where Kitten and I met the man in the wheelchair who got stung by a wasp,' chimed in Harry. 'Did you know that you can escape a wasp if you run in a straight line? If you

zigzag and wave your arms around, the wasp sees a big target.
I tried to tell him, but he didn't listen.'

A peculiar feeling came over me. The major had said the
exact same thing.

I tried to sound casual. 'So that's where you met Major
Gordon? In Dartmouth?'

Harry nodded. 'He had millions of medals and told us all
about his leg being blown to smithereens in the Falklands.'

'And you actually saw him get stung by a wasp?' My mind
was trying to make sense of this bizarre connection to Cassandra.

'Yes,' said Harry. 'He tried to escape. He even got out of
his wheelchair but he couldn't hop fast enough. And then he
bought us ice creams.'

The major had been at the BearFest yesterday. Surely
Harry had to have recognised him.

'The kids weren't there when the whole granny-farming
incident happened,' said Piers as if reading my mind. 'He and
Fliss had appointments at the bear hospital immediately after
your talk.'

'I am sorry I couldn't come,' said Lavinia, furiously blow-
ing her nose into a tissue.

'Excuse me, I must get back to my post.' Harry gave us a
crisp salute that we returned, then left.

'We'd better go,' said Piers.

'Please don't tell Kitten I told you,' Lavinia begged again.

'Don't worry,' said Piers grimly. 'I won't. I'll pick you both
up tomorrow morning at eight sharp. Now go and get dressed
and pull yourself together. And if you don't tell Harry about
his grandfather, I will.'

Lavinia nodded miserably. 'All right.'

We headed to my car. My mind was spinning with the silly wasp story and the fact that Cassandra and the major had met before but it was Delia who had the suitcase. It was all so confusing.

I tried to share my thoughts with Piers.

'Let me handle this,' he said harshly.

'Why should I?' I exclaimed. 'It's my reputation at stake here.'

'You're being paranoid,' said Piers. 'There is bound to be a simple explanation. Stay out of it. You have to trust me on this.'

But as we drove away, I realised that I didn't think I could.

Chapter Twenty-seven

Neither of us spoke again until we got to Bridge Cottage. Piers seemed preoccupied and my mind was spinning with conspiracy theories.

'We'll retrace Father's steps from here.' He pointed to the entrance to the bridleway.

'I think we should start over there, on the forecourt,' I suggested. After all, it was where I had seen Aubrey and Rupert arguing just two days before, as I told Piers.

'So now you think that Rupert is involved?' I caught the sarcasm but didn't bite.

'Go on ahead,' I said. 'I'll take a look around and catch you up.' I turned away and headed to the dumpsite.

I saw the hoof prints straight away.

I rarely saw Rupert on horseback so I was pretty certain it had to be Aubrey. Edith would never have risked Tinkerbell stepping on a nail or piece of glass. In fact, it was pretty foolhardy of Aubrey to venture this way at all. What was he thinking?

The hoof prints continued past mounds of household waste, empty plastic crates, sections of foam and discarded sofa cushions. It was mind-boggling to see what items were thrown away, from rusting metal pipes to sodden cardboard boxes full of old photographs.

The track ended at the bottom of a muddy bank, which had become home to dozens of car tyres that had obviously been hurled down from above. A path had been beaten all the way up through the brambles and brushwood to a ridge. I counted twelve tyres in a heap here, and a pile of horse manure.

It was then that I noticed a muddle of hoof prints and two sets of footmarks all mixed in together. My heart began to pound. I knew this was important, but I wasn't sure why. I was just about to go after Piers when I looked up and saw him heading over.

I waved and shouted. 'Here!'

He broke into a run.

'You found Father's cap?' he said breathlessly.

'No, but look.' I pointed to the prints clearly outlined in the mud. 'I know we don't know if Aubrey actually *did* ride here, but what do you think?'

'What am I looking at?'

'Two different-sized footprints and hoof prints all mixed together.' I picked up a long stick to point them out. 'Do you think Aubrey dismounted?'

'Unlikely,' said Piers. 'He always used a mounting block.'

'Perhaps this time he didn't?'

'What's up there?' Piers pointed to the bank.

'Let's find out.'

We both struggled to clamber up the slope. It was steeper than it looked and the ground was slippery. Brambles grew on either side, leaving very little to cling to. Of course, I fell twice.

Finally we got to the top and stepped into a green lane. There were several places where the brush had been flattened – presumably this was where fly-tippers hurled the heavier items down the bank.

Piers stood with his hands on his hips and surveyed the scene. 'This isn't getting us anywhere. There is no sign of Father's cap at all.'

'No,' I said. 'But I think something happened at the bottom of this bank. Perhaps Aubrey saw someone doing something, dismounted and went to investigate … Wait! Is that a car?'

We both listened. Sure enough, there was a screech of brakes followed by the whine of an engine reversing at high speed. Piers grabbed my hand and pulled me down beside him behind a bush that concealed us from the dumpsite below.

Peering through the branches, we could see that a white transit van had reversed into the forecourt. A man wearing a hoodie jumped out, darted around to the rear to pull open the doors, then scrambled inside. Moments later, out flew cardboard boxes full of junk, a lamp, four broken chairs and finally a portable radiator.

He closed the doors and banged smartly on the side of the vehicle, leaping back into the passenger seat as the driver floored it and the van sped away.

It all happened very quickly.

'I can't believe it!' I exclaimed. 'In broad daylight!'

'Harry drew that van,' said Piers. 'Well, I think we have our answer. Father must have caught them red-handed and was attacked. Perhaps he tried to mount Cromwell but couldn't ...' He didn't finish his sentence. 'My God.'

I knew what he was thinking. It would have meant that Aubrey was dragged for an incredibly long distance. I didn't say a word.

We clambered back down the slope in silence and headed to the bridleway, passing the green bottles – yes, they were Gordon's Gin. Perhaps Delia had seen the transit van dumping the rubbish and got scared. I couldn't think why else she would have left her tote bag.

After two hours of intense searching, we returned to my car. There was no sign of Aubrey's cap anywhere. I could sense Piers's despair.

'Do you want to come back for supper?' I said. 'I can rustle up some scrambled eggs. Maybe watch a movie?'

To my surprise, he agreed.

But as we reached Jane's Cottage, my heart sank. Piers's Mercedes was parked outside. Cassandra got out of the car when she saw us pull up and gave a friendly wave.

I felt a rush of irritation. Piers's expression was stony.

As always, Cassandra looked stunning, dressed in a bur-gundy leather jacket over black jeans and smart button boots. An ice-pink lipstick picked out the streak in her perfectly coiffed hair.

'There you are,' she trilled. 'Any luck with finding Aubrey's cap?'

'Yes,' Piers declared. 'As a matter of fact, we did.'

His lie surprised me just as it seemed to surprise Cassandra, judging by the expression on her face. 'Oh! How lucky. Good. Where?'

'I really don't feel like talking about it if you don't mind,' said Piers. 'It's been a harrowing day.'

'That's why I'm here, darling,' said Cassandra. 'To take you home. We have an early start tomorrow, remember?'

For a split second I felt sorry for Piers. He no longer had the swagger and confidence of a man who was sure of his charm and appeal. He seemed vulnerable and very alone.

'That's a good idea,' I said to Cassandra, even though I thought it a bad one. I just didn't want to fight with her. 'I think we're all tired.'

Piers handed me my car keys.

'He always has to drive,' Cassandra said with a wink. She linked her arm through his and steered him over to the Mercedes before turning to me and waving again.

As I stepped into Jane's Cottage and shut the door, I had a sudden thought. For someone who had just had a spa appointment, Cassandra's hair and make-up looked flawless.

She had lied about being in Devon the week before the BearFest *and* she had met the major before the event. Something didn't add up.

The phone rang. It was my mother. 'Did you find Aubrey's cap?'

'No, but I have things to tell you,' I said. 'Are you up to receiving visitors?'

'I'll pop a Marks and Spencer meal in the oven,' said Mum. 'Their slow-cooked lamb shanks with root vegetables is excellent.'

'I'm going to have a quick shower,' I said. 'I'll be there in an hour.'

It was dark by the time I set off for the Carriage House. Having not eaten all day, I was starving. I was just about to turn into the courtyard when, in the distance, my headlamps lit up a figure on foot.

It *had* to be the mystery man. Our earlier comments about the possibility of his being a witness hit me afresh. But there was more. I was determined to find out what the hell he was doing with his telephoto lens.

Without another thought for my safety, I hit the accelerator. He darted through a gap in the hedge, but this time, he was trapped. It was a sheep enclosure, and even better, an enclosure fenced by barbed wire backed up by a thick hawthorn hedge.

I stopped the car, grabbed my torch and the canister of Mace spray and went after him.

'I know you're there!' I shouted. 'I've already called the police. They'll be here in five minutes.' Which of course was a lie. 'Show yourself!'

To my astonishment, it was Delia who stepped out from the shadows. She was holding a leather suitcase. Shielding her eyes from the light, she whimpered, 'Please don't hurt me.'

Chapter Twenty-eight

'Delia!' I was horrified. 'What on earth are you doing?'

'What? Kat? Is that you? I can't see!' I could hear the panic in her voice. 'Are you alone?'

I lowered the beam a fraction. 'Yes, why?' I said. 'What have you got in that suitcase?'

She hugged it to her chest. 'Stay away from me.'

I knew it! She had the mascot bears! Delia was the culprit after all, not Cassandra. I had been wrong. True, the suitcase looked a little bit bigger than the one I'd seen before, but that was irrelevant. She would have to have six bears anyway – three fake and three authentic.

'You can't get out,' I said. 'It's all fenced in.'

'Leave me alone.'

'You've got those bears in that suitcase,' I said.

'Bears? What are you talking about?'

'You and the major hatched up some crazy plan,' I said. 'Tell me. Tell me right now or I *will* call the police.'

'You told me you already had. And anyway, you can't get a phone signal here.'

'Well I am about to—'

'Please don't call the police,' Delia cried. 'Please let me explain.'

Suddenly a car appeared head-on and we were blinded by the glare of blue slanting headlights. It had to be the Citroën.

Delia screamed. 'It's him!'

Then, inexplicably, the lights went out and the engine fell silent. Delia's panic was contagious.

I heard the sound of a car door opening and spun round to see Delia climbing into the passenger seat of my Golf.

The Citroën's engine exploded into life, then it reversed out of sight and was gone.

I got back into the car and realised I was actually shaking.

'We have to go!' Delia said urgently. 'Please.'

'No. Not until you tell me what is going on.'

'All right!' she shouted. 'But I'll only tell Iris. Please ... please let's go.'

Ten minutes later, we were sitting in Mum's kitchen nursing three large gin and tonics. Delia had the suitcase clamped between her knees.

'I don't want Kat here,' she said.

'Well I do,' said Mum. 'So start talking or we *will* call the police.'

'I haven't done anything!' Delia licked her lips nervously. 'Is the door locked?'

'Come on, out with it,' said Mum. 'We haven't got all night.'

'You've been seen in the walled garden with that suitcase, Delia.'

'I don't want *her* here,' Delia said again.

'I told you. Kat's staying.' Mum pointed to the suitcase. 'What's in there?'

'Nothing.'

I tried a different tack. 'We have a witness who saw you in the walled garden – specifically the ice house.'

Delia's eyes widened. 'I don't believe you.'

'Katherine would hardly make that up.'

'Please, Delia,' I said. 'Just open the wretched suitcase!'

'No!' she shrieked. 'And I'm sick of women like you with all that hair who think they can help themselves to other people's husbands!'

'Excuse me?' I was stunned. Where had *that* accusation come from, and what could it possibly have to do with the suitcase?

'No need to attack my Katherine,' Mum declared. 'It wasn't her fault that David was still married.'

'He wasn't married, Mother,' I said. 'He was legally separated.'

'Rubbish,' Delia cried. 'That's just a lame excuse for an affair!'

'Well I'm sorry you feel like that,' I snapped. 'But frankly it's none of your business.'

Mum suddenly leapt to her feet and grabbed Delia around the chest, holding her tightly against the chair. 'Quick, Kat!'

Delia screamed but couldn't escape my mother's iron grip.

'Get it!' Mum shouted. '*Quickly!*'

I lunged for the suitcase, trying hard to avoid Delia's feet, which were kicking out with such fury that she caught me hard on the shin. I yelped with pain but managed to wrest the suitcase from between her knees.

Delia slumped. 'Go on then,' she said defiantly. 'Open it. See if I care. Get me arrested. That's what you want, isn't it?'

Mum was out of breath and so was I. We took the suitcase to the kitchen counter, surprised that the locks were simple brass closures. No key. No padlock.

I flung open the lid and we gasped in shock. Laid out in neat bundles were dozens and dozens of piles of cash.

It was the last thing I'd expected to see.

'Holy cow!' I whispered.

'Oh. My. God. Did you rob a bank?'

Delia put her head in her hands and slumped on to the table.

'I would hazard a professional guess that there is close to thirty thousand pounds in this suitcase,' said Mum.

'Thirty-three thousand four hundred and fifty to be exact.' Delia took a deep breath. 'Have you ever done something you shouldn't have done?'

'No, never,' said Mum. 'Good grief. Over thirty thousand ...'

'I started telling a lie and ... Lenny ... I couldn't help myself ...'

'Good grief,' Mum said again as she whipped out her Post-it notes. 'You killed him for his life insurance money?'

'Killed him?' Delia seemed horrified.

'I know that Lenny was the love of your life, dear,' Mum

said scribbling God-knows-what down. 'I know, I know, but these things—'

'No!' Delia said angrily. 'He wasn't the love of my life. He was a lying, cheating bastard!' She promptly burst into tears.

'Wait, I'm confused,' said Mum. 'So did you or did you not kill him?'

'Of course I didn't – I mean, I haven't. Lenny is very much alive. The minute he retired from the army, he ran off with the local barmaid, who has hair just like your precious daughter's. Calais, that's where they've gone – Calais!'

'God. Who would want to go to Calais?' Mum said.

'Her name is Genevieve. The trollop is twenty-two years his junior – younger than his own daughter! It's so humiliating.'

'But you told me he was dead,' Mum said stubbornly. 'You and I shared our stories about being widows. Delia, you lied. You lied to *me*.'

'Well he might as well be dead!' Delia exclaimed. 'He's dead to me. I would rather be a widow than a hoodwinked wife with a husband having a mid-life crisis.'

'Isn't he too old to have a mid-life crisis?' Mum said.

'Mother!' I could see how upset Delia was and realised that she was truly suffering. I knew what it was like to be betrayed by someone who you loved with all your heart.

'I spent years following him around the world,' Delia went on. 'Gave up my dream of having my own little knitting shop, and the minute we could start to enjoy our life together, he threw it all away! For *her*! I mean, what can they possibly find to talk about?'

'I doubt they do much of that,' Mum said drily.

'Mother!' I said again. 'Please!' I turned to Delia. 'But where did you get all this money?'

'I cleaned out our bank account.' Delia helped herself to another gin and tonic and downed most of it in one go.

'So you were … hiding the money?' I said.

'But where were you going tonight? Are you on the run?' Mum ventured.

'No. Not at all.' Delia shook her head vehemently. 'I like it at Honeychurch. I just … well, I just have to keep moving it around. Everything was fine until she' – she shot me a venomous look – 'ruined it.'

'What did I do?' I was bewildered.

'I knew that frog was on to me,' Delia went on more garrulously now. The gin was obviously beginning to kick in.

'Lenny?' Mum said.

'No. Not *him*.'

Mum frowned. 'But if it's not Lenny …'

'Of course!' I said slowly. 'It's the man in the Citroën, isn't it? Is he … is he a private investigator?'

'A private *investigator*?' Mum seemed stunned. 'Good heavens.'

'You told us that your husband was in France, so it stands to reason that he would send someone over here.' It was a wild guess, but judging from Delia's expression, the right one.

Mum snapped her fingers. 'Yes, yes! So it's you he has been watching all this time. He's been taking photos of *you*. This has got nothing to do with Kat after all – or Cassandra, for that matter.'

I was relieved but also puzzled. 'But if that's the case, why didn't he just grab the money and have you arrested the moment he found out where you were living?'

'Are you divorced?' Mum demanded.

Delia shook her head.

'Then Lenny's still in love with you. Trust me, I know these things. If it's to do with romance and the human heart, I just *know*.'

Delia looked hopeful. 'Do you think so?'

'And what's more, if he was going to divorce you, the private investigator would have served you with the papers!'

'Maybe he was hired just to intimidate you,' I said. 'In which case, you can return the money and hopefully the whole thing will be forgotten.'

'No. I think he should suffer a little bit more,' said Mum. 'I have an idea. There's this bank in the Channel Islands—'

'No!' I exclaimed. 'No bank! Honesty is the only way to go from here. You have to return the money.'

'I can't,' Delia said miserably. 'I'll be fired. Everyone will know I lied. I lied to the employment placement agency about everything. They tried harder because I said my husband was dead and I was penniless.' A lone tear trickled down her cheek.

'Now we'll have none of that,' said Mum briskly. She thought for a moment. 'So you really *do* like it here at Honeychurch Hall?'

'Of course I do,' Delia said earnestly. 'I love it. I have a cottage that is mine. Something I have wanted my entire life. I never had a chance to put down roots. We were always moving. And now it's all ruined. Lenny has ruined my life. I'm going to jail, where I'll rot in an eight-foot-square cell.' She started to cry.

'I doubt it, dear,' said Mum. 'You can take it on good authority from me. You'd probably get out in six months tops.'

Delia shook her head. 'No. You don't understand. I'm never going back there again!'

'Well in that case, Kat made a good point. You should put the money back – unless …' she thought for a moment. 'You want to keep it somewhere very safe. I know someone—'

'No, Mother!' I knew full well whom my mother had in mind. Alfred.

'Don't let Lenny win!' Mum went on. 'You're young enough to start again. Look at me!'

'But your Frank died,' sniffed Delia. 'You had no choice.'

'And your marriage died too,' Mum said bluntly. 'So pull your socks up. Where's your British phlegm?'

'Gone to the dogs,' Delia whined.

'Dry your tears.' Mum grabbed a box of tissues from the oak dresser and thrust them under her nose. 'No man is worth *that*.'

I thought this a bit rich coming from a woman who had only ever known one man – in every sense of the word.

'Thank you, Iris,' said Delia. 'You're a true friend.'

Recalling Harry's drawings of Delia at the dumpsite, I said, 'But there is one condition.'

'Condition?' Delia looked to my mother for support. 'Who said anything about conditions?'

'What were you were *really* doing at Bridge Cottage the day you left your tote bag behind?'

'I told you the bag was stolen,' said Delia.

'You do know that CCTV cameras have been installed there, don't you?' It was a bluff, of course.

'Good heavens,' Mum said, giving me a sly wink. 'So his lordship really did put them in. Good. He'd been threatening to do that for months.'

Delia turned ashen.

'I think those gin bottles are yours,' I said. 'I also think that the Earl of Denby caught you chucking them out.'

'No.' She shook her head vehemently, then: 'Oh, all right. I admit I threw them out.' She appealed to Mum for support again. 'What do you do with all your empty bottles?'

'I take them to the bottle bank,' said Mum self-righteously.

'Well his lordship is a stickler for recycling,' said Delia. 'And Eric picks up my rubbish to take up to the Hall every week. It's like living behind the Iron Curtain. His lordship goes through everything – a blue bag for this, a plastic bag for that, a brown bin for God knows what. I don't want people going through my rubbish. It's an invasion of privacy!'

'That's all very well,' I said. 'But I *know* you saw something that day and for some reason you are too afraid to tell us.'

'That's rich coming from you of all people!' said Delia with scorn.

'Excuse me?'

'I think we've all had enough now,' said Mum. 'If you don't tell us the truth right this minute, all bets are off. I will call the police and report you for fly-tipping.'

Delia finished up her gin and tonic and set the glass down with a thump. 'Do you really want to know what I saw?'

'Yes,' Mum and I chorused.

'All right. I'll tell you, but you won't like it.'

'Nothing can shock me,' said Mum.

'Oh I think this will,' Delia said. 'Your perfect daughter has been having a fling with the Earl of Denby.'

Chapter Twenty-nine

'Are you out of your mind?' Mum exclaimed. 'You must mean Piers. That's Viscount Chawley.'

'No. I know what I saw,' said Delia. 'Ask her!'

The idea was so ridiculous I actually laughed. 'You need your eyes tested,' I said. 'I was happy that my mother had found someone that she liked spending time with.'

'What?' Delia seemed appalled. 'Iris? You and ... that horrible old man?'

'He wasn't horrible at all,' Mum protested. 'He bought me jewellery!'

'They called him the hanging judge, you know,' Delia said. 'If you ask me, you had a lucky escape.'

'That's not what you thought yesterday,' Mum retorted. 'I saw you flirting with him at the BearFest.'

'Me? Flirting? Never. It's *you* who needs her eyes tested, not me.'

'Steady on, Delia – and you, Mum.'

'You told me that you would never look at another man,'

Delia fumed. 'You told me that Frank was the love of your life. You told me that no one could ever come close to replacing your wonderful husband. That's why we got along. We were both broken-hearted. Destroyed by losing the men we truly loved; unable to go on living without them. Bereft. Lost.'

'Hold that thought, dear, because I must ask you,' said Mum. 'Are you a fan of Krystalle Storm's books by any chance?'

Delia seemed momentarily startled, but then: 'I *love* Krystalle Storm! All my friends in the army love Krystalle Storm. We have read all her books – especially the Star-Crossed Lovers series. I have read *Forbidden* four times!'

'Ah, but not her latest one,' said Mum with a hint of triumph. 'It won't be published until December. Just in time for Christmas.'

'Lovely,' said Delia. 'Do you know the title?'

'*Betrayed.*'

'Oh – betrayed.' Her shoulders slumped. 'How true.' She reached for the gin bottle but Mum deftly whipped it out of her reach.

I, however, was not going to get sidetracked. It was something Delia had said earlier on. 'What did you mean when Mum was talking about prison and you said you were never going back there again?'

'I said no such thing.'

'Yes you did,' Mum and I chorused again.

Delia lifted her glass but realised it was empty. She slammed it down on the table. 'Are you calling me a liar?'

'Yes,' we chorused yet again.

'I wondered why you asked me how often Aubrey came to Honeychurch Hall,' Mum mused. 'And now I know. You *had* met him before, hadn't you?'

'Why am I under attack?' Delia pointed to me. 'She's the one who should be questioned, not me.'

I looked to Mum helplessly. 'I have no idea what she's talking about.'

'I saw you on Saturday, late afternoon,' said Delia.

'I don't see how,' I said. 'I was clearing up the Emporium. And then I went to see the major—'

'Who Kat found dead, by the way,' said Mum.

'Yes, I know. You already told me that.'

'Ah yes, but did you know he had two legs?'

'Two legs!' Delia started to giggle. 'You're joking, aren't you?' I could see that my mother didn't think it was very funny. Nor did I.

'You're drunk,' Mum said with disgust. 'Your poor friend was found with a broken neck and you find it amusing?'

'He was no friend of mine,' said Delia. 'I'd never met him before in my life.'

'You didn't know the major?' I was confused. 'But you must have done!'

'Nope.' Delia seemed to brighten up considerably. 'And what's more, the army is very small. We all know each other, and I can tell you something. Whatever the major said, he never served in the Falklands.'

Given the major's story about his missing leg, he probably had lied about everything else as well. It was so depressing. Were there no honest people left in the world?

Delia rose somewhat unsteadily to her feet. 'I'd better get back.'

'I don't think so,' said Mum. She grabbed Delia's shoulders, pushing her back down in her chair. 'I think Kat has a few more questions that need answers.'

'I do?'

'I've said all I'm prepared to say.' Delia folded her arms and sulked. 'You can't keep me here against my will.'

Mum thought for a moment. 'You like your job, don't you?'

'Yes. Why?'

'And Shawn said everyone likes you too,' said Mum. 'Which is a pity, because it looks like I'm going to have to tell his lordship the truth about your past.'

'Go ahead. I dare you.'

Mum gave an imperceptible nod. 'Good. In that case – Kat?'

I went to the phone and pretended to dial the Hall. 'Hi, Cropper, it's Kat here—'

'No! No!' Delia shrieked. 'All right, I'll tell you whatever you want to know.'

I put the phone down. 'You'd better start at the beginning,' I said. 'Let's say, when you *thought* you saw me at Bridge Cottage. Why did you think that?'

Delia gave a heavy sigh. 'Because I recognised your hair.'

'What time was this?' Mum demanded.

Delia shrugged. 'I don't remember. Late afternoon?'

'When I was still at the Emporium,' I said.

'So you saw someone with hair like Katherine's?' Mum suggested.

'Oh yes. *That* kind of hair is hard to miss,' said Delia. 'Genevieve has hair like yours. Long, beautiful hair.'

'I'm sorry, Delia, but I'm going to have to ask you a very personal question,' Mum said gently. 'You wear a wig, don't you?'

'A wig? Me? Of course I don't.'

Mum rolled her eyes. 'Do you think we're blind? It's too *perfect*, too … done.'

'Have you no heart?' Delia's face crumpled. 'I have alopecia.'

'Oh!' Mum reddened. 'I am so sorry. I had no idea. The wig is a lovely colour.'

'I've always had thin hair, and that's why …' Delia struggled to keep her composure, 'it was why Lenny's betrayal was even harder to bear. Genevieve is everything I am not.'

'And you are everything she is not,' I pointed out.

'I'm so sorry, dear. I know you must be suffering,' Mum said. And I was sorry too. In fact, I felt ashamed at how insensitive Mum and I had been. We'd even joked about Delia's wig. My hair *was* my trademark look and I took it for granted. No wonder Delia had been upset about my long tresses. I must have been a constant reminder of Lenny's infidelity.

'So where *exactly* were you when you thought you saw Katherine?' Mum said.

'Over by the fence—'

'Where you left the gin bottles and where I found your tote bag?' I asked.

Delia nodded.

'Did you see what kind of car this woman was driving?'

'No,' said Delia. 'She came down that bank from the lane

above. She had a black dustbin bag, but she wasn't dumping stuff.' She frowned. 'She had one of those litter sticks and was picking things over and putting them *into* the bag.'

Mum looked at me. 'Do you think it could be Cassandra?'

I had thought the exact same thing.

'And you're positive you didn't see the car she was driving?' I asked again.

Delia shook her head. 'And she never saw the earl until he tapped her on the shoulder.'

'The earl?' Mum said sharply. 'He was on foot?'

'Not to start with,' said Delia. 'When I realised who it was riding past Bridge Cottage, I hid. I suppose that's when I dropped my tote bag. It was a very windy day.'

I could hardly draw breath, I was so gripped by her story.

'I think the earl had been watching her for quite some time. I saw him dismount and then lead the horse along the path. She didn't hear him coming.'

'How could she not have heard him?' marvelled Mum.

'It was … it was …' Delia started to get agitated. 'It was very upsetting.'

Mum took Delia's hand and squeezed it. 'You're doing a good job. You're among friends here.'

'I heard raised voices but I didn't know what was said,' Delia went on in a trembling voice. 'She kept trying to hug him, trying to make him hold her, but he wouldn't have any of it.' She shot a look at me. 'I thought they were having a lovers' tiff.'

'Just to be clear,' said Mum. 'This was at the bottom of the bank on the other side of the dumpsite.'

'Yes, otherwise perhaps I could have helped …' Delia took

a deep breath. 'The earl went to mount his horse. I'm not sure what happened, but the wind suddenly picked up and blew a huge sheet of blue plastic across the ground. I suppose the horse got startled. I saw the earl lose his balance because he only had one foot in the stirrup. He tried to stay on, and I think he would have done, yes.' She nodded to herself. 'But then … that woman took the litter stick and poked the sharp end in the horse's rump.'

Mum seemed horrified. 'Oh good heavens!'

I felt sick. Cassandra had *struck* the horse. How vindictive! She had actually made it bolt. I couldn't believe it. Neither, it seemed, could my mother, only Mum was of a different opinion. 'How could you have stood there and done nothing?'

'I was too far away!'

'Why didn't you tell this to the police?' Mum demanded. 'You've had every opportunity.'

'You don't understand,' Delia said miserably.

'You witnessed a *murder*!' Mum shouted.

'I'd get the blame! You don't *understand* what it's like once you've got a criminal record.'

'Let's hear it then,' said Mum. 'God, getting the truth out of you is like getting blood out of a stone.'

'It was for drink-driving, if you must know,' Delia said defiantly. 'Banned for life and six months in prison.'

'That can't have been your first offence,' Mum said. 'How many times have you been convicted?'

'It's none of your business!'

And then I guessed. 'The earl was the judge, wasn't he? He was the man who convicted you.'

'Oh good Lord!' Mum regarded Delia with suspicion. 'Maybe you're making all this up about the woman and the litter stick. Perhaps it was you who killed the earl.'

'No!' Delia said. 'I didn't do anything wrong.'

'I don't know whether I believe you,' said Mum.

Delia slumped forward again. 'I knew you wouldn't.'

'Tell us the truth!' Mum cried. 'Stop all these deceptions!'

I glowered at my mother, who had to be the queen of deceptions.

'As part of my sentencing, I was supposed to go to Alcoholics Anonymous,' said Delia. 'I was supposed to get a sponsor and—'

'You didn't,' Mum finished for her.

'I went a few times, but then ... Anyway, somehow the earl found out I wasn't going. When he saw me yesterday, he cornered me and told me he would have me back in his courtroom if I didn't do as I was told. Not only that, he had found out where I worked and was threatening to tell his lordship. So you see, if anyone had a motive to see him dead, it's me.'

'Well, I don't know what to believe,' said Mum wearily. Nor did I.

'I knew that if the truth came out, I'd be fired,' Delia went on. 'I love my job. So you see, if I came forward, it would be her word against mine.' She looked up, her eyes bright with tears. 'You have to believe me. Please help me. It's my second chance. Everyone deserves a second chance, don't they?'

Mum leaned back in her chair. 'What a to-do.'

'What if we got proof,' I suggested. 'I'm not sure how exactly ...'

'I think I have an idea,' said Mum slowly. 'But we will need your assistance, Delia.'

Delia's confession had been deeply disturbing. I knew now that Cassandra was a clever and dangerous woman. She had adored the earl. She had looked up to him and regarded him as a father figure. There was no predicting how she would act now. But what was baffling to me was why she had done it. It made no sense. What had he said to her yesterday afternoon to make her lose her mind?

'We want you to take a look around Cassandra's room when you go in to clean it,' said Mum.

'*Cassandra?* You mean her ladyship's best friend?' Delia seemed genuinely shocked. 'Whatever for?' And then it was as if a light went on. Her jaw dropped. 'You think ... you think she's got something to do with it?'

'Yes,' I said firmly. 'And tomorrow she will be in London all day with the viscount and Lady Lavinia.'

'That's right.' Delia nodded. 'I overheard her saying to her ladyship that she expected to inherit quite a lot of money from the earl.'

Perhaps that had been Cassandra's motive. Maybe when Aubrey caught her at the dumpsite, everything changed. After all, she was the campaign manager for EcoChamp. He must have wondered what on earth she was doing there in disguise.

'Good, then the coast will be clear,' said Mum.

'It's true, I clean her room,' said Delia slowly. 'And even if someone else saw me – like little Harry – no one would suspect anything.'

'Good,' said Mum again. 'At last we are making some progress.'

'All right. I'll do it. I don't like her very much, I have to say. She calls me Evans. Who does she think she is? Lady Mary from *Downton Abbey*? Everyone else calls me Delia. I don't need to be talked down to just because I've fallen on hard times … What exactly am I supposed to be looking for?'

'A wig!' Mum declared. 'Like Kat's hair.'

'And an orange tweed flat cap.' Aubrey must have lost it at the bottom of the bank when he had come off the horse, or at the very least, somewhere along the bridleway. Piers and I had combed the area thoroughly yesterday but had come away empty-handed. Cassandra *had* to have taken it.

'And what about those teddies?' Mum said. 'May as well look out for those too.'

'See if you can find a small tan suitcase,' I said.

'Speaking of suitcases,' said Mum. 'Perhaps you should leave yours here.'

Delia hesitated. 'Why?'

'You know that sooner or later that little Poirot out there is going to knock on your door and search the premises.'

'Poirot wasn't French,' I pointed out. 'He was from Belgium, and besides, I think he would have solved the whole thing by now.'

'Well … it would take a weight off my shoulders,' Delia admitted. 'Where are you going to put it?'

'I won't tell you, and that way, if he asks you, you won't know,' said Mum.

'He's not exactly going to torture her into a confession,' I couldn't help but say.

'All right. But I know exactly how much is in there, Iris.' Delia got up and headed for the door. 'Wait. You said that everything had been recorded on a CCTV camera. Can't the police use that?'

'No,' I said quickly. 'The thing is, you mistook Cassandra for me, so obviously, the footage would imply the same and we'd be back to the beginning: her word against yours – and mine, for that matter.'

'Quite right,' Mum chimed in. 'Plus it's not very reliable. His lordship told me only yesterday that he thought it had been vandalised by some youths from … wherever they are from. He didn't specify.'

'There is something else that could be a problem,' said Delia. 'Cassandra could blame it on a white transit van.'

'You've seen it?' I swear my heart skipped a beat.

'Yes. Three times now, throwing out all kinds of stuff. Always late afternoon.'

'You saw the man in a hoodie?' I said.

'And a woman.'

'A *woman*?' I exclaimed. 'I only saw the man.'

'She's the driver,' said Delia. 'She had to help shift a mattress, and I can tell you that their language was … shall we say, colourful? I've not heard the like since my army days.'

'I suppose you were too far away to hear anything useful,' said Mum with a tinge of sarcasm.

'On this occasion I had to seek refuge behind a fridge freezer,' said Delia. 'I think she called him Tom.'

'Tom?' The name meant nothing to me.

'Or Trey.' Delia shrugged. 'Maybe it was Troy. I don't know, but he did call her Mum.' And with that bombshell, she left the kitchen.

'I think it's Elsie King.' I couldn't believe it.

Mum looked blank.

'Someone who has everything to lose and nothing to gain.'

Chapter Thirty

'Who?' Mum demanded.

'Crown Haulage and Clearance,' I said, 'Remember the skip that was delivered to the Carriage House?'

I went on to explain how I had met Troy and Elsie at Riverview retirement village when I had gone to visit the major the first time.

'But … you mean they're running an illegal racket on the side?' Mum was appalled, and so was I.

'It's obviously a front,' I said. 'Whenever someone dies at Riverview, Elsie offers to help them clear the house – especially if there are no surviving relatives.'

'So you're saying that this Elsie keeps the valuable stuff to sell off and dumps the rest?'

'It sounds like it.' I remembered how Elsie's home was crammed with furniture. It had seemed like a warehouse. No wonder she'd asked if I would do a valuation! That way she could cherry-pick the items she thought worth selling at auction and get rid of the rest.

'If anyone is granny-farming, it's her!' Mum exclaimed. 'But there can't be that much turnover at Riverview. I mean, if they're dumping furniture every week … is someone dying there every week? Good grief! You don't think she's knocking off the residents, do you?'

'God! I hope not. No, I think she trawls the obituary columns just to see who has died and what their circumstances are.'

'Singling out grief-stricken families. That's wicked,' Mum fumed. 'Preying on people who can't face dealing with sentimental possessions after a death in the family.'

'I'm going to call Shawn in the morning,' I said.

'Can't he just go and arrest them?'

'You know how it is,' I said. 'They need hard evidence. Perhaps now he might put a surveillance team there.'

'They should put Harry on the payroll …'

'Or *we* should be on the payroll,' I said.

'Quite.' Mum gave a heavy sigh. 'Aubrey would have been happy to find the culprits. Oh well, let's hope Delia comes up with something.'

I was having second thoughts about Delia getting involved, and shared them.

'You've got nothing to worry about,' said Mum. 'She's got all day to snoop. They're leaving bright and early and won't be back until Tuesday morning. Are you staying for dinner tonight?'

'No, I'm tired.'

'Pity. I thought we could watch you on the telly.'

'Telly?' I echoed.

'The *West Country Round-Up*'s arts and entertainment segment.'

'That,' I said, 'is the last thing I feel like watching.'

That night I was tempted to call Piers just to check and see if he was OK, but I knew he'd call me if he wanted to talk.

The following morning I left yet another message for Shawn – who seemed to be as elusive as Piers – and told him that we had not found Aubrey's cap. As for my suspicions about Cassandra's involvement in the earl's death, I'd keep those to myself until Delia had done her sleuthing. Things had got very complicated.

After getting my wing mirror repaired in Totnes, I spent the rest of the day at the gatehouse playing catch-up and following a surprising number of leads from the BearFest. Despite the entire mascot bear fiasco, I'd garnered a dozen or more new clients anxious for valuations.

I tried not to check my fan mail, but in the end, my curiosity got the better of me. Although there were a handful of insulting emails accusing me of granny-farming, most seemed to believe that the major was senile. I did not, however, watch the footage of his accusation that had gone viral on YouTube.

I contacted Jean Grogan of Little Scruffs and asked her if she had had a request for a special order of mascot bears recently, but she had not. She recommended a few other bear makers, who I called but with no luck. Unless Delia found the bears in Cassandra's bedroom, they had gone for good.

I was in the galley kitchen boiling the kettle for my four o'clock cup of tea when I heard a knock at the door. It was Shawn.

'I got your message,' he said. 'May I come in?'

'I didn't recognise you out of costume,' I teased.

'Shall I go home and put it on?' He seemed in a good mood and I wondered why.

'You're just in time for a cuppa.'

He followed me into the gatehouse and took in the showroom, making admiring noises. I sometimes forgot how lovely it was.

'I haven't been in here since Albert Jones was the gatekeeper,' he said. 'I like it.'

'I use this side as a showroom and the other gatehouse for storing my stock,' I said. 'The dowager countess has been very generous.'

Shawn stood in the kitchen doorway and watched me make the tea. I could sense his eyes on me and began to feel self-conscious.

Finally he spoke. 'I thought you'd like to know that losing a leg was not the only thing Major Timothy Gordon lied about.'

I hesitated. Did this mean Shawn had spoken to Delia? I knew she'd been terrified of being questioned by the police. 'What did Delia say?'

'Oh, we probably won't need to talk to her after all,' said Shawn. 'I assume she'll just confirm what we already know. We got the report back from the military service records this afternoon. You'll never guess—'

'Please don't make me guess,' I said. 'My mother does that.'

'All right. I'll put you out of your misery.' Shawn wore a cat-that-got-the-cream expression.

'Go on,' I said. 'It's obviously good news.'

'The Walter Mitty Hunters Club calls his kind "bloaters".'

'Bloaters? What are they?'

'Men who grossly exaggerate and fabricate their role in the army.'

'So he was in the army?'

'He served as a chef in the Army Catering Corps from 1971 to 1974 before being discharged for running a little business on the side.'

'Wow. I would never have thought that.'

'He was able to live on his ill-gotten gains along with a generous disability allowance from the council and whatever he bought and sold online. I suspect the major – or should I say *Private* Timothy Gordon – preferred to be regarded as a war veteran as opposed to a man who had been caught with his fingers in the cookie jar.'

'But what about the photographs that were all over his house? And his medals?'

'All bought on eBay.' Shawn smiled. I detected that something had changed about him, but wasn't sure what. He seemed warmer towards me today.

'What about his daughter in New Zealand?' I asked.

'There is no daughter in New Zealand.'

Why was I not surprised? Elsie King hadn't known everything there was to know about her residents after all. 'So he was all alone. That's rather sad.'

'There is something else …'

'Oh dear,' I said. 'You have that look on your face.'

'Well …' Shawn seemed sheepish. 'Elsie King told me that she saw you visiting Gordon earlier in the evening. Hours before you raised the alarm.'

'I thought we'd already confirmed that I wasn't there.'

I was just about to tell him that Delia had thought she'd seen me at the dumpsite, too, but realised I couldn't. To my dismay, I found I was suddenly protecting Delia. 'But I do have a lead for you,' I said.

I went on to tell him about the white transit van dumping goods at Bridge Cottage in broad daylight.

Shawn whipped out his notebook and pencil and started scribbling. 'And you think it could be Elsie King and her son?'

'I'm convinced of it.'

'I'll ask DC Banks to keep an eye open. Excellent work! If ever you decide to give up your antique business, I'm quite certain you'd make a good detective.' He grinned. 'But in the meantime, I must caution you not to take matters into your own hands. These people can be dangerous and I would hate you to get hurt.' He looked deep into my eyes. 'Will you promise me that?'

'Um. Yes.' I could feel my face growing warm at the lie, since I was quite sure that at this very moment, Delia was ransacking Cassandra's bedroom looking for clues, and if she was found out, it would be my fault.

'So what's the next step?' I said. 'Do you still believe the major's death is suspicious?'

'Not any more,' said Shawn. 'Now that we realise he has two legs, it looks like he did, in fact, fall down the stairs.'

I wasn't convinced and told him so.

'There was no sign of forced entry and we have nothing concrete to go on,' he said.

'What about the mascot bears that he brought to the BearFest?' I said. 'They weren't there.'

'Hardly proof of foul play.' Shawn drained his mug and

carefully rinsed it out in the sink. 'Any more sightings of your stalker and the black Citroën?'

'Um. No.' I couldn't believe it. I had had to lie to protect Delia, *again*!

'I've already asked DC Banks to keep an eye out for the car in the village.'

I swiftly changed the subject. 'It was nice to meet your mother-in-law.'

'Lizzie thought you were nice too.' He gestured for me to walk ahead of him as we left the kitchen. I became very aware of how close he was standing behind me. 'Yes, she thought I should invite you out to dinner. There was a place that was a favourite of Helen's that I thought you might like …'

'Really?' Was he mad? Why would I want to go to a place that reminded Shawn of his dead wife? Fortunately I was saved by a beep from my iPhone. The screen lit up with Piers's name.

Want to see you tonight, chica!

Of course Shawn must have seen it too. I could practically hear him breathing over my shoulder.

I sidestepped away. 'It's probably about finding his father's cap.'

'Yes, you should definitely focus on finding his father's cap,' said Shawn, suddenly all business. 'I'm sorry to have taken up so much of your time. Goodbye.'

And with that, he strode quickly out of the gatehouse, leaving me feeling guilty. But it was just as well that he'd gone, because the next text that popped up said, *Girls staying at club. Driving back now. 99% positive will be back by eight.*

I texted back, *Great!*

That gave me some time to shower and tidy up, but it was only when I was upstairs grabbing a clean towel that I noticed the stack looked crumpled. I was obsessive about organising my airing cupboard, and yet I couldn't be certain. I checked my chest of drawers, and sure enough, my perfectly paired socks looked slightly askew.

Someone had been in my house. My thoughts went instantly to the French detective. He had seen Delia get into my car last night with her suitcase. Perhaps he thought she had given the money to me for safe keeping?

Now I wished I *had* told Shawn the truth. How on earth had I allowed myself to get caught up in all these deceptions? After tonight, I resolved, I'd never do it again.

Piers eventually texted me at 8.05: *Found Father's cap! Meet me at Falcon's Nest in thirty*.

Great! I texted back again.

Then, to my astonishment, he wrote, *I love you*.

For a moment I was flummoxed. Piers had said he was crazy about me and that he adored me, but he'd never texted, let alone told me to my face, that he loved me.

I didn't know what to do. Eventually I zipped off a heart emoticon. He'd have to be satisfied with that for now.

No sooner had I done that than my mobile rang. I didn't recognise the number.

'Kat? Is that you?' It was Mum.

'Where are you calling from?'

'Delia's cottage. You've got to come quickly. Hurry!' she gushed. I could hear the excitement in her voice. 'Have we got a surprise for *you*!'

Chapter Thirty-one

'I've got five minutes,' I said to Delia, who answered the door beaming. Her face looked flushed and it was obvious she'd been drinking.

'Come in, come in!'

'I hope that's Kat and not a kitten,' I heard my mother shout. 'We're in here!'

I walked into the small sitting room and stopped. Horrified.

Six mascot bears lay on the coffee table. My heart sank. 'Where did you find them?'

'Tucked inside shoe bags in Cassandra's suitcase under the bed.' Delia seemed triumphant. 'I couldn't find the little case you mentioned. Maybe she got rid of it.'

'But …' I was dismayed. 'You should have left them there! You should never have brought them here!'

'You wanted proof.' Mum rolled her eyes at Delia. 'She's never satisfied, Delia.'

'Yes, proof, but … you've got to take them back right now.'

Even as I said it, my mind was racing. Cassandra and the

major *had* known each other and been in this together from the start, but I found it unbelievable that she would go to all that trouble to embarrass me.

'And I found this.' Delia brandished a brochure for the Dart Marina Hotel and Spa. 'See?' Inside was a receipt for Cassandra's stay. She had checked in a full week before she turned up at the Hall, plenty of time for her to get all her proverbial ducks – or should I say bears – in a row.

'And this!' Delia presented a receipt from a company I hadn't heard of before – Lila's Bear Magic – for three mascot bears. Cassandra had spent three hundred pounds on rushed copies.

For the first time, I felt a wave of fear. She had been cold-bloodedly planning this dangerous deception for quite some time. She had even had the foresight to get her father to sponsor the event in order to wangle her way in as a valuation expert.

'This is not going to prove anything,' I said.

'Nonsense. Delia found them in Cassandra's room,' Mum insisted.

'But don't you see?' I was exasperated. 'Cassandra could easily accuse her of planting them there.'

'No, there's more! Go and get it, Delia.'

Delia scurried out of the living room and into the kitchen. A few moments later, she popped her head around the door wearing a luxurious wig.

'Rapunzel!' she grinned.

'Good grief!' I exclaimed. 'Oh dear. Delia, everyone knows that you wear wigs. This could so easily be one of yours.'

'But it's not.'

'I see what Kat means,' said Mum slowly. 'You'll have to put it all back.'

'And straight away,' I said.

'Why?'

'We haven't caught Cassandra physically wearing the wig, and she could claim the bears were planted.'

Delia's face fell. 'But she's guilty.'

'Poor Aubrey,' Mum whimpered. 'And Delia said she couldn't find his cap. I told her she couldn't have looked hard enough.'

'I resent that. I did look hard enough,' said Delia hotly.

Of course, Piers had just told me that he'd found the cap, but I kept this to myself for the time being. Mum would only ask questions, and as yet, I didn't know the facts.

'I risked my life going through her room,' Delia went on. 'And what thanks do I get?'

'I know, I'm sorry, and of course we're grateful,' I said. 'I just didn't expect you to bring it all here.'

I felt depressed about everything.

It was just as well that Piers had found Aubrey's cap. Unless Aubrey's death was also deemed an accident like the major's, right now Delia could be the prime suspect. Harry had drawn her at the dumpsite; I had found her tote bag there, and I was pretty certain other people at the BearFest had witnessed her altercation with Aubrey on the Saturday afternoon.

Delia was right. Who would believe her word as a convicted criminal against that of a much-loved society celebrity from *Made in Monte Carlo*? Had Cassandra set Delia up to take the fall just in case she couldn't pin any of it on me?

But it wouldn't come to that, would it? The police had already decided that the major's death was an accident, and the same would be true of Aubrey's. Cassandra was going to get away with it.

'Can't you tell Piers?' Mum said.

'I don't think he would believe me.' And I didn't. 'I must go.'

'Where are you going?'

'I have things to do!' I didn't want to tell her I was meeting Piers. In fact, in light of all this, I was having second thoughts about going at all. I needed time to think about what to do with all this new and incriminating information.

'Well, let's regroup in the morning,' said Mum. 'Delia's going to take it all back now whilst they're still away, aren't you, Delia?'

'All right,' said Delia grudgingly.

As I headed to my rendezvous with Piers, I was in a dilemma. How could I not tell him what Delia had found? But if I did, I had no idea how he would react. It was hopeless telling Shawn. I already knew what he'd say. There was absolutely no proof that it was Cassandra. And besides, hadn't she been with Piers on Saturday late afternoon and early evening? Mum had seen them together in his car. Yes, Cassandra was free and clear.

I spotted the Mercedes in the driveway of Bridge Cottage, so I parked on the road. It was a dark night with a half-moon that only occasionally peeped through the heavy clouds. Grabbing a torch from the glove compartment, I set off down the bridleway towards Harry's tree house. In the distance I could see lights twinkling in the trees. Piers must have lit the tea lights that Harry kept inside the hut.

I reached the bottom of the tree and shouted a hello but got no answer. Leaving the torch on the ground, I began to climb the rope ladder.

'Hello?' I called out again as I drew level with the deck.

Suddenly, a hand reached down to grab mine. All too late I saw the perfectly manicured fingernails.

It wasn't Piers. It was Cassandra.

Chapter Thirty-two

'Come on up,' Cassandra said cheerfully as she hoisted me aboard. She was dressed all in black. 'Don't look so disappointed.'

I tried to adopt an expression of casual interest, but deep down I was scared. 'Not disappointed at all,' I said lightly. 'Just surprised.'

I grabbed on to a nearby branch. The platform seemed narrower tonight in the darkness.

Gesturing to the upper level I said, 'Is Piers up there?'

Cassandra looked incredulous. 'Seriously? You must be more naïve than I thought.'

'Well, I saw the Mercedes,' I said steadily. 'I assumed you both drove back from London together.'

'Nope. I sneaked off this afternoon.' Cassandra seemed to be thoroughly enjoying herself.

My stomach lurched when I thought of Delia. Luck had been on her side when she'd searched Cassandra's room, but would it still be there when she went to put the things back?

I realised it was critical to keep Cassandra talking for as long as possible. Delia had promised to do it this evening, but who knew when.

'Isn't this fun?' Cassandra went on. 'Harry's little girlfriend Fliss has made the hut so cosy. The pair of them are just like Piers and me when we were small, although our tree house wasn't as good. Ours was just a plank across a few branches, but we loved playing up there.'

'Piers sent me a text, Cassandra,' I said. 'Where is he?'

'Ta-dah!' She produced an iPhone from her jacket pocket. 'It was me.'

So no one knew that I was here at all. I tried to stem the rising feeling of panic.

'Piers is always losing his phone,' Cassandra went on. 'He's so silly. But you wouldn't know about things like that. He's frightfully forgetful – oh, and for the record, he didn't find Aubrey's cap after all. Lavinia blurted it out.' She frowned. 'He's never lied to me before – so … you must have it. Where is it?'

'I don't have it,' I said.

'I looked in Jane's Cottage. You've made it rather nice. I like the little bedroom at the top of the spiral staircase. Quite the love nest.'

So I was right, someone had been in my house. 'I told you, I don't know where Aubrey's cap is.'

'But I couldn't get into the gatehouses,' Cassandra continued. 'You've got quite a security system set up there, haven't you?'

'What's this really about, Cassandra?'

'I thought we'd have a friendly chat, just to get the lie of the land. Shall we sit down?'

'I'm OK standing here, thanks.'

Cassandra sighed. 'Well. I'm not very happy. I *was* happy – Piers and I were happy … but when you came along, you ruined everything.'

'If this is about your relationship with Piers, that's between you and him,' I said. 'He and I are just good friends.'

'But he wants more,' said Cassandra brightly. 'The fact that you and he have not had *carnal* – such a horrid word – relations is an obvious indication that he wants you to marry him.'

'As I said—'

'No! Let me finish!' she shouted. 'You see, I can't allow that to happen. Ever.'

It was then that I finally snapped. 'You know what, Cassandra? You're a selfish cow and I'm sick of your childish games. Do you really think I didn't guess what you were up to? You went through my rubbish. I suppose it was you who sent that photograph of me fly-tipping to the *Dipperton Deal*?'

'Guilty as charged,' she beamed. 'So simple. A touch here and a touch there and *voilà*! Even an idiot can do a bit of Photoshopping if you know how.'

'Personally, I thought it was a very sloppy job.'

'But it did the trick, didn't it? If anyone was sloppy, it was the newspaper. They published it without even checking where it came from.'

'You're unbelievable.'

'Golly. Do I detect a little anger there? Maybe you're not as perfect as Piers thinks you are. He'll be so disappointed.'

'Oh shut up,' I said, and edged my way back to the top of the rope ladder. 'I'm leaving.'

'Wait – don't you want to hear how I did it?' Cassandra exclaimed. 'Don't you want to know how I persuaded the major to do my dirty work?'

Of course I did. 'OK. Tell me.'

'The bears belonged to my great-grandfather, on my mother's side,' she said. 'The story goes that he found them on the battlefield and kept them.'

'So you got them copied?' I said. 'That's a lot of trouble to go to.'

'But worth it,' said Cassandra. 'Every time I replay that moment when the major accused you of granny-farming, I laugh. I couldn't believe how quickly my clip went viral.'

'So it was *you* who posted it online?' Why was I not surprised? 'I thought you'd left with Aubrey.'

'I knew there would be a bit of hoopla after the major's accusation, so I told Aubrey to go and get his car just ten minutes before the shit – pardon my French – hit the fan. Aubrey would have been all over it.'

'Risky,' I said.

'Yes, I was a teeny bit worried, but it worked out in the end.'

'Lila's copies were good.'

'I thought so too,' said Cassandra. 'I got the idea when Piers told me you'd had a copy made of Harry's Steiff bear, Edward … Wait, what did you say?'

All too late I realised I had let slip the name of the bear maker. 'I said they're obviously copies when put next to the real thing.'

'No,' said Cassandra slowly. 'You mentioned a name.'

'No I didn't.'

'Yes you did. I took great care to snip the labels out …
Well, never mind,' she went on. 'The only person who knows
the truth is the major, and let's face it, he can't talk. Poor man.
What a tragic accident.'

'Just like Aubrey's fall,' I said quietly.

'Another tragic accident and nothing to do with me.
Besides, I was with Piers on Saturday night and your mother
saw us. You should have seen the look of surprise on her face.
So I have a cast-iron alibi – oh, and Piers knows all about my
fly-tipping prank. He thought it was hilarious, especially the
incontinence pad – what was it called again? Tena Lady?'

'I don't believe you.'

'Believe it! Piers and I play jokes like that all the time. You
know what he's like – but wait, you don't really, do you?'

But Cassandra was wrong. I did. What was more, I'd had
first-hand experience with Piers's jokes – such as the time he im-
personated an Air France in-flight magazine food critic to get us
a free meal at Nine, a Michelin-starred restaurant in Plymouth.

Piers had told me that he and his old school friend Roger
Matthews played pranks like that all the time. He'd never once
mentioned Cassandra. Maybe Cassandra was right after all.
Perhaps I didn't really know him.

'If Paddington Bear suspects any foul play, the only person
who was seen leaving Riverview retirement village was you.'

'Ah yes,' I said. 'The wig.'

'I got the idea from the housekeeper. Everyone knows
Evans wears a wig … Hang on, how did you know about *that*?'

'There was a witness,' I said.

'Ha! I assume you're talking about Harry's drawings. They'll hardly stand up in a court of law.'

'I'm not talking about the drawings,' I said. 'Delia was at Bridge Cottage. She saw everything.'

'So what!' Cassandra remained defiant. 'Who is going to believe the housekeeper, especially given her criminal record? If anyone has a motive, it's her. They had a fearful row at the BearFest. Aubrey told me everything about her convictions. We were very close.'

'So close that when he caught his lovely Kitten at Bridge Cottage dressed in disguise and sifting through the rubbish, he must have wondered what you were doing.'

'You can't prove anything.'

'I think Aubrey – who treated you like a daughter – confronted you and there was an argument—'

'Stop it, stop it!' she shouted. 'It was an accident. I swear it was an accident. I didn't think the stupid horse was going to shy – he just lost his balance ...'

'But you did nothing to help him,' I said.

'I couldn't! I tried, but I couldn't get close enough to the horse to grab his bridle.'

'So instead you poked him on the rump with your litter stick.'

'Rubbish! I did no such thing!'

'Nor did you go after him – you just let him ... let him ... Aubrey could have been alive, Cassandra! How can you not have cared?'

Cassandra gave a girlish sigh. 'All right. Yes, you're quite right,' she said. 'I was always Aubrey's special girl. He much preferred me over Lavinia.'

'Which made his discovery of your subterfuge all the more devastating,' I put in. 'Piers will never forgive you.'

'Piers will never know,' said Cassandra simply. 'And even if he found out, he would never believe you. You can't prove a *thing* about Aubrey or the major.'

'You're right,' I said. 'I can't. You've won.'

'I have, haven't I?' Cassandra laughed. 'Sometimes I find it hard to believe I'm so clever.'

'And the major?' I said. 'How did you persuade him to switch the bears?'

'Oh yes, that! Serendipity! Harry and I were walking along the promenade in Dartmouth when we saw him in his wheelchair with a little sign asking for money. Harry insisted we go and talk to him – you know how that boy loves anyone in a military uniform.'

'Yes, he does.'

'Of course the major recognised me immediately from *Made in Monte Carlo*,' Cassandra went on. 'He wouldn't stop talking. He bored me rigid about his army service and how he lost a leg. We just couldn't get away! And then he started droning on about his military memorabilia that he wanted valued. What do I know about military memorabilia? My role on that stupid reality show was scripted!'

I made a mental note to tell Mum that she had been right about that.

'He kept asking for my phone number, but I wouldn't give it to him. He seemed a bit creepy actually. Anyway,

I took his and said I'd make some enquiries. Then, all of a sudden ...' she started to laugh again, 'this wasp came along and landed on the major's cheek, and he actually *jumped* out of his wheelchair to try and get away. It was hysterically funny.'

'I am sure the major didn't think it was funny.'

'Naturally, he tried to cover it up by hopping about. Seriously. Did he think I was an idiot? It was only later that I had a brilliant idea. Do you still want to hear all this?'

'Yes, I'm riveted,' I said drily.

'This really is your own fault, Kat,' said Cassandra. 'I realised that Piers was mad about you and I suppose I just wanted to show you up but I couldn't think how.'

'Wasn't the fly-tipping enough?'

'Not really.' Cassandra sighed. 'So ... I called the major and offered him two hundred and fifty pounds to do a little job for me, in exchange for which I'd keep quiet about his so-called disability. I mentioned my relationship with the Earl of Denby and that definitely did the trick. I had no idea Aubrey had such a formidable reputation.'

'So you blackmailed the major.'

'No. It was an assignment for which he got paid,' said Cassandra. 'All he had to do was show you the fake bears and then, at the BearFest, he would show me the real ones to value on camera. Everyone was happy.'

'And the tan suitcase?' I said. 'I'm curious. What do the initials stand for?'

'F. H. B. Francis Horatio Bowden,' said Cassandra with a hint of pride. 'My great-grandfather. I must admit, I was a little concerned that you would ask the major about that, but luckily, you didn't.'

And that was when I guessed. 'The major didn't want to give you the real bears back, did he?'

'He had the nerve – the absolute *nerve* – to ask for a thousand pounds otherwise he would go to the police and tell them what I had asked him to do! He tried to blackmail *me*! He seemed to like you for some reason. Said you had been kind to him. Everyone seems to like *you*.'

I thought for a moment. 'But how did you get to the retirement village? By taxi?'

'Rupert's Land Rover, of course,' she said. 'The keys are kept in the tack room. Alfred was working in the walled garden, Lavinia and Edith were at that Pony Club thing and Rupert was out. I got back without anyone being any the wiser.'

'How very convenient.'

'If only the old fart had done what we'd agreed,' said Cassandra with a sigh. 'He told me he would go upstairs and get them and that I must wait downstairs. But of course I didn't. I followed him and … well, you know the rest.'

'He threatened you with a gun?'

'No. He made a phone call. To you. I managed to distract him, yet he *still* refused to give me my bears,' said Cassandra. 'It was so infuriating. Then he had the nerve, *again*, to order me off the property! You could say there was a little scuffle, but all I did really was give him a little … PUSH!'

And with lightning speed, Cassandra shoved me off the platform.

Chapter Thirty-three

I don't know how long I had been unconscious. I came to with a blinding headache, wedged in a criss-cross of branches peppered with thorns so sharp that they pierced my skin like needles.

The hawthorn hedge had saved my fall.

As I tried to throw myself sideways, a white-hot pain shot through my left arm and took my breath away. *Please God, don't let it be broken.*

Fear hit me afresh. How could I have been so stupid?

Cassandra was a cold-blooded murderer.

She had pushed the major down the stairs; she had watched as a man whom she had always regarded as a father figure was dragged to his death … and she had thrown me out of a tree hoping I'd plunge to mine. Who would be next?

I'd tried to cover up the fact that I knew the name of the bear maker, but Cassandra was clever. She knew, I was sure of it. I had to warn Delia.

Finally I was able to hurl myself sideways and toppled to

the ground. My arm hit it first. A wave of nausea swept over me but I managed to struggle to my feet, grateful that it was just an arm and not a leg.

I looked around for the torch but couldn't see it. Luckily Cassandra hadn't thought to ask for my mobile. Maybe she'd thought the fall would break my neck and I wouldn't need it. But it didn't matter. There was no way I could climb up the rope ladder to raise the alarm with one hand.

I had to get back to my car – but what if she was waiting for me there, just in case? I couldn't risk it. I needed to reach Honeychurch Cottages as quickly as possible.

There was a footpath that cut through the opposite field and then snaked through the pine forest, coming out eventually at the rear of the walled garden. Cradling my injured arm, I set off at a jog, only stopping when I reached the tall double gates.

Cautiously I opened one of them a crack and peered out into the service road to make sure the coast was clear.

I was in luck! Mum's Mini was still outside Delia's cottage and there was no sign of the Mercedes.

But as I approached number 3, I stopped. Something wasn't right.

The front door was open.

Had Cassandra guessed and got here first after all?

Inside, Delia's sitting room was a scene of disarray. There were signs of a struggle – a broken lamp, an upturned chair and what looked like a bullet hole in the ceiling. The bears, the wig and the receipts were gone.

With rising panic, I searched the rest of the cottage. Delia's bed had been turned upside down and her wardrobe doors were open, clothes and shoes strewn across the floor. Drawers had been emptied out and books swept off a little bookcase next to the bed.

I knew exactly what Cassandra had been looking for – Aubrey's cap.

Had she taken Mum and Delia hostage? With Cassandra, anything was possible.

Desperately I searched for a telephone, but when I found it, it lay smashed on the ground.

I hammered on the Croppers' front door, wondering if they would even hear my knock given the volume of the television blasting from beyond.

Finally Mrs Cropper appeared. For a brief moment I thought I had come to the wrong house. Gone was her pink-striped pinafore and white mob cap. Tonight she wore her grey hair down in a single plait and was dressed in a plum velour tracksuit.

'Please can I use your phone?'

'Good God!' Mrs Cropper exclaimed. 'Whatever happened? Your face! It's covered in scratches. Are you hurt?' She noticed me cradling my left arm. 'A fall?'

'Please let me use your phone,' I said again. 'I need to call my mother.'

'What's Iris done *now*?'

'This isn't the time for your feud.' I was close to tears. 'Mum's Mini is outside but neither of them are at the cottage and … There's been some sort of … incident.'

'I always say that a cup of tea is the answer,' Mrs Cropper said. 'Come on in.'

Seth Cropper didn't even look up as I walked into the small sitting room. Dressed in striped pyjamas, he was engrossed in a game show that involved a lot of clanging bells and cheers from the audience.

The phone was on a side table.

I rang the Carriage House first, but the answering machine picked up. I left a message. I tried twice more, but I knew deep down that I was wasting my time. I caught a glimpse of myself in the ornate mirror above the table and was shocked to see the angry welts that raced across my cheeks. My hair was stuck with leaves and twigs and my face was deathly white.

Mrs Cropper emerged with a mug of tea. 'Drink this.'

'I can't,' I said, but took it all the same. 'Did you hear anything strange coming from next door?'

'Can you say that again?' Mrs Cropper said. 'I can't hear you.'

'Never mind.' I put the mug on the side table and reached for the phone again. My wrist had swollen to the size of a golf ball. At least it wasn't my arm as I had thought at first.

Mrs Cropper gasped. 'You need to get to the hospital. Oh dear! Eric's not here to drive you – darts night at the Hare and Hounds …'

I dialled Shawn's mobile and left a message, feeling a surge of annoyance. Why did he never answer? But someone picked up on his home number.

It was Lizzie. She told me that Shawn was out this evening and that she was babysitting. I had to ask her to repeat herself twice because I couldn't hear above the sound of the television, but I gathered that she'd give Shawn the message the moment he got home.

I suddenly felt utterly exhausted and could feel tears spilling down my cheeks. Mrs Cropper watched me with concern. 'Is there anything I can do?'

I thought about raising the alarm at the Hall, but then remembered Alfred. Good old Alfred. He was always home in his little flat above the stables. He'd know what to do.

'I'll get Alfred to drive me to the hospital.' I took a gulp of the hot, sweet tea and handed back the mug. 'Thank you.'

The minute I was outside, I realised I had left my Golf at Bridge Cottage. How could Alfred drive me anywhere without a car? But then I remembered Mum's Mini.

For once, I was glad that she persisted in leaving her car keys in the ignition.

Unfortunately, the car was facing in the wrong direction. The stable yard was barely a quarter of a mile away, but I couldn't reverse that far with one hand, and since the car had a manual gearbox, making a three-point turn in the narrow lane would be too difficult.

I could feel panic rising again. *Pull yourself together, Kat!* I'd have to exit the tradesmen's entrance, zip along Cavalier Lane and enter the main drive. Yes, that was what I would do.

But as I turned into Cavalier Lane, my headlights picked out a large mound in the middle of the road and – to my horror – a mangled bicycle. The rear wheel was bent; the front handlebars twisted.

I slammed on the brakes and got out.

Delia was lying on her side with her arms splayed. Her

right leg was twisted at a sickening angle. Shards of bone were protruding through her thick tights.

I dropped to my knees, desperately searching for a pulse. It was there – faint, but there. She was alive, but unconscious.

Perhaps my mother had made a run for it on foot whilst Delia had tried to escape on her bicycle. It was possible. Yes, maybe that was what had happened.

'Hello, Katherine.'

Cassandra's voice chilled me to my core. I hadn't heard her footsteps. There had been no sound of a car. How long had she been standing in the shadows watching me?

Suddenly something cold and hard was pushed into the small of my back. Instinctively, I knew what it was.

A gun.

'I think you and I should take a little drive.'

Chapter Thirty-four

'In you go,' said Cassandra as she opened the passenger door. She'd parked the Mercedes a little way up the hill and out of sight. 'Now no funny business. Otherwise I'm afraid things could be frightfully grim for your mama.'

My stomach lurched. 'What do you mean? Where is she? You'd better not have hurt her.'

'Or what? I don't think you are in a position to make threats, do you?'

It was when Cassandra slid into the driver's side that I saw the gun illuminated by the overhead light. It was an antique – a pre-war German Mauser.

'Lovely, isn't it?' said Cassandra. 'And yes, it fires. Our fraudulent major would have made sure of that. But if you're very good, I won't have to use it. I've always been an excellent shot. Learned how to fire a gun when I was a child. Of course I wasn't as good as Hugo – not that … Never mind,' she said quickly. 'You see, Piers and I often go on shoots together. We like country pursuits. Not like you. A townie.'

She leaned over to pull the seat belt across my chest, catching my damaged wrist. I cried out in pain.

'Oops, sorry. That must hurt. Is it broken? Did you have a nasty fall?'

I didn't answer.

Cassandra turned the key in the ignition. 'I must admit, I was surprised to see you standing over the housekeeper's dead body like that. It was quite a drop, but obviously not high enough.'

Good. She doesn't know that Delia is still alive.

'I was lucky,' I said. 'The hedge broke my fall.'

'Hence the nasty scratches on your beautiful face.'

'You really think you're going to get away with everything?'

'Of course,' said Cassandra. 'I have the perfect alibi. I told Lavinia and Piers I wasn't feeling well – the shock of losing Aubrey, you understand – and needed rest.'

'You think of everything,' I said, not even bothering to mask my sarcasm.

'I *know*!' said Cassandra. 'We're all staying at the club. I'll be back there in time for breakfast with no one any the wiser.'

'Not even Piers?'

'No, not even Piers,' said Cassandra sadly. 'Funnily enough, him banning me from his bed has worked out rather well in this case, don't you think?'

'But why did you kill Delia?'

'Who? *Moi*? I have no idea what you're talking about. It was obviously a hit-and-run. Everyone knows she's a frightful drunk. She probably overbalanced into the path of an oncoming car.'

I'd watched enough forensic programmes to know that paint residue from any accident could be matched, but I wasn't going to remind her of that.

'But why?' I said again. 'What did she do?'

'It's awfully naughty to steal someone's personal effects, you know,' said Cassandra. 'I realised what had happened the minute I sneaked into my bedroom to change.'

So she must have known *before* she summoned me to the tree house.

'I could see the corner of my suitcase sticking out from under the bed,' she went on. 'To quote Piers, I was probably eighty-five per cent certain it was the housekeeper, but then you confirmed it.'

'I did no such thing.'

'You think I'm deaf as well as stupid?' she exclaimed. 'What did you say to me – *Lila's copies?* Like I said, I'd taken great care in snipping out the labels on those fake bears.'

'So you went to Delia's cottage …'

'And sure enough, the bears were all there!'

She eased the Mercedes down a twisty narrow lane. My heart started thumping again. 'Where are we going?'

'You'll see. I know all the hidden places. Piers told me that he guessed I'd had something to do with the mascot bears. I thought he would have found it hilarious, but he was actually quite cross with me.'

My heart sank. 'He knew about the bears as well?'

'Surprised?' Cassandra gloated.

I couldn't believe it. Piers had known and yet had said nothing to me. For a moment, my acute disappointment outweighed my fear of being in a car with a woman who was clearly insane.

'It sounds to me as though you are perfectly suited,' I said. 'And I'm glad.'

'Me too, although ... After dropping Harry and Fliss back at the Hall, he said he desperately needed to talk to me. We stopped at a pub – I can't remember which one – and I thought it was a date. Don't you hate it when that happens? A man buys you flowers and then promptly tells you he is going to propose to someone else.'

I didn't know what to say, so I said nothing.

'But I took no notice,' Cassandra went on. 'He'll come to his senses soon enough when he doesn't have you as a distraction ... Ah, we're here.'

She eased the car down a steep hill. And there, at the bottom, was Bridge Cottage. 'Told you I know all the short cuts around here.'

She drove the Mercedes through the gateway and stopped on the forecourt, turning off the engine and cutting the lights.

'What are we doing here?' I whispered, hoping she couldn't hear the thumping of my heart. A horrible feeling of déjà vu washed over me. It hadn't been that long ago when my mother and I had been trapped inside Bridge Cottage moments before it caught fire.

Tonight, the blackened shell seemed even more sinister than usual. Mounds of rubbish cast eerie shadows under a half-moon that peeped through the rain clouds.

'This is the end of the road.' Cassandra leaned over and unbuckled my seat belt, deliberately nudging my swollen wrist again.

'Where's my mother?'

'You'll see.' She opened her door and slid out, then came around to my side and opened mine. 'Quite feisty, I must say, and her language … it shocked me. Not particularly ladylike, but then one expects that from the working classes.'

I scrambled out of the car just as a police siren sounded in the distance.

Cassandra stiffened. 'Did you call the *police*?'

'How could I have done?'

Then … it faded away.

'You see? They've gone.' I just prayed that Lizzie or even Mrs Cropper *had* managed to raise the alarm and that an ambulance had come for Delia.

'Move!' Cassandra gave me a vicious push and I fell to my knees.

'Get up!' she screamed. 'What's wrong with you? You're pathetic!'

Fear gripped me again. What was she planning? I had to do *something*, say *something* to bring her to her senses – and then: 'I don't know how I passed muster with Squadron Leader Bigglesworth, do you?' I said lightly. 'As you said, I'm so pathetic.'

'What?' Cassandra seemed confused. 'Who?'

'Biggles. Harry Honeychurch, your godson,' I said. 'I'd be dismissed in an instant, wouldn't I?'

Cassandra didn't answer. I couldn't see her face – it was too dark – but I sensed her hesitate.

'I know you love him just as much as I do – probably more,' I said quickly. 'And I know he idolises you.'

'Leave Harry out of this,' she said roughly.

'Have you thought what will happen when he discovers that one of his absolute favourite people in the world has gone to prison for murder?'

For a moment I didn't think she'd heard me, but then she laughed. 'Oh, that's not going to happen. He'll never know. No one will ever find out.'

'What are you going to do?'

'I thought you wanted to see your mama?'

'What have you done with her?' I cried.

'Shut up and move.' Cassandra poked the gun into my ribcage. 'Follow that path.' She gestured to a narrow track that snaked around the ruins of the old house. 'And if you try to run, I *will* shoot you.'

We stopped next to a sodden mattress that lay on the ground amidst the rubble of what used to be the kitchen.

'Move that,' she commanded.

'I can't!' I said helplessly. 'I've only got one hand.'

'Do it!' She flapped the gun at me. '*Do* it!'

'Kat? Kat? Is that you?'

'Mum!' I looked to Cassandra in horror. 'Where is she?'

'Help!'

My mother's voice seemed to be coming from beneath my feet.

'What have you done to her?' I demanded.

'Oh, don't worry. She's fine. A bit dirty perhaps.' At my confused look she added, 'She's in the coal cellar. Why else do you think I'm asking you to move this stupid mattress?' She kicked it with frustration.

I tried to process exactly what Cassandra had said. I had to keep calm, but not only was my arm throbbing, my heart was racing so quickly I thought I would collapse.

'Help me move the mattress,' I said. 'I promise I won't run. Please don't hurt my mother.'

'Why would I hurt her?' Cassandra seemed incredulous. 'In fact, I wish I'd had a nice mother like yours—'

'Help!' Mum cried out again. 'Down here!'

'Shut up!' shouted Cassandra – then her mood changed and she became calm. 'Where was I? What was I saying? Oh. Yes. You see, the thing is, you have everything and I have nothing. Even my father doesn't care about me.'

'Help!' Mum cried out yet again.

'Shut up, shut up!' screamed Cassandra and again her mood flipped. 'Do you know what it's like not to feel wanted? No, of course you don't. Piers wanted me. And then you came along …'

'I've told you,' I said steadily. 'Piers and I are just friends.'

'OK. Enough of talking about me.' She put the gun in her jacket pocket. 'As I said, one false move and your mama will be no more.'

Reluctantly – and painfully – I helped her heave the mattress aside. Underneath were two sheets of corrugated iron laid flat.

'And those as well,' Cassandra said.

Struggling, we managed to flop them over to reveal the mouth of a dark hole, with steps leading down to the old coal cellar.

I froze in horror and tried to back away, but Cassandra was ready.

She shoved me hard. 'Down you go,' she said as I tumbled once more into darkness.

Chapter Thirty-five

Miraculously I had instinctively twisted my body to the right to save landing on my injured wrist, but I was winded and my right shoulder hurt.

'Kat,' Mum sobbed. 'Please talk to me, Kat! Please.'

'I'm OK,' I managed to whisper. 'Really. I'm OK.'

The cellar was dark but a square of light above helped my eyes adjust until a coarse grating sound followed by a crash plunged us into darkness again.

Cassandra must have replaced the corrugated iron sheets *and* the mattress.

We were trapped.

'We're going to die down here,' Mum whimpered.

'Don't be silly,' I said. 'Where are you?'

'I can't move. She's tied me to an old pipe.'

I struggled to my feet and promptly cracked my head on the low ceiling, sending my head spinning.

'Be careful,' said Mum. 'The ceiling is very low.'

'I think I found that out,' I gasped. 'Keep talking. I'll make my way over to you.'

'Over here,' she said from behind my right shoulder. 'That woman is insane. It's all that inbreeding in the upper classes.' She promptly burst into tears.

I felt like crying too, but one of us had to stay calm. 'It's OK, Mum,' I said. 'We'll find a way out.' Stooping down, I gingerly shuffled towards her voice over pieces of coal and other rubble and debris. Even though the fire had happened months ago, there was still a smell of smoke.

'She's a cold-blooded killer,' my mother went on. 'Oh Kat, if you saw how she ran poor Delia off the road. She slammed her foot down on the accelerator. I'll never forget the thud. She actually laughed!'

'Delia is going to survive,' I said. 'I heard the ambulance on its way when Cassandra kidnapped me. I think Mrs Cropper raised the alarm.' It made me feel better even if it wasn't true.

'Finally that old bag has done something useful.'

'I'm sure she feels the same way about you,' I said, relieved that my mother seemed to be rallying. 'And believe me, there will be traces of paint on the fender of the Mercedes. She'll be caught.'

Unless she drove back to London and got rid of the car. Anything was possible with Cassandra, but I didn't want to share my fears with my mother quite yet.

'But by then we'll be dead and eaten by rats.'

'There aren't rats down here,' I said, although it was definitely possible. 'Tell me what happened.'

'Cassandra knocked on the door,' said Mum. 'I thought it

was you. I can't work out how she knew. She was supposed to be in London.'

'Delia didn't cover her tracks very well.'

'It was too late to hide everything,' Mum went on. 'It was all displayed on the coffee table like meat on a butcher's slab. The Croppers must be stone deaf. We screamed. We shouted. Delia swung a lamp at her, but it was still plugged into the wall – she'd had a few drinks ...'

'I think I've found you,' I felt for her face with my one good hand, then ran it down her arm. Her hands were tied with binder twine. 'At least you aren't handcuffed. It could have been worse.'

'Delia fell on to the coffee table and it collapsed.' Mum started to giggle, but I knew it was from nerves. 'It was like a scene from Monty Python – ouch! That's my foot – and then Cassandra pulled out a gun. I thought it was a child's gun, one of Harry's, and just told her to stop being a silly girl and put it down ... Can't you go any faster?'

'No.' I was struggling to work the knot free.

'That's when Delia made a run for it and Cassandra fired the gun! She didn't care about me!'

'Oh Mum, I'm just glad you weren't hurt.'

'She held the gun to my head and dragged me around Delia's cottage demanding I open all the cupboards and drawers.'

'She was looking for Aubrey's cap.'

'Really, Kat, can't you go any faster?'

'I only have one good hand, Mum – there, all done! You're free. Let's make our way back to the steps.'

Our eyes soon adjusted to the inky darkness, but progress

was still slow. Twice Mum hit her head. At last we reached the steps.

'There's only room for one of us,' I said, 'so it looks like it's going to be you. Go up on your hands and knees.'

'OK. This is ruining my clothes.'

'I'm right behind you if you fall.'

There was a scattering of pebbles and a lot of spitting. 'Disgusting! Disgusting! Coal dust!'

'Keep your mouth closed!' I exclaimed.

There was some grunting and groaning and then: 'It's no good,' Mum gasped. 'It's too heavy! What did she put on there? The coal bunker?' She yelled at the top of her lungs: 'HELP!'

'You're wasting your breath.'

We both sank back on to the filthy floor, utterly defeated. For once, my mother said nothing.

As I stared into the darkness, a pinprick of light flashed across the far wall and then went out. Car headlamps? The Mercedes, perhaps?

And then ... was it remotely possible?

'Mum?' I said slowly. 'Didn't we have a coal cellar in Tooting?'

'Yes, we used it for storage.'

'Weren't there *two* entrances? One inside the house and another from the driveway?'

'Yes! A coal chute!' Mum cried. 'Clever, clever you.'

'I saw a tiny bit of light over there ...'

'Yes! I thought I saw something too! I know exactly what you're thinking – let's hope that it's a chute and not a hatch ... fat lot of good a hatch would do.'

'We need a stick or a pole or something,' I said as I groped around blindly.

'Seriously, Katherine? I can hardly see my own hand … Oh, wait. I think this will do.'

'Ouch! Be careful!' I cried as I felt something hard strike my shoulder.

'Argh! Get off my foot,' Mum gasped, and then accidentally hit me again.

'I'm sitting down,' I said. 'It's too dangerous.'

'Collateral damage,' she grunted as I heard the stick strike the walls and ceiling with frenzied muffled thumps.

And then … the sound changed to a hollow metal twang, followed by splintering wood.

Moonlight flooded the cellar, illuminating nuggets of coal and mounds of coal dust.

'Thank God!' my mother exclaimed. 'We're alive!'

'Mum, you look … good heavens.' All I could see were the whites of her eyes. Her face was completely covered in coal dust.

'What?' Then she saw me and sniggered. 'We're like chimney sweeps from *Mary Poppins*! Up you go. I'll push you out first.'

The chute was narrow, steep and hard to get a foothold on, but with Mum wedging her shoulder underneath my rear end, I managed to haul my way up to the surface. I turned to help her up and we both collapsed in a heap on terra firma.

'Shh!' I whispered. 'Listen! Can you hear something?'

'There's someone here … Help—'

'No!' I pulled her back into the shadows. 'Over there – see, by the gate … it's the Mercedes!'

The car was still parked on the forecourt.

'Oh good grief, she's still *here*!' Mum exclaimed. 'Why? To make sure we're dead?'

'Stay where you are,' I said. 'I'm going to see what's going on.'

I crept stealthily towards the car, which was fortunately shielded from view by an abandoned sofa. Reaching the forecourt, I took cover behind it.

To my astonishment, the black Citroën was parked across the gateway, neatly blocking Cassandra's escape. I couldn't see if the driver was there or not, but I assumed he couldn't be.

Cassandra was frantically clearing mountains of rubbish away from the dilapidated wooden fence. Every few moments she would scream out an obscenity.

'It looks like Poirot has come in useful,' Mum whispered in my ear.

'I told you to stay put.'

'She's going to try to drive through that fence,' Mum went on. 'What does she think she's driving? A snowplough?'

Cassandra gave the Citroën's tyres a vicious kick before stomping back to her own car, and yanking the driver's door open.

In a flash, Mum sprang forward holding an empty gin bottle aloft. In three quick strides she came up behind Cassandra and crashed it down on top of her head.

Cassandra crumpled into a heap.

'Mother!' I was horrified.

'Serves her right!' Mum fumed.

I hurried over and dropped to my knees, feeling for a pulse. 'She's breathing!'

'Of course she is,' said Mum. 'She'll live. People like that always do.' She picked up a glass shard.

'No! What are you doing?'

'This!' She sank it viciously into each of the Mercedes's tyres. 'Better to be safe than sorry.'

'I thought for a minute that you …'

'Seriously? You thought I'd actually kill her?'

A sudden movement in the shadows startled us both. A man with heavy-rimmed glasses and wearing jeans and a black leather jacket emerged from the undergrowth.

'*Bonsoir, madam, mademoiselle*. Claude Moreau,' he said with a smile. '*Est-ce que vous allez bien* – you are OK?'

'Yes thank you,' I managed to say.

'Although we could have done with your help a bit earlier in the evening,' Mum declared. 'Wait? Do I hear the cavalry?'

'Yes!' I cried as the sound of an approaching siren grew louder and the sky was alight with blue and white flashing lights.

'*Excusez-moi*,' said the Frenchman, and with a nod of his head, he hastened back to the Citroën and sped away.

The panda screamed to a halt and Shawn scrambled out, followed by Detective Constable Clive Banks, whose black beard seemed to have a life of its own.

'It's Paddington Bear and Captain Pugwash!' Mum's cheers turned to cries of alarm as Cassandra struggled to get to her knees.

I sprinted forward, but Clive beat me to it. He knocked Cassandra back down and rolled her over on to her chest, swiftly snapping on the handcuffs. 'You've been nabbed, missy.'

Cassandra fought back, kicking and spitting.

'Not so ladylike now, are you?' Mum declared.

'I want to speak to Piers! Get off me!' Cassandra screamed as Clive bundled her into the back of the panda. 'You can't prove a thing. I'm innocent!'

'Kat! Thank God you're safe.' Shawn tried to hug me, but I cried out in pain.

'My wrist!'

'Sorry,' he said.

'How did you know where to find us?' Mum asked. I'd wondered the same myself.

'I'll tell you everything tomorrow,' said Shawn. 'Right now, we need to get Kat to hospital.'

Chapter Thirty-six

'**I brought blueberry muffins,**' **said Shawn when I opened** the front door the next morning. His smile turned to embarrassment. 'Sorry! I thought you would have been awake by now.'

'I should have been up hours ago. The painkillers knocked me out.' I forced a smile. I felt horribly self-conscious dressed in my pyjamas and a white towelling robe that now had distinctively sooty cuffs. I'd been ordered not to bathe, so I had done the best I could with a warm flannel.

'Come on in.' I opened the door wide to let him pass through, catching a whiff of musky lime aftershave. This was unusual for him. I'd only ever inhaled banana fabric softener before.

It had been almost two in the morning by the time my mother and I got back home from A&E at Torbay and South Devon Hospital.

My wrist was finally in a cast, having been fractured quite badly – although I didn't get too much sympathy from my mother, who claimed that when she broke her hand over a year ago, the pain was far worse.

'What would you like to drink?' I said now.

'Let me make it.'

'I have to wear a cast for six weeks,' I grumbled as we went to the kitchen. 'It's so infuriating.'

'I'm just so relieved that you're all right.'

I perched on a bar stool whilst Shawn moved around my tiny kitchen with confidence. Other than relying on his mother-in-law for after-school care, he did most of the cooking for his twin boys. I liked that about him.

We didn't speak until we were sitting at the counter sipping mugs of coffee and devouring the blueberry muffins.

'These are delicious,' I said.

'Thanks,' he said shyly. 'One of Helen's recipes.'

'It sounds like she was a good cook.'

'She was the best.'

Great. Of course she was. 'You said you had news.'

'At roughly eleven hundred hours, after you went off in the ambulance, a white transit van pulled up at the dumpsite.'

'I don't believe it!' I exclaimed.

'Clive and I had waited behind to secure the crime scene,' said Shawn. 'We heard the van coming and hid from sight. The idiots didn't even notice our car! Caught them red-handed.'

'That's brilliant!'

'Crown Haulage and Clearance have *two* transit vans,' Shawn went on. 'One operated as a bona fide business ...'

'Yes, Mum used them.'

'The other van was stored in a lock-up behind Riverview

retirement village,' said Shawn. 'They used the lock-up as an illegal transit station.'

'How convenient.' Of course! I'd noticed the storage units when I first went to visit the major to value his bears.

'Elsie King was the mastermind,' Shawn continued. 'She had a lucrative racket going on – enough to be able to buy a house for cash in Menorca. Up until a couple of months ago, the pair used another dumping ground, but when the council installed CCTV, they had to go elsewhere.'

'Bridge Cottage,' I said.

'Exactly,' said Shawn. 'Apart from suggesting to the families of her own deceased residents that she could help clear out their possessions, she also studied the local newspaper obituary columns.'

I recalled seeing Elsie with her red pen, sitting at the dining room table on the day the major died. 'I thought so.'

'You don't seem surprised.' Shawn seemed put out. 'She liked to focus on the elderly who lived in retirement facilities who had either no family or family who lived too far away.'

'That's despicable!'

'The more expensive pieces she kept for herself to sell on eBay or put in an auction. The rest she'd dump – family photos, sentimental mementos, everything.'

'So if anyone was granny-farming, it was Elsie!' I was astonished. 'But wait – what about her cats and the canary? What will happen to them?'

'The entire menagerie is at my house at the moment,' said Shawn. 'The twins are delighted. We'll find good homes for them – or keep them.'

'You're a good man,' I said, and meant it.

'Now, for the best part.' Shawn looked smug. 'You'll never guess—'

'Please don't make me guess.'

'We found this.' Shawn reached inside his trench coat and pulled out a Ziploc bag containing an orange tweed flat cap.

I gasped. 'That's Aubrey's! Where did you find it?'

'On Troy King's head.'

'He was *wearing* it?' I was confused. 'But I didn't think he was there when Aubrey came off the horse – Delia would have said so.'

'Ah … but we implied that he was,' said Shawn. 'How else do you think we managed to extract so much information from him? He's not the sharpest tool in the shed.'

'Where was the cap?'

'He took me to the exact spot. It had fallen behind a refrigerator.'

'Why on earth would he want to wear someone else's hat?'

'It seems he's a bit of a hat collector.'

'It's no wonder that Cassandra couldn't find it.'

'With no witnesses, and a criminal record, Troy could easily be seen as the prime suspect,' Shawn went on. 'The earl had fined him on three previous occasions for fly-tipping. A fourth conviction would almost certainly mean a prison sentence. An excellent motive for manslaughter.'

'Oh dear,' I said. 'Surely you don't think there's a chance that Troy *could* become the prime suspect?'

'Ah, now it's funny you should say that,' said Shawn. 'Were you aware of Cassandra Bowden-Forbes's mental health issues?'

'Excuse me?'

'Cassandra suffers from bipolar disorder.'

'I thought she was a bit irrational, but no, I did not know that.'

'In fact, she had just discharged herself from a luxury private clinic in Switzerland—'

'She said she went to Greece!'

'When she was brought in for questioning, she told us that her doctor had changed her prescription and that she had not been acting in a rational manner; that anything she may have said to you should be disregarded.'

'That's … that's ridiculous!'

'And as she pointed out, there were no witnesses who could place her at any of the scenes.'

'But that's not true!'

'I'm afraid it's her word against yours,' said Shawn. 'She has hired a top QC, and Viscount Chawley will be giving her a character reference.'

I felt as if I had been punched in the stomach. Piers was going to speak up for Cassandra? I refused to believe it. 'But that means she could get away with *everything*!'

'I'm afraid it looks like that, unless you can get your … *boyfriend* to say otherwise.'

'What are you talking about?'

'He's provided her with an alibi for Saturday. They drove home from the BearFest and according to Piers were together for nearly all of the evening.'

'What? Piers said that?' I was gutted.

'He refuses to believe that Cassandra would ever harm his father.'

'You've spoken to him?' Piers had not been in touch with me at all.

'By phone early this morning,' said Shawn.

'How does he explain Cassandra's secret drive down to Devon whilst he and Lavinia were staying at their club?'

'Apparently she has a sleeping disorder.'

My jaw dropped. 'You mean she drove two hundred miles and didn't remember?'

He had the grace to look sheepish. 'Something like that. He insisted there was a perfectly reasonable explanation.'

'Unbelievable.' I was growing increasingly angry. 'What about Cassandra running Delia off the road? My mother was in the car. She was *there*! She saw it happen!'

Shawn looked uncomfortable. 'Well, now let's just think this through and imagine your mother on the witness stand at the Old Bailey.'

'Meaning?'

'The defence team will obviously look into her background. Certain details would come to light …'

'Oh. I see what you mean.' Of course I did – my mother's pseudonym as Krystalle Storm, her secret offshore account and all her other lies would not make her a credible witness. It could even destroy her career.

'Cassandra claims that Delia was drunk when she was riding her bicycle and fell in front of the car,' said Shawn. 'And there is something else – we have since discovered that Delia

Evans has stolen a vast sum of money.'

'Who told you? The French detective?'

'He was most generous with his information. Wait – you *knew* about the stolen money?'

'It's her money from her marriage.' I sounded like my mother.

'You deliberately withheld important information?'

'Yes. I suppose I did. Her husband ran off to Calais with a barmaid—'

'Calais! I could think of more romantic places.'

'Delia was going to return the money – well, half of it.'

'In the eyes of the law, it's still a crime.'

I hated it when Shawn got all self-righteous.

'What about the major?' I refused to accept that Cassandra was going to get away with that. 'She admitted to me that she pushed him down the stairs. She stole his gun!'

'As I already mentioned, Cassandra is denying that now. The only witness we have is Elsie King, but as you know, she identified you as being there that afternoon and now claims she can't remember the exact time.'

'But it wasn't me!' I said angrily.

'I'm sorry,' said Shawn. 'I'm just telling you what happened.'

'And I suppose you're going to tell me that Cassandra claims that my mother and I just happened to be strolling through a dumpsite late at night and fell through the floor into a coal cellar?' I said, not bothering to disguise my sarcasm.

Shawn looked down at his shoes.

'How will she think up an explanation for *that*?' I went on. 'After all, that's exactly where you arrested her.'

'Cassandra claims that she was having one of her manic episodes … Look, I'm sorry.' Shawn reached out to touch me, but I slid off the bar stool and stepped away.

'I need to think,' I said. 'She can't be allowed to get away with this.'

Shawn came up behind me. 'Kat, there is something I need to tell you.' He gently took my shoulders and turned me around to face him. 'When Lizzie told me you were trying to reach me, I knew something bad must have happened. And then my grandmother called and confirmed my worst fears.'

'Mrs Cropper didn't know any details,' I said somewhat rudely. 'I just asked to use her phone.'

'She told me that your face was covered in scratches.' He looked intently into my eyes. 'That you'd broken your arm—'

'It was my wrist, and I didn't know I'd broken it at the time.'

'I was worried sick.'

'Really?' I was hardly listening. I wasn't sure what was making me angrier – the very real chance that Cassandra could get away with it, or Pier's compliance in all of this.

'Look, I had rehearsed a speech … Kat! I'm talking to you!' Shawn said sharply.

'I'm sorry, I'm too upset.'

He gave a heavy sigh. 'This is not actually going the way I planned.'

'Planned? What do you mean, planned?'

'I need to know if you and Piers are a couple,' he blurted out.

'You're asking me this *now*?'

'I'm only asking because I would never step on the toes of another man. And then, of course, you went to Paris.'

'Nothing happened in Paris!'

'Seeing you with … seeing you with *that* man, who … I don't think he could ever make you happy. I know it's none of my business, but he is immature and … I've known him since I was a kid. He's older than me, but—'

'Nothing happened in Paris, Shawn,' I said again. 'And no, we are not a couple.'

Not now. Nor would we ever be.

I saw a glimmer of relief in his eyes. 'It's been five years since Helen passed away—'

'Shawn, I'm sorry,' I said abruptly. 'I just can't do this right now. I can't. I'm upset about Cassandra. I'm tired and in pain. And to be honest, I'm really confused.'

'Kat,' Shawn persisted. 'I'm new at this. I know we've tried to date before and things never quite worked out – but will you have dinner with me on Saturday night?'

I looked at him in dismay. Had he not heard a single word I'd said?

'No, no!' He put his hand up as if stopping traffic. 'My mistake. Forget I asked. Sorry. Better get on.'

He marched out of the kitchen. I went after him. 'Shawn! Don't be silly—' but he was already at the front door.

Piers stood on the doorstep holding a bouquet of red roses. 'I see my timing is terrible.'

Chapter Thirty-seven

'**This isn't what you think,**' **I** said as **I** pulled my robe closer, cursing myself for saying something so clichéd even though I was innocent.

'Well, it looks like you've both been busy,' Piers said coldly.

'In case you haven't noticed, I have a cast on my wrist. I was in A and E.'

Piers's eyes widened. 'Oh Kat! I had no idea. Are you OK?'

'She's fine,' said Shawn.

Piers scowled. 'Did *he* give you my message?'

'No. What message?'

'It must have slipped my mind,' said Shawn mildly.

'I told him I was taking a taxi from London – Lavinia stayed up in town. I couldn't call you because Kitten had my iPhone.'

'Yes, I know that,' I said. 'She texted me pretending to be you.'

'I wondered if she was doing something silly,' Piers went on.

'*Silly?* My mother and I could have died.'

'She didn't mean anything by it,' said Piers.

I felt my jaw drop in astonishment.

'When I realised my phone was missing,' Piers went on, 'I used the computer at the club to track it. You can imagine my shock when I realised it was back in the Devonshire countryside.'

Still I said nothing.

'And then when Kitten wasn't in her room and my car had gone, I guessed she had ...'

'She had ... what?' I prompted. 'What did you think she was going to do? Invite me for tea?'

'I don't know ... Wait, what's that?' Piers suddenly caught sight of Aubrey's cap in the Ziploc bag. 'Where the hell did you find it?'

'At Bridge Cottage,' said Shawn.

Piers's eyes narrowed. 'Kat and I went through that place with a tooth comb on Sunday afternoon. It wasn't there.'

'When we have more information, we'll be only too happy to share it with you,' said Shawn.

'I suppose you planted it. You're determined to pin the blame on Kitten.'

'Piers – she's not who you think she is,' I said.

'I'll tell you right now that there is no way she would ever have hurt Father,' Piers declared. 'She idolised him!'

'Now calm down, sir,' said Shawn in a rather patronising tone. 'We have a witness—'

'Ha! You mean the *housekeeper*? She's a known drunk! If anyone wanted to hurt Father, it would be her.'

'Forensics are examining your Mercedes right now,' said

Shawn. 'We're confident we'll have proof that the car struck Mrs Evans's bicycle, and we know that Ms Bowden-Forbes was driving it at the time.'

'Kitten suffers from somnambulism,' said Piers. 'She wouldn't have known what she was doing.'

'Really,' I muttered under my breath.

'Yes, *really*.' Piers was growing angrier by the minute.

I was incredulous. 'You want us to believe that she drove all the way from London whilst she was asleep?'

'Yes! And I'll take that.' Piers snatched the Ziploc bag from Shawn's hand.

Shawn snatched it back. 'I don't think so.'

Piers pushed him and grabbed it again. 'Don't you touch me!'

Shawn darted forward and wrestled the bag from Piers's grasp, then promptly thrust it down the front of his trousers.

'You idiot!' Piers shoved Shawn again.

Shawn shoved him back.

It was madness. 'Stop this!' I shouted. 'Or I will call the police … yes, the *real* police, in Dartmouth!

Shawn froze. '*Real* police?'

'I didn't mean it quite like that,' I stammered.

Piers grinned. 'Nicely put.'

'I give up.' Shawn threw up his hands and turned away. He was halfway back to his car when he stopped dead. He spun on his heel and stalked back to Piers, who was standing there gloating. Prodding Piers's shoulder, he said in an icy voice, 'You've just assaulted a police officer.'

'I'm not scared of Paddington Bear.'

'Stop this!' I said again. 'You're not children!'

'Keep out of it, Kat,' Shawn snarled. 'I've been wanting to do this for a very long time.'

'Oh really?' Piers jeered. 'Come on. Up with them!' He raised his fists and began bouncing around Shawn on the balls of his feet. 'Come on, come on!'

Shawn's face was purple. He removed his trench coat, carefully folding it with the lining outside, and thrust it at me. 'Hold that.' With painstaking slowness, he then rolled up his sleeves whilst Piers continued to dance around him throwing air jabs.

'Come on, come on,' Piers said again. 'Don't pussyfoot around.'

Suddenly Shawn roared and charged towards him, drawing his right hand back in a clumsy fist and swinging it at Piers's head.

Piers ducked, Shawn overbalanced and only just managed to stay on his feet.

'Ha ha!' jeered Piers. 'I suppose they didn't teach you to box at Paddington Bear school, did they?'

Shawn took another run at him, but Piers was ready with a vicious right hook to the chin. Shawn went wheeling backwards and landed on his bottom in a large muddy puddle.

'Stop! Please stop!' I shouted.

But Shawn was too angry. He scrambled to his feet, and in one dirty move ploughed into Piers and took him down in a rugby tackle. They fell into the topiary planter by my front door, careened into the little wicker table on the veranda and landed in my favourite hydrangea bush.

'Enough!' I yelled.

Piers must have hit his head on the corner of the table, because he didn't fight back when Shawn deftly flipped him over and snapped on the handcuffs.

'You're under arrest for assaulting a police officer,' gasped Shawn. 'You have the right to remain silent—'

'Oh shut up, you pompous fool!' Piers moaned. 'Kat, you saw what happened. He started it.'

'No I didn't!' Shawn cried.

'Yes you did!'

I regarded these two pathetic specimens covered in mud and leaves. Shawn's chin was red and it looked like his eye would be closed up by the morning.

I should have felt flattered that they had been fighting over me, but instead I thought *no thanks* to both of them. I returned to the house, slamming the door behind me.

There were a few more outraged shouts of protest, but I didn't bother to look out of the window. Finally I heard the panda car drive away with the siren on full blast.

Shawn really *had* arrested him.

As I righted the wicker table – which now had a broken leg – and stared at my mangled hydrangea, I wanted to cry.

The events of the last few days had certainly taken their toll, and last night's escapade had reminded me all too well of another time when I was trapped in a very dark space fearing I would never see daylight again. But really what I felt was acute disappointment in both men. I knew that neither was right for me.

Piers's history with Cassandra was so rooted in loyalty that she would always be a problem, and strangely enough, the same was true for Shawn. When he'd arrived with blueberry muffins, he'd brought Helen in the bag too.

The phone rang. It was my mother.

'How are you feeling?' she said briskly. 'I hope you're not all maudlin.'

'Sort of,' I said. 'You?'

'Well – do you promise not to judge me?'

I gave a heavy sigh. 'I promise.'

'Of course I'm very sad about Aubrey's death – such an awful way to go – but to be honest, I've been giving it a bit of thought and it would never have worked. All he talked about was recycling and … the fluffy mules … well, they weren't exactly *me*.'

I laughed.

'I think I was flattered by the attention,' Mum went on. 'It was nice to know that at my age I still have some allure.'

'I've come to a similar conclusion,' I said, and went on to tell her all about the schoolboy fight between Shawn and Piers.

Mum roared with laughter. 'Good grief. Alfred should teach Shawn how to box properly. I wonder why they loathe each other so much.'

'I have no idea and I really don't care,' I said. 'Oh Mum, do you remember when I was little and you used to wave your magic wand and all my problems would go away?'

'I still have that wand, you know.'

'Can you wave it now?'

'I'll do better than that,' she said. 'We're going to visit Delia in hospital. I have a surprise for you. Be ready in twenty minutes.'

Chapter Thirty-eight

'**I can't believe she's actually got herself a private room,**' Mum said as we reached Delia's door, having stopped off at Marks & Spencer to buy flowers and chocolates. 'Bit extravagant, don't you think?'

'Be quiet, she'll hear you.'

I knocked and we went in.

'Oh lovely!' Delia said happily. 'Meet my nurse.'

Delia's nurse happened to be an attractive balding man in his late sixties. He was plumping up her pillows and fussing over the blankets that covered a cage protecting her broken leg.

Despite her face being a rainbow of yellow, purple and brown bruises, she looked radiant. She was also not wearing a wig, and even though her hair was a little on the thin side, it was a beautiful silvery white and brought out the colour of her eyes.

But it was when the nurse kissed her gently on the forehead that Delia grinned. 'This is Lenny.'

Mum's jaw dropped.

'Oh.' I was taken aback. 'How lovely to meet you.'

'I thought you were in Calais with Genevieve?' Mum said coldly.

'She wasn't even French,' Delia laughed. 'She was plain old Jennifer Piles.'

'I know, I know you must hate me,' said Lenny. 'I was a silly bugger. Don't know what I was thinking.'

'I suppose it all happened in a fog?' Mum sneered.

'Mum,' I said in a low voice. 'Let's keep out of it, shall we?'

'No, I shan't keep out of it.' Mum plonked the flowers and chocolates on the bedside table. 'You've tormented your poor wife, broken her heart – and what did she do to deserve all that?'

'Well, she cleaned out our bank account,' Lenny said drily.

'He's not pressing charges,' said Delia.

'And why should he!' Mum seemed outraged.

Lenny had the grace to look ashamed. 'I'm not proud of what I did, but Delia's forgiven me,' he said. 'And I understand you've been a good friend to her, and I like that.'

'Do you now!'

'The truth is, I knew the minute I got on the ferry that I'd made a mistake, but by then, Delia had vanished. I couldn't find her anywhere.'

'He hired a private detective.'

'Yes, we know that, Delia,' Mum said. 'He scared Kat half to death. She thought she was being stalked by a serial killer.'

'Well, not exactly …'

'I just wanted to make sure she was all right,' said Lenny.

'You wanted to make sure you knew where the money was!' Mum declared.

Lenny looked to Delia and grinned. 'I like her. I like a woman who speaks her mind and is loyal to you. You've never had a proper friend because we've always moved around so much.'

'Please, Iris,' Delia said desperately. 'Give him a chance to make amends.'

'You really are taking him back?' Mum seemed stunned. 'A man who did that to you?'

'Mum, it's Delia's life,' I said gently.

'We're going to give it a go,' said Lenny. 'Start courting again. I'm not going to be sleeping at the cottage. I've taken a room at the Hare and Hounds. I'll do whatever it takes to win her back. I love her. I know she's forgiven me, but I don't know if I will ever forgive myself.'

'Well don't do it again, otherwise there will be trouble,' Mum scolded.

Delia and Lenny shared a glance. 'Excuse me a moment,' he said, and left the room.

'Be happy for me,' Delia pleaded. 'He's riddled with remorse.'

'Good!' Mum cried.

'Kat – I have something for you.' Delia pointed to her tote bag, which was hooked over a chair. 'Can you pass that to me?'

I did as she asked, and she pulled out a large brown envelope.

'Lenny asked me to give this to you to give to Shawn.'

'What is it?' I said.

'You'll see.'

Inside were dozens of incriminating photographs of Cassandra that had been taken through a telephoto lens.

'Surveillance photographs!' I exclaimed. 'I don't believe it.'

'Yes.' Delia nodded. 'Our little Poirot came up trumps.'

I was euphoric. 'Proof at last! But why would he do this?'

Delia shrugged. 'He got bored just watching me all the time. Once he knew that the money I'd taken—'

'Half of which belonged to you,' Mum reminded her – I could tell that unlike Delia she was not going to completely forgive Lenny immediately.

'Yes, I know, Iris,' said Delia. 'Anyway, once Claude knew that the money was safe, he realised that Cassandra was behaving very oddly and was up to no good.'

'Poirot saved our lives,' said Mum suddenly, and went on to tell Delia about what had happened that night at Bridge Cottage.

'Claude is willing to testify,' Delia went on happily. 'So you see, if Lenny hadn't left, I wouldn't have come to Honeychurch Hall and then Cassandra would have got away with—'

'Murder!' Mum and I chorused.

Lenny re-entered the room. 'Here she is!'

'Oh! Guy!' Delia exclaimed. 'My lovely boy! What a surprise!' She looked at Mum and winked.

I turned around and my heart skipped a beat. A tall man with piercing grey eyes and a military crew cut stood in the doorway bearing the same flowers and chocolates from Marks & Spencer that we had bought.

'Mum!' he smiled. 'Well … I admit I've seen you look better.'

He kissed her cheek and then turned to his father. 'Glad you know what's good for you, Dad.'

Mum whispered in my ear, 'What do you think?'

I suddenly realised why she had insisted I come with her to see Delia today. 'Did you know he'd be here?'

'Who? Me?' she said, feigning innocence.

Delia's son turned to greet us. 'I'm Guy, and of course you must be my mother's best friend, Iris, and you … are Katherine.'

'Call me Kat.' I took his outstretched hand and felt a jolt of electricity that took me completely by surprise. Astonishingly, I felt my face grow warm.

'Lovely to meet you, Guy,' said Mum smoothly. 'I am sure we'll be seeing more of you now you're stationed nearby. If you'll excuse us, we'll leave you all to it.' She grabbed my arm and steered me out of the room.

'Oh, goodbye!' I said, and couldn't help but steal a look over my shoulder. Guy was watching me and smiling. I smiled back, then, once we were out in the corridor, whispered, 'Mum, why are we going?'

'Trust me,' she said. 'It doesn't do to look too keen.'

'Was I that obvious?'

'Well, you were beginning to drool.'

'Mother!'

'Guy really belongs on the cover of one of my books,' Mum mused as we walked back to the car. 'Don't worry. You'll see him again. He's on leave for a week or two.'

'Not that I'm interested,' I said quickly.

'Of course not, but if you ever want to borrow my Ann Summers lingerie, just let me know.'